D0984521

AT THE LAKE
OF
SUDDEN DEATH

AT THE LAKE
OF
SUDDEN DEATH

Timothy Holme

MYST
H
||

Walker and Company
New York

First published in the United States of America in 1987 by the Walker Publishing Company, Inc.

Library of Congress Cataloging-in-Publication Data

Holme, Timothy.
    At the lake of sudden death / Timothy Holme.
        p.   cm.
    ISBN 0-8027-5682-4
    I. Title.
    PR6058.O45355A8 1987   87-18801
    823'.914--dc19   CIP

Printed in the United States of America

10 9 8 7 6 5 4 3 2 1

To George Hardinge, with gratitude

Part One

DEATH BY WATER

CHAPTER 1

A pebbly stretch of beach on Lake Garda early one July morning. The holiday-makers are not yet up, but the sun is and its rays make the water dazzling silver as it laps the beach, its calm in deceptive contrast to the storm of the previous night. A little way back from the shore cypresses reach majestically towards an azure sky while, further away still, olive trees dress the rising hillside with silvery green. On the air there is a barely perceptible hint of a scent of lemon.

Only one thing mars this idyllic scene: a human body, face downwards, with long red hair stirring in the water as though it had life of its own. It is young, female and shapely, dressed in a yellow t-shirt, jeans and gym-shoes. With its face still unrevealed, the nose rubbing delicately against a pebble, it awaits discovery.

This is not long in coming. An early rising boy rounds a corner on to this particular stretch of beach. He is entirely taken up with the skimming of pebbles on the smooth surface of the lake and he does not see the body until he is nearly on top of it. When he does, he starts backwards in alarm. Then, curiosity getting the better of him, he moves a cautious step forwards and bends down to examine it more closely. He has never seen a dead body before and he is still young enough to be quite detached about the experience. He would like to see the face, but as well as a certain reluctance to touch the body he suspects he would be in trouble with grown-ups if he did so.

After a minute or so he decides that action is called for and, with a last look at the water-shifted form to fix it in his memory for describing to friends, he turns and runs across the beach towards a narrow path leading to the village.

A few minutes later he is back with half a dozen grown-ups. He points excitedly at the body, shouting in Italian. 'There it is! You see? I told you.' Obviously the adults have been in two minds as to whether he was to be believed.

A couple of the men move with some reluctance towards the

3

water's edge. The women cluster round, their expressions a mixture of fascination and horror. The body is pulled from the water and laid upon its back on the beach. Even death and a so far undetermined period of time in the water have not altogether obliterated the fact that the young woman was beautiful.

One of the women crosses herself and she is followed by the rest of the group, including the small boy. A jacket, the most suitable thing to hand, is laid reverently over the dead face and then, after some hasty muttering, two of the group set off down the path leading to the village.

They are gone somewhat longer than the boy was and when they return they are accompanied by two carabinieri and a black-cassocked priest. As the priest stands over the body, his head bent and his lips moving in prayer, the elder of the two carabinieri – a permanently cynical looking brigadiere who appears to have seen more than his share of drowned corpses – pulls off the jacket and studies the face of the dead woman with professional calculation. 'Out in last night's storm probably,' he says to his colleague. 'Some of them just ask for trouble.'

More people start to arrive and crowd in on the tragedy, gawping, whispering, gloating. They are shooed to a respectful distance by the second carabiniere.

Then a single man appears and stands at the point where the path meets the beach, staring at the scene with a sort of horrified premonition. He is dark, southern looking with sharp, black eyes, capable of moonlight tenderness, and very white teeth. After a couple of seconds he starts to walk reluctantly, almost with dread, towards the body, his moccasins crunching the pebbles.

At his approach the brigadiere looks up sharply, ready to send him about his business, but then, apparently recognising him, his manner becomes unpleasantly oily. 'Dottor Peroni!' he says. 'I didn't know you were on the lake.' He stops short, struck by the southerner's expression as he looks down at the dead face. 'Did you know her?' he asks.

For a moment the man called Peroni does not reply. Then he shakes his head. 'No,' he says, 'no . . .'

'I thought for a moment . . .' says the brigadiere and then changes his mind. 'Funny that you of all people should turn up now,' he says instead. 'I mean just at the moment a body appears. But this isn't in your line, Dottore – just another accidental drowning. At this time of the year they're as common as road accidents round here.' He looks down again at the body. 'Foreigner by the looks of her,' he says. 'Daft lot they are.'

Commissario Achille Peroni would have been hard put to it to explain why he had lied about knowing Cordelia. He had nothing to fear in their all too innocent relationship being known and still less to gain in its being kept secret. The denial had been instinctive, probably due to a reluctance to uncover such a vulnerable spot under the indifferent gaze of a carabiniere who had recognised him by chance. Besides, he had been taken dangerously off balance.

He had slept badly, hag-ridden, it almost seemed, by premonition. Earlier, before even going to bed, he had heard the storm beginning to rumble out on the lake, but it was not a bad one and after what had happened three nights before it did not in itself alarm him. Nevertheless fear continued to assail him like an insistent nightmare. Finally, having got up early, he had set out to walk along the lake, his empty stomach lurching with the same sense of impending disaster. After some time – twenty minutes? Half an hour? – he came to a narrow path leading down to the lake and took it. Then emerging on to the beach he at once recognised not immediately the body, but the situation: the murmuring, unusually solemn crowd grouped about sudden death, the carabinieri with a messy, unpleasant job to do. And almost immediately his own heart and a glimpse of red hair told him the body was Cordelia's.

Had he sensed impending tragedy throughout their brief acquaintance? Common sense would say no, but common sense had never been a strong suit with the Neapolitan gutter urchin who all too often erupted within the rational commissario of police.

The series of events leading up to this morning had started when Peroni – now stationed in Venice – had been unexpectedly allotted ten days' leave in the sought-after month of July. This so took him aback that he was at a loss to know what to do with the time. Finally he had decided to accept an invitation from his sister, Assunta, and her husband, Giorgio, who were holidaying at the camping site near the village of Garda on the lake of the same name. The couple's adolescent children, Anna Maria and

Stefano, were there, too, but as they both preferred the nitty-gritty of camping life in tents with their friends, there was ample room in the caravan for Peroni.

He didn't like it. Caravans were too small for even the most rudimentary of life-styles. He disliked squatting on a tin lavatory made for midgets and trying to wash in a bathroom the size of a chess-board, but he disliked even more slopping blearily across to the public services and queuing up with his hearty, gibbering fellow campers. He also objected to eating out of doors, as Giorgio insisted on doing, on a camp stool that collapsed if you even looked at it and off a miniature table that wobbled however skilfully you adjusted the legs. And then he met Cordelia and decided that there were circumstances in which the discomforts of Purgatory would be negligible.

He had sneaked off to the village one morning five days before to steady his camping-shattered nerves with an early aperitif, leaving the children sweating profusely at tennis, Assunta cooking the lunch and Giorgio seated outside the front door, a handkerchief over his head and reading the local paper, as at peace with the world as the Israelite under his palm tree when, having taken a table outside one of the *caffé* in the village's miniature harbour, he had become aware of a head of enticing red hair bobbing up and down at knee level at the table next to him, and he realised that there was nothing to stop him practising the only sport that interested him, even at the lake.

'Can I help you?' he said in the atrociously accented English of which he was so proud, having noticed that there was a copy of *The Times* beside the fruit juice on her table.

'Yes,' she said, drawing herself up and blinking in his direction, 'you can help me look for a contact lens I've dropped.'

Peroni could say, or believed he could say, more or less anything he liked in English, but the trouble, he had to admit, arose when it came to understanding what the English said in reply to him. So now he had failed to understand a single word she had pronounced in answer to his offer of help. 'I beg your pardon?' he said.

'You can help me', she said, this time in flawless Italian, 'look for a contact lens I've dropped.'

'Ah, yes, of course,' said Peroni, resigning himself to Italian, too, but consoled that a relationship had been so easily struck up. He then crouched by her table, searching the ground for the

6

contact lens, at the same time taking the opportunity to examine her legs, of which, since she was wearing shorts, there was a delicious abundance, and they were of a grace to make a sculptor gasp with admiration. He forced himself to concentrate on the missing contact lens and then, having found it, took one last, avid look and, re-emerging, offered it to her in the palm of his hand.

'Thank you,' she said. 'Excuse me while I put it in.' This she did efficiently and quite unself-consciously, then went on, 'I'm quite blind without and too vain to wear spectacles except for work.'

'Work?'

'Well, studying.'

'You're a student?'

'That's right.'

With complete naturalness, neither brushing off nor beckoning on, she picked up *The Times* and engrossed herself in the crossword puzzle. Peroni, while she did it, studied her face. It was an interesting one, frank and open, with candid blue eyes and a light dusting of freckles beneath them. Her chin was delicately cleft and there was a clear hint of stubbornness in the set of her lips. She wore no make-up.

From her face he looked down to her right hand, which was moving with surprising rapidity over the puzzle, and, shifting to get a better view, he saw that she was in the process of finishing it. He watched as she filled in the last clues.

'Too easy,' she said, putting down the paper. Then her expression became suddenly business-like. She looked at the man's watch she was wearing, finished her fruit juice and stood up. 'I must be off.' She hitched on to her shoulder a light blue canvas hold-all she had with her.

'So soon?'

'I have an appointment.'

'Can I see you again?'

She looked at him for a second, the blue eyes thoughtful. 'Are you married?'

Peroni goggled at her; he wasn't accustomed to such reactions. He looked for an amusing comeback, failed to find it. 'No,' he said.

'Very well then.'

'Dinner this evening?' She thought briefly, then nodded.

'Which hotel are you staying at? I'll pick you up.'

She put down money for her drink. 'Don't worry. I'll be here at half past seven.'

And without further ceremony she turned and left. Peroni looked after her. In spite of her candour there was something about her he couldn't define. It perplexed him.

CHAPTER 2

'I recommend the risotto. It's made with tench following a recipe that's been in the family for over a century.'

'Risotto then, with pleasure.'

She had turned up at the harbour with what Peroni considered to be unfeminine punctuality wearing, to his slight surprise and considerable pleasure, a long dress of the darkest of blues which dramatically highlighted her tumbling cascade of red hair. There was also a suppressed exhilaration in her manner which he had realised with irritation was not due to him. 'How did your appointment go?' he asked, aiming at what seemed the probable cause.

'Fine,' she said and then deftly and politely changed the subject.

Peroni was illogically jealous that she should be holding something back from him, but he had suppressed the feeling as best he could and driven her to the nearby village of Lazise where, in another miniature harbour, they sat at a restaurant table by the water's edge.

'You're on holiday?'

'That's right.'

'With your family?'

'No.' She looked mildly surprised at the question. 'Alone.'

'Oh . . .' Peroni was taken aback.

'You're shocked.' She sounded mildly amused. 'You don't approve of a woman roving the world on her own.'

'No, no, no!' Peroni was alarmed at the accuracy with which she had hooked his thought. 'I was just a bit surprised – I mean why here in particular?'

He had the distinct impression of unexpectedly rounding a corner and realising that something has been whisked away only just in time to prevent him seeing it. His curiosity pressure went up several degrees.

'Why ever *not* here?' she said. 'It's a famous holiday resort, the climate's perfect, the views are stupendous and the lake is ideal for yachting. So what's surprising about it?'

'Nothing,' said Peroni, more than ever convinced that she was holding something back. 'Let me pour you some wine.'

She let him and they drank it in silence, watching a shoal of baby fish swarming, apparently aimlessly, in the water below them. Then the risotto came.

'Where are you at university?' asked Peroni as they ate.

'Oxford. And there's no need to look so impressed.'

'What are you doing there?'

'History.'

'I thought it would be languages. Your Italian is perfect.'

'Thanks for the compliment. Languages are a family thing: we don't consider them as work, but fun.'

Peroni raised his eyebrows, wishing he could say the same thing about his English. 'How many do you speak?'

'Oh, French, German, Spanish, the usual, plus Greek and Russian. And I'm learning Hebrew. I'm sorry – that sounds like showing off, but I can only repeat that I was brought up to consider languages as a game. But look here, we're falling into much too conventional a male–female pattern with the some-what older, but very good looking man asking all the questions and the flattered, fluttering female pouring out the answers. Let's break it up a bit. What do *you* do for a living?'

For some reason Peroni felt reluctant to tell her he was a policeman. 'I work for the Ministry of Home Affairs,' he said, dodging the question neatly and truthfully.

'You don't look like a civil servant.'

'I don't feel like one.'

'And you're on holiday, too?'

'Yes.'

'Alone?'

'No, I'm staying with my sister's family.'

'Uhum. Well, now we've got the unimportant facts out of the way, maybe we can start getting to know each other. You're right – this risotto is delicious.'

Peroni felt oddly disconcerted. He was not accustomed to women like this. She was alarmingly clear-sighted and she kept on saying things he didn't know how to react to. The fact that she was evidently a feminist threw him off balance, too. He didn't like feminists. But he did like her.

He liked her more and more as the evening went on. He liked the way she laughed and the way she made him laugh. He liked the way she ate and drank (amazing how many women had put him off by fussy eating or silly drinking). He liked the way she treated him as an equal and he found himself growing to like the off-beat things she said, even when they cut the conversational ground from beneath his feet.

The evening passed too quickly. When he had taken her back to Garda, he said as he had done before, 'Can I see you again?' and she, as on the earlier occasion, looked at him for a moment speculatively.

'I don't see why not,' she said finally, 'provided that one thing is clear.' Peroni waited for it with some apprehension. 'I'm not promiscuous and I don't intend to go to bed with you as the rather trite phrase has it. If you accept that condition I should like to see you again very much.'

The lecherous *scugnizzo* within staggered from the blow, but Peroni did his best to put a good face on it. 'I accept,' he said. In the darkness she could not see that the index and middle fingers of both his hands were crossed.

'Fine. I'm going sailing tomorrow morning. Can you sail?'

'Well, yes and no.' Peroni didn't like admitting that he couldn't do things.

'I'll teach you if you like.'

'Yes, I would like.'

'Seven o'clock here then. All right?'

That meant a six thirty a.m. rise. Quite out of the question. 'All right,' said Peroni.

'See you then.' She gave him her hand, a firm, cool grip, then turned and was gone before he had time to suggest taking her home.

Peroni floated back to the camping site on a high cloud of sheer euphoria, fell into a sweet, dream-sprinkled sleep and was up the next morning with the effortless high spirits of a young bird in time to meet Cordelia at the harbour where they walked out on to the jetty under a bright, already hot sun. Towards the further end she stopped in front of a cheeky, adventurous looking little two-sailed craft.

'Meet the *Spaghetti Western*,' she said. 'Not my choice of name. She already had it when I inherited her from a friend of mine who was out here last year. She's very high-spirited, but she responds perfectly to the right handling. In you get.'

And in, a little gingerly, Peroni got; the *Spaghetti Western* scarcely looked robust enough for the two of them. Cordelia cast off and boarded in a graceful flow of movement.

For Peroni the next couple of hours were a generous mixture of Paradise and Purgatory. The Paradise was Cordelia's presence and the constant, inevitable physical contact with her necessitated by the handling of such a small craft. The Purgatory was provided by the sheer, gruelling effort she imposed on him. She was a good teacher, but a ruthless perfectionist, and she harried, admonished and abused him uninterruptedly. When they sailed back into the harbour, Peroni was limp, sweating and aching all over, but he already felt he could handle a yacht.

'I'll make a yachtsman of you yet,' she said. 'And now,' looking at her watch and hoicking her light blue hold-all out of the *Spaghetti Western*, 'I must go.'

Disconcertingly she had switched him off and was concentrating on whatever mysterious business she was about at the lake. He wanted to question her, but instinct told him this wouldn't be well received. So he asked instead when they could meet again.

'I expect to be busy for the next couple of days,' she said, 'but I should be free towards evening tomorrow. I'll meet you at the bar here – say, eightish – and we can have a drink and another lesson.'

Peroni had to be content with that.

'The body of a woman was washed up on the shores of Lake Garda earlier today. She was identified as a twenty-one-year-old Englishwoman, Cordelia Hope, who was spending a holiday at the village of Garda.'

Peroni sat numbly listening to the tinny sounding transistor radio behind the bar, thankful only that he was alone.

'Carabinieri have ascertained that she took her yacht out on the lake some time last night, as had been her custom to do most nights. A sudden storm took her by surprise and, being an inexperienced yachtswoman, she was swept from the deck of the craft into the water and drowned. The woman was the lake's third victim this season . . .'

It was impossible. Peroni had reason to know it was impossible.

At eight o'clock sharp on the evening after his first lesson he arrived at the harbour bar, but there was no Cordelia. Half an hour and two Chivas Regals later she still had not come. He ordered a third and reflected on what to do. He was not accustomed to waiting for women; it was they who waited for him. His southern male vanity was badly pricked. Honour demanded withdrawal. There were more fish in the lake.

Quarter to nine and still he lingered. If and when she chooses to turn up, he told himself, let her seethe in her own disappointment. If she finds you meekly waiting after nearly an hour she'll know she's got the upper hand and she'll never let you forget it. Let her writhe.

At nine o'clock he was ruefully admitting into a fourth Chivas Regal that she was not the type to writhe. Far too self-possessed. And in that case, he admonished himself, you're better without. Go and pick up some willing Scandinavian trollop slavering for a Latin lover and forget Cordelia.

She came at ten past nine. 'I'm very sorry to have kept you waiting,' she said, 'but something cropped up. You shouldn't have waited.'

'Oh, that's perfectly all right,' said Peroni hypocritically. 'I didn't mind in the least.' She was looking unusually dejected. 'Is something the matter?'

'No, no – I'm probably just hungry. Let's have a pizza. My turn to pay. Then we'll go for a sail.'

'Won't it be a bit late?'

'Nonsense. Sailing by night is best of all.'

It was nearly eleven and already dark when they glided out of the little harbour with the *Spaghetti Western*. Peroni felt a little nervous, but the weather was perfect and the lake as smooth as a mill pond and, he wondered, who could say what changes a night trip on this velvety water might not bring about in her stubborn and so far quite inflexible insistence on chastity?

'You take over,' she said.

Peroni obeyed. Fortunately there wasn't a great deal to do

and, still wrapped in her unexplained dejection, she chivvied him less about his blunders. Then suddenly she seemed to snap herself out of it and began talking. It was frothy, but brilliant, talk and ranged from politics (she dissected the Italian political corps with feather-light incisions) to food (she conjured up a meal of Oriental extravagance which she promised to prepare for Peroni one day) to books (there seemed to be nothing she hadn't read) and the differences between England and Italy ('It's like a sort of eternal battle between the sexes with the difference that you can never be sure at any one time which particular sex either of the countries belongs to').

'Do you know,' said Peroni when there was a brief pause in the conversation, 'I haven't the slightest idea where we are. I mean, apart from the fact that we're on the lake.'

'I have.'

'You would,' said Peroni and she grinned at him in the darkness. 'Where?'

'The lights over there are Sirmione and that's Desenzano.' Then she sighed with sudden feminine rapture as though she were looking into a particularly tempting shop window. 'Isn't it beautiful?'

It was. A spectacle by day, the southern shore of the lake was a fairyland by night. Peroni viewed it with pleasure as they glided over the water.

'Look at that villa,' he said, 'that one standing in its own park. I could live there. I wonder who owns it.'

'I know that, too. Hang on a minute – we'd better catch that wind. Let me take over a minute.' He did so and watched the flow of her body with delight as she moved about to swing them into a fresh wind and away from the shore. 'Yes, that villa,' she went on when she was satisfied with the change of direction, 'it's one of those ultra-expensive geriatric clinics – the sort where the nurses all glide instead of walking and have built-in smiles and the guests are treated as reverently as though they were priceless pieces of porcelain. If I were that old I think I should almost prefer the knockabout down-to-earthness of an old fashioned workhouse. I mean, at least it's real life.'

'I'm not sure I don't agree with you. But how do you come to know your way about the lake so well?'

'I haven't been wasting my time this last week.'

They were dangerously near the subject of her mysterious

activities on the lake and Peroni wondered whether, in the intimacy of the lake by night, she might not be a bit more amenable to enquiries. He decided to risk it.

'What is it you do when you go off by yourself?' he asked and then, as she opened her mouth to say something, he went on adroitly, 'All right, you don't have to tell me if you don't want to. But mightn't it be good to have someone to discuss it with – whatever it is? I might even be of help – assuming you want help. After all, it can't be anything illegal.'

Again she grinned at him in the night. 'Who says it isn't?'

Peroni was almost as taken aback as if she'd used an obscenity. 'Now I've gone and shocked you again,' she went on. 'You are so easily shockable. That's what comes of being a man and a southerner as well. Why shouldn't I be involved in something illegal? Because I'm a well brought up young lady and an undergraduate of Oxford University to boot?' She had divined Peroni's thought so exactly that he could do nothing but goggle at her in the darkness. 'Let me tell you,' she went on, 'that outside the rose-tinged fantasy of masculine imagination there are few limits to what seemingly respectable female undergraduates may not get up to.' She paused, brooding. 'Though in fact,' she said at length, 'I'm not quite sure about the ethics of it myself. Legally wrong, morally OK might just about sum it up.'

'But what is it?' said Peroni, exasperated.

'An adventure.' She broke off and when she spoke again there was an echo in her voice that sounded shockingly like despair. 'An adventure that seems to have taken a wrong turning. Or got lost altogether.'

'What sort of adventure?'

She hesitated, obviously uncertain as to whether to take the irrevocable step of confiding in him, hovering on the brink. Then suddenly something else caught her attention. He was aware of it, but couldn't identify it.

She moved quickly to adjust the foresail and it seemed to him as though presences, too far off for more specific identification, were moving towards them across the water and singing with high voices as they came.

'What is it?' he said.

'Dirty weather.'

Then he realised that the presences were clouds racing

towards them at terrifying speed and the voices were their carrying winds.

'Just hang on tight,' said Cordelia, 'and don't panic.'

The first part of her instructions he obeyed fervently, but the speed with which the clouds were massing towards them and the howling of the wind's crescendo made the second part impossible.

The water below and around heaved and swelled furiously, dashing over the bows and hull so that Peroni was soon wet through. Clouds, distance or both had cut off any reassuring glimpse of shore so that they were quite alone with the teeming, murderous monster the lake had so rapidly become.

It played with the *Spaghetti Western* like a giant feline, throwing her up in the air, catching her, spinning her round, flicking her to and fro.

As tight as Peroni was able to cling on, the force of the onrushing waves that engulfed him was so great that he expected from one wave to the next to be swept into the lake. And in spite of his terror at the prospect, he couldn't help marvelling that Cordelia, who didn't seem to be holding on at all, remained in the yacht. She was everywhere at the same time, effortlessly adjusting her body to the furious pitching and tossing, apparently unaware of Peroni's presence, entirely absorbed in her single-handed battle with the lake.

The darkness was terrifying, but Peroni soon realised that even that had its advantages when a violent and prolonged streak of lightning, simultaneous with a doomsday peal of thunder, lit up the surrounding scene, confirming his worst fears. The waves were even more mountainous than he had imagined.

Somewhere in his mind an idiot voice kept piping something he had once heard somewhere and unwisely forgotten. 'Lake storms can blow up in no time at all and they're really terrible. Even the most experienced fishermen are terrified of them.'

A particularly gigantic wave smashed into them making the *Spaghetti Western* buck, shuddering, and tilt right over so that for an instant Peroni seemed to be looking down on the raging water. She had capsized.

'St Januarius!' Peroni screamed inwardly, invoking the patron saint of Naples, a medalet of whom he always wore round his neck. 'Get us out of this and I'll have the biggest candle in the world lit for you in Naples Cathedral!'

Whether St Januarius found this offer irresistible or whether Cordelia's yachting skill managed to achieve the impossible there was no telling, but somehow the *Spaghetti Western* righted herself and, a short while after, slipped out of the ferocious eye of the storm which immediately proceeded to forget all about them and rampaged off in search of other prey.

It was raining and the waves were still fairly high, but death no longer roared in Peroni's ears and the lights of the shore twinkled consolingly.

'Well, that was fun, wasn't it?' Cordelia had the nerve to say. 'But we'd better make for harbour just the same. We don't want to run the risk of a return performance, do we?'

Perhaps the storm had made Cordelia change her mind about sharing her secret with Peroni, but she didn't raise the subject and he was too shaken to insist. They sailed into Garda harbour, tied up and said goodnight with a handshake.

CHAPTER 3

'Buon giorno, Dottore,' said the cynical looking brigadiere, receiving Peroni with phony, overplayed deference. 'Take a seat. What can I do for you?'

'The girl on the beach this morning—'

'Ah yes, the young Englishwoman who was drowned in the storm . . .'

The brigadiere's eyes were fishy and indifferent and he was obviously making mental calculations about the motive for the visit. Peroni looked at him wearily. It had been all too evident from the radio announcement that Cordelia's death was considered accidental. But someone who had handled a yacht with such consummate skill only three nights previously could not have been just swept overboard in what had been a far less violent storm. Peroni had immediately decided that the carabinieri must be disabused of the accidental death theory. But already he was beginning to suspect that this was not going to be so easy.

' . . . wouldn't believe it,' the brigadiere was going on, 'but they do it the whole time, these foreigners. If they don't drown themselves swimming after a six course meal, they go and fall off their boats. Doesn't anyone teach them anything where they come from?'

'But she didn't fall off her boat.'

'What?' The wily, unintelligent eyes narrowed.

'She didn't fall off.'

'How do you know?'

Peroni realised that he couldn't answer the question without admitting that he had lied on their previous encounter, which was, to say the least, a humiliation. But it was a necessary humiliation if he were to convince the brigadiere.

'I told you I didn't know her,' he said. 'I was upset at coming upon her like that unexpectedly and the denial was spontaneous. But I did know her. I was with her during a storm on the lake only three nights ago. She handled the boat perfectly.'

'I see. You realise, of course, Dottore, that if it was anybody but you I should have to charge you with giving false information to the authorities?'

'Yes, of course, I—'

'I suppose you struck up a holiday friendship with her?'

'You could put it like that—'

'I see.' Peroni knew exactly what the man thought he could see and the image of Cordelia in his mind made the routine lubricity of it unbearably repulsive.

'You don't see,' he said, 'but never mind that. What I'm trying to tell you is that it's impossible she was accidentally drowned.'

'Just because she *wasn't* accidentally drowned a few nights before? It doesn't really make much sense, Dottore, does it? And even assuming you're right, what alternative does it leave us with? That she let herself go into the water? Is that what you're suggesting?'

Suicide? The idea had never occurred to Peroni. He remembered the echo in her voice just before the storm when she had spoken of 'an adventure that seems to have taken a wrong turning'. She was capable of despair, he thought. But then he remembered the next day . . .

'Ready for the high seas?'

'As a matter of fact, I thought—'

'Cold feet, eh? And all on account of a mini-blow like last night. Oh no, my boy – it's like falling off a horse, the only thing to do is get straight back on again.'

There was a barely contained exhilaration about her and Peroni decided to risk an enquiry. 'Has your adventure got found again?'

'Maybe. I have hopes. In you get.'

Apparently she was not to be drawn. With a brief, wary glance at the horizon Peroni got in. The weather, he was relieved to observe, was as near to perfect as it could get.

'You take her out of the harbour. Then we'll go out a bit and follow the coast line towards Malcesine. If you're good I'll buy you an ice-cream when we get there.'

'Aye aye, Admiral.'

They sailed for a while in silence except for brief instructions from Cordelia.

The July afternoon was perfect and they both exulted silently in it, content to follow their separate trains of thought.

'Why don't you want to tell me?' said Peroni at length.

She studied the question. 'For various reasons,' she said after a moment. 'For one thing I'm possessive about it. For another, if there *was* anything really illegal involved I wouldn't want to get you mixed up in it. And for a third – well, I'm sort of superstitious. I'm afraid that if I told you it might sort of wither up and die on me.'

'Will you ever tell me?'

She looked at him in a new way which was a mixture of appraisal and amusement and something else which he couldn't define, but which he liked. 'One day perhaps, when it's all over. One way or the other.'

'You're very independent.'

'I need to be.'

She was squatting close to him and her very clear blue eyes were looking straight into his with what he took to be a challenge. He responded. For a long while their mouths did no more than touch gently. Then Peroni drew her closer to him. She made an effort to pull away, then relaxed and a glowing animation began to instil the kiss.

Eventually she withdrew her mouth from his and touched his cheek with the fingertips of her right hand. 'I liked that,' she said, 'very much. But I don't want it. There is a difference you know.

18

Like I said, I need to be independent. Besides,' she went on, suddenly smiling and standing up, 'you're meant to be concentrating on your sailing. Our ice-cream is thataway.'

And that was all for that day.

'Suicide?' said Peroni. 'No.'

'Murder then?' The word seemed to jump from the brigadiere's mouth like a toad.

'It's possible.'

'What grounds have you got for saying that?'

Just in time Peroni recognised the danger. What grounds had he got? The knowledge that Cordelia had been engaged on some unspecified business about the lake? The brigadiere would make short work of that. Somebody altogether higher up was required.

'No grounds,' he said, trying to look humble.

'You see?' said the brigadiere with the expression of an older man whose head was screwed on properly. 'Of course it's quite understandable you should react like that – any man would who's been shacking up with a girl and suddenly found her dead like that. Only human. So we'll call it quits, eh, Dottore? You forget about murder and I'll forget about false information.' He held out his hand and Peroni reluctantly took it.

There came a knock at the door and, on the brigadiere calling out 'Avanti', it opened to admit a ruddy, fiftyish, vigorous looking man with a sunburnt pate and abundant, fluffy duck's wings of white hair over his ears. He was elegantly dressed, but had a home-made look about him which suggested that he would have been more comfortable tramping about the country with a gun and wearing wellingtons, corduroys and a baggy old jacket. At the sight of this character the brigadiere shot up out of his chair to attention like a rocket and saluted.

'Buon giorno, Signor Sindaco!' he said. The mayor, thought Peroni, that explained the deference.

'Sit down, Brigadiere, sit down – you'll break the cobwebs if you jump about like that.' He spoke in heavy dialect – an affectation of the upper classes in the Veneto – and the brigadiere sat down, cracking his mouth into a dutiful smile at the little quip. 'You'll forgive me interrupting your busy social life,' the mayor went on, nodding genially at Peroni, 'but I've had a request for information from the British Consulate in Venice concerning a poor young woman who was drowned during the night and as I was passing by I thought I'd call in and save you from overdoing yourself with a visit to the town hall.'

'Very good of you, Signor Sindaco. I've got the file in front of me now if you'd care to look at it.' He gave Peroni a quick foxy look. 'This is Dottor Peroni of the *Pubblica Sicurezza*,' he went on. 'He called in to see me about the woman, too.'

Peroni caught the note of warning and decided docility would be politic.

'I just happened to meet her a few days ago,' he said, 'and I wondered if there was anything I could do.'

'Peroni, Peroni, Peroni,' said the mayor, ignoring this and looking at him over half-moon spectacles which he had perched on a large, mottled nose, 'I've heard that name somewhere. Got it! The Rudolph Valentino of the Italian police! The copper who does his sleuthing over the bodies of beautiful women and swings from rooftop to rooftop like Tarzan. That's more or less the form, isn't it?'

Peroni smiled politely and nodded. He had once been vain as a peacock of the Valentino epithet, but now that he could no longer get rid of it he loathed it heartily.

'Bombarone,' said the mayor, thrusting out his hand, and as he took it Peroni remembered that he had often heard that name when he had been stationed in Verona. Bombarone was a prominent local Christian Democrat with his fingers always in half a dozen political pies at a time. He was a fixer, a kingmaker, an *éminence grise*. And this realisation awakened an ambition that had been prowling about in Peroni's fertile mind over recent months and had only been temporarily lulled by the meeting with Cordelia. Maybe Bombarone was just the man he needed. And then the thought of Cordelia made him feel guilty at this primping of personal ambition. But maybe Bombarone was just the man he needed for her as well. Maybe Bombarone could be helpful in more ways than one.

'Why don't you come along to my office and we'll open a bottle of wine,' the mayor went on, playing in nicely with Peroni's project. 'Not often that we get a famous figure like yourself round here. Where is it you're stationed now – Milan, isn't it?'

'Venice.'

'That's right – Venice, Venice . . .' Tunelessly he started to sing 'La Biondina in Gondoleta' and then broke off after a couple of lines to say, 'Yes, well . . . If you'll excuse me while I take a few notes for the British Consulate we'll be off.' Then having taken his notes he put his arm round Peroni's shoulders and started to steer him towards the door. 'Come along, come along,' he said, 'we'll leave the good brigadiere to resume his interrupted slumbers and go and open a bottle of genuine Bardolino – none of your supermarket muck, but pure wine from real grapes. Off we go then.' The brigadiere stood to attention again and the mayor waved at him genially as they went through the door.

A Land-rover was waiting for them outside. 'Excuse the transport,' said the mayor as they climbed in, 'but I have more than my share of sleek limousines when I have to go down to Rome.'

The drive to Garda town hall was brief. As they got out of the Land-rover and made their way into the building Bombarone waved, patted shoulders, squeezed hands and joked all the way.

'Sit yourself down,' he said when they got to his large, first-floor office. 'I shan't be a minute.' He then went out and returned a minute or so later with a dusty, unlabelled bottle, a corkscrew and two glasses. Having unceremoniously pushed aside a mass of official looking documents on his desk – 'Bumf, bumf, bumf!' – he deposited the glasses and set to opening the bottle.

'Well, what do you say to that?' he went on when Peroni had tasted the wine.

'Excellent indeed,' said Peroni. 'There isn't even a touch of preservative chemical in it.'

'Now there's a palate for you,' said the mayor, slapping his leg in appreciation. 'Not more than one person in ten thousand could tell that. No wonder you're a detective! And I'll give you a tip if you keep it under your hat. If you'd care to get hold of some of this, go and see General del Duca in Bardolino. He makes it and he'll let you have a case or two if you tell him I sent you. A remarkable old man, General del Duca.'

The telephone on Bombarone's desk rang and, waving to Peroni to help himself to more wine, he picked up the receiver. Peroni followed the conversation at first idly, then with increasing attention, and fitting together the content with the Christian name Bombarone was using he had no difficulty in deducing the surname. It made him gasp inwardly. The mayor was high in the nation's councils indeed. The restlessly pacing ambition in Peroni roared for satisfaction. But how to approach the subject?

'Friends in low places,' said Bombarone deprecatingly when he finally put the receiver down.

'I've been thinking lately,' said Peroni, having decided that a direct approach was best, 'of standing for Parliament.'

'Well, well, well!' said Bombarone, giving him a shrewd, amused glance as he refilled their glasses. 'Have you indeed? The Rudolph Valentino of the Chamber of Deputies, eh? Mark you, it's a dog's life.'

'Do you think I might stand a chance?'

'Why not? Why not? What sort of party were you thinking of representing?'

'The *Democrazia Cristiana*, of course,' said Peroni, mildly shocked.

'There's no of course about it. We might have slotted you in very nicely with the Communists or the Fascists. Still, all things considered, the DC is probably the best choice. An interesting idea. Leave it with me for a few days, will you, and I'll come back to you.'

Once again the telephone rang and Bombarone with an air of mock martyrdom picked up the receiver. '*Pronto, pronto*. Ah Signora, *buon giorno*. I was just about to ring you back.' He cupped his hand over the receiver and mouthed to Peroni, 'British Consulate in Venice – about the girl who was drowned. Yes,' he went on, 'I have the details in front of me now. Swept overboard in a storm last night, poor girl. Yes, terrible, terrible. Oh yes, quite accidental, no question about that. She arrived here on the third of July and was staying in a hired room at Via Mazzini three . . .'

Peroni made a mental note of the address. The rest of the details were meagre and he learned nothing new except that Cordelia's body was to be flown back to England when the formalities had been concluded.

'There we are,' said Bombarone as he put the phone down. 'Tragic waste. Young life. Sad, sad. Let me fill your glass. You said you knew her?'

'I met her four days ago.'

'It must be a sad blow for you. If only these inexperienced

22

young people would realise that the lake can be treacherous.'

'She wasn't inexperienced.'

Peroni's tone made the mayor look at him sharply. 'No?' Then he relaxed. 'Though of course accidents can always happen – even to the most experienced yachtsmen.'

'I'm not entirely convinced it was an accident.'

'You're not?' Worry escalated into alarm. 'Surely you're not suggesting . . .' he looked about as though to make sure nobody was listening '. . . murder?'

As toad-like as before the word jumped into the silence. Was that, Peroni wondered, what he was really suggesting? He remembered the last day and that curious impression . . .

It was a strange chess-board of a day with the squares hidden until you moved on to them so that you never knew whether the next hop would take you to black or white. It was nearly two o'clock when they met and before she even opened her mouth he recognised that her mood was unusual. She was by turns exhilarated and depressed, switching from one to the other practically in mid-sentence. Had she reached a conclusion, achieved some sort of goal? And if so, of what possible nature that it should produce such conflicting emotions? Delicately but firmly she avoided all his questions.

They lunched late under the trees by the lake and Cordelia drank more wine than he had ever seen her do, for she was naturally abstemious, and when he mentioned it she just said, 'Maybe I have cause to celebrate. Or maybe I have sorrow to drown. Maybe both.'

It was while they were having coffee that Peroni first had the impression that they were being watched. He looked round, but could see nobody taking particular interest in them, though this was hardly surprising as the village was swarming with holiday-makers. He mentioned it to her, but she made light of it. 'Anything that's female and foreign in Italy gets stared at all the time.'

They lingered over lunch, then went on to the beach where Cordelia said, 'If you'll excuse me for a while,' and then before Peroni had time to work out what she meant promptly fell sound asleep. She slept like a child, breathing softly and regularly and he watched her as she did so, marvelling at the glow of her complexion and the cascade of red hair, wondering at the same time what strange contradictions were lodged in her mind.

Again he had the sensation of being watched and this time he actually made a brief patrol of inspection, but with no more results than before.

She awoke with the same dappled mood of sorrow and joy and they walked for a long while by the lake, stopping eventually for a pizza. When they finally left the pizzeria it was dark and already late.

'I'm going sailing,' said Cordelia.

'I'll come with you.'

'No . . .' She put a hand on his chest. 'Not tonight. I want to be by myself – me and the lake and the *Spaghetti Western*. Do you mind very much?'

'Yes, but I'll have to put up with it.'

'Thanks.'

'Tomorrow?' said Peroni as they walked to the yacht.

'No.' Her voice in the darkness went suddenly tense. 'I'm leaving tomorrow. It's better if we say goodbye now.'

'Leaving?' The announcement was like a physical blow. 'Just like that?'

'All holidays have to finish,' she said getting into the boat. 'But listen – whatever happens don't you dare waste our lessons. I'm docking the *Spaghetti Western* here, so take her out whenever you can. She'll appreciate it.'

'Without you—'

'You must go on sailing.'

'But shan't I ever see you again?'

'Stop being so melancholically Latin. *Chi non muore si rivede* as the proverb has it: whoever doesn't die will meet again.'

'But when?' Already she was casting off.

'Who knows? Maybe sooner than you expect.'

'But I shall be leaving myself in a few days—'

'Just like a man – all this fuss because a woman takes the initiative.' The *Spaghetti Western* started to move away from the jetty. 'Don't worry,' she called to him, 'I'll find you – wherever you are. And I'll come and see you.'

The *Spaghetti Western* sailed out of the harbour mouth into the night.

'No,' said Peroni slowly, 'I'm not suggesting anything.'

24

The toad was still there even if Bombarone couldn't see it, but now Peroni had decided that he would have to find out for himself who had spawned it. The facts at his disposal – if you could describe anything so tenuous as facts – were no more sufficient to convince the mayor that Cordelia's death had not been accidental than they had been to convince the brigadiere.

Bombarone poured the last of the bottle into Peroni's glass. 'Well, I won't try to hide from you that I'm relieved,' he said. 'You had me worried. I mean if a visitor was murdered here it would be very bad for our tourist business.'

For an instant Peroni thought this was another of his jokes, but a glance told him that for once the mayor was entirely serious.

CHAPTER 4

The house in which Cordelia had lodged turned out to be something of a surprise. You reached it via a courtyard and a flight of outside steps, and when Peroni had rung the doorbell and been admitted by a wrinkled old woman dressed all in black he found himself in a little world quite remote from the Garda of boutiques, discos and fancy bars, perhaps the only corner of the village left untouched. And that, he reflected, was probably why she had chosen it. The place was dark and chilly, despite the July heat outside, with stone floors, sparse, elementary furniture, ancient photographs and holy pictures.

He introduced himself as a friend of the signorina *inglese*, which caused a lot of commiserative clucking, and asked if he might look through her things. The old woman said she would make him a cup of coffee while he was doing this and showed him into Cordelia's room.

A small, spartan room with a window looking away from the lake towards the hills, the green of which was smothered by tourist development. There was a cupboard with her clothes, and grief clawed at Peroni when he saw the dark blue dress she had worn for their first supper together. He had to detach his mind forcibly from the links with her alive (toothbrush, comb that

25

combed the red hair, mirror that reflected those candid blue eyes) as he went over the rest of the contents. But he found nothing to indicate what her business at the lake had been.

He went to the kitchen where the coffee was grumbling furiously in the espresso machine.

'She told me in a letter,' he lied glibly from long experience, 'that she was searching for something here at the lake, but she didn't say what, so as I'm trying to clear up her affairs a bit I wondered if you had any idea of what it might be?'

'She said she was writing a book.' The old lady said this with reverent incomprehension.

A book? Peroni sipped the coffee she had poured for him. 'Did she say what it was about?'

'Oh no.' Her expression said clearly that she would never have understood it even if Cordelia had done.

'I suppose she was out a great deal?'

'She mostly only came here to sleep.'

'Have you any idea where she went?'

'She didn't tell me and I didn't ask her. She was a pleasant young lady and she paid her rent without any fuss. That was all that concerned me.'

'Did she have any friends, acquaintances on the lake?'

'If she had, she didn't bring them here.'

'Delicious coffee.' Peroni gave her a sunny Neapolitan smile.

'Splendid,' she said and it took him a second to realise that she was supplying him with the brand-name of the coffee. 'Except for the first day.'

'I beg your pardon?'

'Except for the first day. I know where she went the first day because she asked me the way.'

'And where was that?'

'San Vigilio.'

San Vigilio is a small peninsula jutting out into the water on the Verona side of the lake. You leave the main road and walk down a path until you reach gates leading into the grounds of a magnificent private villa. At this point, if you are not a guest, you can fork off right down to the public beach or left, down some steps, to a miniature harbour complete with bar and hotel. Peroni decided to start his enquiries here, so he went into the bar and ordered himself a Campari soda.

26

He was served by a superior looking gentleman with cavalry twill trousers, a blazer and what looked like an English public-school tie.

'I wonder if you can help me,' said Peroni pleasantly.

'If I can, sir.' From the tone it sounded as though he thought it highly doubtful, and the 'sir' at the end was like a suspicious looking fairy at the top of a swish Christmas tree.

'A friend of mine, an English girl who was drowned in the lake last night – maybe you heard about it? – well, apparently she was engaged in some form of research here and her family have asked me to find out all I can about the progress she had made as they are anxious to have it continued in her memory if possible.' His mind on the improvisation, he was not consciously aware that he was transforming himself into the sort of international, wealthy aristocrat who would be perfectly at home in these surroundings, and he was surprised to observe that he was being listened to with respectful attention. 'I understand that she called here immediately after her arrival,' he continued, 'and I wondered whether the visit had any connection with her research. She was in her twenties, very attractive, with golden-red hair.'

'Yes sir, I remember the young lady. I spoke to her myself.' Peroni was surprised by the cordiality, then became aware of the act he had slipped into and hitched up his jet-set trousers. 'But I was unable to give her any information myself for her book about Vivien Leigh.'

About whom? Vivien Leigh? Wasn't that *Gone with the Wind*? Peroni remembered clearly how her beauty had enflamed his adolescent urges after he had made his way illicitly into a Neapolitan fleapit cinema through the emergency exit. That was one thing. But Vivien Leigh as the motive for Cordelia's mysterious comings and goings on the lake was quite another. Confucius could hardly have been less likely.

'The hotel at the time was owned by an Englishman by the name of Walsh,' the gentleman was going on, 'but he has been dead for some years now. So the best I could do was refer the young lady to the only person who was employed here at the time Signorina Leigh was a guest. She then thanked me warmly and left.'

'Who was it you referred her to?'

'A girl who was working here as a maid at the time and now

runs a bar in Garda called the Capri. She is known as Signorina Alice.'

Peroni also thanked the gentleman warmly, paid for the Campari and walked back up to his car.

The Capri huddled sulkily in one of the back-streets of Garda as though it knew its name made it about eight hundred kilometres geographically displaced. Receiving none of the lake breeze, it was hot and airless, which probably explained why it was also deserted except for one of the village's chorus of mock fishermen in an alcoholic stupor over a carafe of wine, and an enormous lady, all pouches and folds and mounds, who was bulging out of the cash-desk like a gluttonous Jill-in-a-box.

'I should like to speak to Signorina Alice,' said Peroni going up to her.

Quick, cunning little eyes looked at him from within their pouches of flesh. 'I am Signorina Alice,' she said.

Peroni was taken aback. The man at San Vigilio had said a girl. Then he realised that enough time had passed to allow a girl to grow into the mountainous female before him. He told her his business.

'Well, as to that,' said Alice, 'I haven't got time to waste talking to strangers. It's the height of the season and I'm run off my feet.'

The near deserted bar made her real meaning all too apparent and Peroni got out a couple of ten thousand lire notes which she eyed suspiciously before clipping them into the till. 'The young woman did come here,' she said, 'and she did ask me about Vivien Leigh.'

'What did you tell her?'

'Oh, what she did when she was at the hotel.' She said this with an unpleasantly knowing air.

'And what was that?'

She told him. As scandal magazine gossip went, it was spicy enough, but hardly sufficient to occupy the mind and energy of a girl like Cordelia. More than ever Peroni felt there was something out of place. 'Did she ask you anything else?'

The little eyes flicked to the pocket where he kept his wallet. 'She might have done.' Stifling a sigh, Peroni got out another twenty thousand, wondering how much bulgy Alice had got out of Cordelia. 'She asked me about other famous people who

28

stayed at the hotel while I was there,' she said when the notes had been safely clipped in on top of their predecessors.

'For example?'

'Oh, all sorts,' she said with a cunning look. 'The hotel was famous and Mr Walsh could pick and choose his guests.'

'Anyone in particular?'

A sly smile stirred beneath the pouches of her mouth. 'Well,' she said, 'for example there was Winston Churchill.'

Peroni's mind snapped taut. Churchill, he knew, had stayed at the lake some time after the war. Ostensibly for a painting holiday, but there had been rumours about some sort of search. Whatever the truth of it, this at last was something worthy of Cordelia's attention. And something she might have been murdered for as well.

'She asked you about him?'

'If you ask me, it was him she was really interested in.'

That made sense, too. If Cordelia had been on to something really important, the Vivien Leigh story would have been no more than a smoke-screen. 'What did she ask you?'

'What he did, where he went, the people he met. But there wasn't much I could tell her. They kept everything about him very quiet. We knew he was on holiday and he went out painting practically every day. That was all.'

But something in her tone suggested there was more. 'Are you sure?'

'Well,' said Alice after a brief display of hesitation, 'there was just one thing.'

'Yes?'

'I used to help carry his paints and easels and things out to the car and one morning I happened to hear the man who was always with him – an Englishman, a sort of policeman, but he spoke very good Italian – I heard him telling the driver where to go.'

'Where?'

This time she looked quite steadily at his hip-pocket. And he did not attempt to stifle the sigh; sixty thousand lire was a lot of money with no expenses rebate. But it was for Cordelia. He handed over the notes.

'Villa Mimosa,' she said.

CHAPTER 5

The Villa Mimosa stood high in the hills above the village of Albisano, surrounded by stone walls and commanding a magnificent panorama of the lake, now burnished gold in a flamboyant, late-evening sun. Peroni parked his car outside the wrought-iron gates, got out and rang the bell of the intercom. A starched female voice answered and he asked to see Count Attilio Remigi – who Signorina Alice had generously informed him was the owner – at the same time stating his business as succintly as he could. Without comment the gates were opened and Peroni drove up to the front door. This was already open and a woman whose appearance was in keeping with the voice was waiting for him. From behind her there came a mighty roar of the Beethoven Fifth and Peroni could not tell whether her disapproving expression was for it, for him or for both.

'Count Attilio will receive you,' she shouted over the music. 'Please follow me.'

They walked the gleaming paths of the villa towards the source of the music and stopped outside a door from behind which the last movement at full volume was emanating. Superfluously, since the inmate could not possibly have heard, she knocked and then opened the door to usher Peroni in.

It was a magnificent studio, overlooking the lake, hung with modern paintings and abundant in books. The occupant – a handsome man in check shirt and corduroy trousers with leonine hair – was swaying gently in the middle of the room conducting an invisible orchestra. A bottle of whisky stood on the table beside him in imminent danger of being sent spinning by the man's flailing right hand.

Peroni coughed, then realising that would get him nowhere shouted into the thunder, '*Mi scusi!*'

The man looked round blinking and focused on him. 'Ah yes,' he said, 'Signorina Adelaide told me. A relation of the red-headed journalist who was drowned. Hang on a second.' He turned down the music and gestured Peroni to an armchair.

'Whisky?' he said and, without waiting for an answer, poured out two generous measures. 'Chin chin!' he said. 'You know why I drink?'

'Because it's there?' suggested Peroni.

The count squinted at him. 'Clever,' he said, 'but no. I drink because it's the only thing I can do really well. If I could conduct like Karajan I wouldn't need to. However, don't let it worry you. What can I do for you?'

'My cousin, Cordelia—'

'But she was English.'

'My aunt married an Englishman.'

'I see. Please go on.'

'I understand that she came to see you shortly before she died.'

'The two events are in no way connected.'

'I'm not suggesting they are. But I've been asked by the family to find out all I can about the last days of her life—'

'And so you want to know why she came here. Simple. She wanted to know about one of my family's many glorious hours – to be precise, the one in which our ancestral home had the honour to be visited by the late Sir Winston Churchill.'

'For a book?'

'That's what she *said*.'

Behind the whisky and the eccentricity, Peroni recognised, there was shrewdness. 'What other motive could she have had for wanting to know?' he asked.

'The Mussolini gold.'

'What?'

'Don't tell me you haven't heard of it. It's the name given to the treasure which our beloved Duce is said to have dumped in the lake some time before his ill-fated attempt to escape to Switzerland at the end of the war. People have been trying to get their hands on it ever since. And if you ask me that was what your delightful, red-headed "cousin" was after, too.'

The inverted commas were so unmistakable that Peroni felt almost physically as if a rug had been twitched from beneath his feet. The count was looking at him with a malicious, but not unfriendly grin. He decided to tell the truth. 'You're right,' he said.

'I usually am.' The count waved deprecatingly. 'But this time it didn't require an excessive mental effort to recognise the famous Commissario Achille Peroni. I've seen your photograph

31

in a magazine at my dentist's. You're a living legend, which is a very enviable thing to be. Why bother to go incognito?'

'Because I disagree with the official theory that the girl's death was accidental. I believe she was murdered, but I don't want to go round muddying the waters by letting everyone know I'm making enquiries.'

'I shall respect your secret. Fortunately, not everybody goes to my dentist, and even if they did they certainly aren't such good physiognomists as I am. Do you think that I might have killed her?' The interview was getting out of hand, but how to keep the count under control? 'As suspects go,' he was rambling on, 'the odds on me must be pretty good. I winkled out her secret and I might have found out something more as well. And if that were so, she would have been standing between me and the Mussolini gold, in which case I might well have murdered her.'

'Did you?'

'A Pirandello-esque question. Whatever I answer you can always believe the exact opposite.'

'How would you go about salvaging the gold?'

'That should be no great problem for anyone who knows its location. But Garda is the largest lake in Italy and, if the treasure's there at all, it could be anywhere. That's why the numerous attempts that have been made to find it have all failed – nobody has the faintest idea where it is. But I apologise,' he went on, refilling their glasses. 'I'm taking an unfair advantage of my initial upper hand. From now on I shan't speak until I'm spoken to. Ask all the questions you want.' He took a gulp of whisky and leaned back looking expectant.

Having the ball dropped with such unexpected suddenness into his hands, Peroni hesitated for an instant over what to do with it. He concentrated. 'Perhaps,' he said, 'you would be so kind as to describe your interview with her.'

'Well, she spun her tale about a book and I nodded sagaciously and played along with her. She was very pretty and I was curious to see what she was getting at. She said this book was about Churchill's mysterious comings and goings in Italy after the war and as she understood he had been a guest at this house she wondered whether I could tell her anything about the visit.'

'And could you? You must have been very young at the time.'

'Thirteen. But I had good reason to remember the visit. For

one thing, the appearance in a young boy's life, however brief, of a figure like Winston Churchill is not easily forgotten. And for another I had played my own little part in that day's doings. I can still remember how extraordinarily hot it was that morning ...'

Usually its position high up above the lake ensured the Villa Mimosa of a cool breeze on even the hottest of days, but not today. The sun beat down ruthlessly, the dogs lay about like corpses and the servants, preparing for the shameful visit, went about their work listlessly, limiting movement to the minimum.

Attilio perched on a shady branch high up in his tree, safely hidden from any lurking partisans or English or American troops, waiting for the arrival of the Enemy. Attilio was one of the few remaining Fascists in Italy and what he lacked in age and authority he made up for in fervour. He intended as soon as possible to revive the Fascist party which he would then lead himself to take over the Government and restore to Italy the vanished imperial glory which had so nearly been within her grasp in the days of the Duce.

Unfortunately, he was obliged to keep his plans secret as his father and the whole life and society founded on the Villa Mimosa were still, four years after the war, passionately anti-Fascist. Count Remigi had been a partisan and his activities had done much to favour the entry of the Allied forces into Italy. It was, indeed, reaction against his turbulent and domineering father that had determined Attilio's choice of politics, but he was still too young to realise this.

When his initial sense of outrage at the announcement of Churchill's imminent arrival had passed he found himself in some perplexity. His first idea had been to assassinate the former British premier, but there were disadvantages to this. For one thing, it might prove difficult – Churchill would be sure to have an escort – and for another, apart from the momentary satisfaction, it wouldn't really do a great deal of good. Whether you liked it or not, the British and Americans had by now won the war and there was no going back on that. Besides, Attilio could hardly hope to get away with it and bang would go his chances of leading a new Fascist party to glory.

No, a subtler approach was called for. Maybe if he went about it cunningly enough Attilio might find out something that would be of use for his future political plans. For instance, what was Churchill coming here for in the first place? The count said that the visit was a purely social one, but Attilio wasn't wearing that. Why should the former British leader bother to come all the way to an isolated villa way up in the hills? It wasn't enough to suggest, as the count did, that the visit was a tribute to his partisan activities; Italy was crammed to the seams with ex-partisans who had contributed towards the so-called liberation. Churchill would hardly have picked on one for a special visit. And such a very secret visit, too.

Obviously there was more to it than the count was letting on.

The solution to the riddle, Attilio was fairly certain, was linked with the more general problem of what Churchill was doing at the lake at all. The official story that he was on a painting holiday was no more convincing than the count's story of a social visit.

Four years previously, immediately after the war, Churchill had spent another so-called painting holiday in Italy – that time at Lake Como. And now here he was back on Lake Garda. By a strange coincidence Mussolini's headquarters during the last ditch Republic of Salò had been set up at Gargnano – on the shores of Lake Garda. And then towards the end of April 1945, following an unsuccessful meeting with Cardinal Schuster in Milan, he had moved to Como with plans, so it was said, for setting up his own resistance in the mountains. And the last two nights before he had finally been captured by the partisans had been spent at Como.

Putting these facts together, it seemed probable that Mussolini had left something behind before setting off on his last and fatal journey towards Switzerland. And whatever that something was, Churchill was eager to get his hands on it. So eager that he had come out to Como immediately after the war assuming that as it was Mussolini's last stopping place he would have left whatever it was there. But the trail, it seemed reasonable to assume, had led nowhere and Churchill had gone back to London empty-handed except for his canvases.

And now here he was back again – this time at Garda, headquarters of the Republic of Salò. Could he have learned something to suggest that what he was after had been left behind, not at Como, but at Garda? Attilio believed so. And that would explain today's luncheon party: Churchill wanted some-

34

thing from the count. But what? At that point Attilio's deductions came to a dead end. But if he kept his eyes and ears wide open today he just might find out.

His leafy vantage point commanded a maximum panorama of the country toppling giddily down towards the burnished lake and he now saw, rounding the corner of a white and dusty road far below him, a large, black limousine heading purposefully up the hill. The Enemy.

Attilio started to scramble down the tree. Then he made his way across the lawns to the large gravelled forecourt in front of the villa. By the time he got there a reception party had already been formed. The count, immaculate in his country gentleman's clothes, was standing at the foot of the steps, his chin jutting out in a characteristically heroic attitude. The countess was just behind him, looking a shade anxious but extremely elegant in a beige costume that she normally kept for royal occasions. And standing in a line at the top of the steps, very much on parade, were the servants, rigidly suffering in their most formal uniforms.

'Attilio!' exclaimed his mother, horrified. 'You haven't changed or even washed!'

The count's haughty eyes summed up the situation at a glance. 'Too late to do anything about that now,' he snapped, 'Mr Churchill has seen worse in his time than a scruffy little boy. Attilio,' he went on, switching to terse English, 'when we go into the drawing room you will go upstairs and make yourself respectable for luncheon. Is that understood?'

'Yes, Papa.' No point in arguing the toss when the count asked if something was understood.

The general attention, momentarily distracted on to Attilio, now returned to the bend in the drive beyond which the sound of an approaching car engine could already be heard. Seconds passed and a majestic bonnet with gleaming silver radiator rounded the bend and the car crunched its stately progress up to halt in front of the count. Immediately the front passenger door was thrown open and a young man in a dark suit jumped out. He then opened the rear door and stood respectfully to attention.

The Enemy emerged from the car with the slow deliberation of a great cloud. On his head he was wearing a monstrously wide-brimmed hat and from his mouth there jutted an equally larger-than-life-size cigar. He shook hands with the countess and the count and civilities were exchanged in English. Then the awful blue eyes fell on Attilio.

'My son,' said the count.

The Enemy humphed in acknowledgement, the blue eyes still on Attilio. 'I do believe,' he rumbled, 'that the boy's up to mischief.'

The countess laughed politely. The servants, though they couldn't possibly have understood, smiled dutifully. The count showed his teeth. And then Churchill, escorted by his hosts and the young man who had opened the car door for him, climbed the broad steps and went in through the front door, followed by the servants.

Attilio brought up the rear and peeled off from the main party to go up to his room. There he washed quickly and put on his best suit. When he was ready he went downstairs just in time to join the party as it made its way into the dining room, a sumptuous room at the back of the villa with a gleaming eighteenth-century table laid with the heavy embossed pieces that constituted the family silver. The count and countess glanced briefly at Attilio and then, satisfied with his appearance, paid no further attention to him, which was just what he wanted.

An elderly maid glided behind the chairs proffering a large silver platter with asparagus risotto. The countess usually had pasta served, but on this occasion, Attilio imagined, she had probably wished to spare the Enemy any possible fork-twirling embarrassment.

The conversational wheels turned effortlessly, oiled no doubt by the constant replenishing of Churchill's and the count's glasses. It was led by the countess who, as Attilio knew from many boring social occasions, was a mistress of the art. Skilfully she steered it along appropriate avenues: her guest's well known hobby of painting, the beauties of Lake Garda, the long and colourful history of Anglo-Italian friendship, the cuisines of the two countries, and so on. It was, of course, all in English, but this gave Attilio no difficulty as he had been brought up with English as a second language. The problem lay in discerning anything that might be of interest. It was all just slick, grown-up cackle and, although the Enemy played his part in it politely enough, Attilio had the impression that his mind was on other things.

36

On it went through the main course and into the fruit salad and ice-cream, at which stage Attilio's attention was caught by Churchill's escort, who had not uttered since the meal began. He was good-looking with smooth, fair hair and quick, watchful grey eyes in a boyish, very Anglo-Saxon face. For a moment Attilio wondered what it was in the young man that had caught his attention and then he realised that it must be the fact that the escort was following the conversation as closely as he was himself. Was that so surprising? It was his job to follow what went on. And yet Attilio couldn't quite shake off an impression that the escort's interest was more than professional.

But if so, he certainly couldn't have got any more satisfaction from it than Attilio himself, for they got to the end of the coffee and brandy without anything of moment being even hinted at.

'Perhaps you'd care for a stroll, Mr Churchill?' said the count as they rose from table.

'A most felicitous suggestion,' rumbled the Enemy, 'and one well calculated to induce good digestion to wait on the appetite stimulated by your superb luncheon, Contessa.' The countess smiled prettily, obviously not having quite followed the rolling prose but catching on to the compliment. 'And as for you,' the Enemy went on to his escort, 'no assassin's knives can be lurking in such a remote paradise as this, so if you care to relax your vigilance for a brief repose, you have my authority to do so.'

'Very kind of you, sir,' said the escort.

Attilio watched the count and Churchill as they went out through the French windows into the shimmering heat. So that was it. The real business was to be discussed in the grounds privately, without even the escort. It must be really hot. He muttered something at his mother, who was anyway far too concerned about the progress of the visit to worry about him, and ran back up to his room, which commanded a good view of the grounds. There were the two men – one massive, bulky and slightly hunched, the other tall and slim – strolling across the lawn deep in conversation followed by the count's favourite Irish setter, Arrigo. Churchill was doing the talking and the count's head was bowed as he listened in silence. Goodbye to all hopes of learning the secret – and there would never be another chance like this!

But then the unexpected happened. The two men came to a dense clump of trees by the artificial lake and sat down, the

37

Enemy still talking, on a stone bench. There was still a chance. If Attilio ran round by the greenhouses he would reach the other side of that clump and then he could wriggle his way Indian-style to within earshot, remaining completely hidden by the trees.

Fingers crossed that he wouldn't be stopped by his mother or some other busybody, he raced down the stairs and out of the villa by a side door. Nobody was about and he reached the trees without interference. Silently he went down on to his stomach and started to slither forward with a delicacy that came of long practice in war games.

He hadn't gone far before he was able to catch the characteristically inflected rumble of Churchill's speech, but he was not yet close enough for words to be distinguished. A twig cracked beneath his weight and he went dead, but the talking went on unchecked and after a couple of seconds he began to crawl again. Then just as he was straining to catch the sense of what was being said, Churchill stopped talking and the count began in a lower, more monotonous tone. Carefully Attilio wormed his way closer.

' . . . Fascist families living reasonably near the lake,' the count was saying. 'Oh, of course everybody was Fascist at that time as you must be very well aware. But I mean of the standing that would be likely to meet your specifications – high up in the hierarchy, trustworthy and, of course, in a position to do what you say.' (What *had* he said?) 'One of them was the del Duca family and the other was the Pagani.'

'How do you spell them? I never can get my ear wrapped round your Italian.'

It was while the count was obliging that Arrigo started to bark. 'He must have flared something,' said the count. 'He never barks without good reason. Maybe it's a rabbit.'

That's it, a rabbit, Attilio willed his father to go on thinking as, at the same time, he about turned and started to wriggle his way back as rapidly as he could, hoping against hope that Arrigo wouldn't take it into his head to try to set the rabbit up.

He reached the edge of the clump in safety and was just reckoning that he could risk a crouched spring over to the rear of the greenhouses and safety when something that felt like a pouncing eagle landed on his shoulders and he felt himself being pulled up to look into two remorseless grey eyes.

'What are you up to, young man?' said Churchill's escort.

'I was playing!' said Attilio, trying to sound indignant. 'I always play here!'

'We'll see about that!'

And Attilio was carried in an implacable grasp round the clump of trees to the lakeside where his father and Churchill were sitting on the bench. Arrigo, Attilio noticed furiously, had the nerve to wag his tail.

'I found this young man wriggling his way out at the other side of the trees,' said the escort.

'I am rarely mistaken about this sort of thing,' said the Enemy, bulldog jaws clamped and something in the blue eyes that Attilio couldn't interpret. 'The very moment I set eyes on this boy I knew that he was up to mischief.'

With overwhelming relief Attilio realised that what he hadn't been able to interpret was a twinkle.

'Not long after that famous visit,' said the count, coming to the end of his story, 'my mother engaged a new maid by the name of Serenella and I fell passionately in love with her, which seemed on the whole much more interesting than restoring Italy to the glories of ancient Rome, so I forgot all about Churchill's secrets.'

'And those two families your father mentioned?'

'Well, I presume Churchill went to see them, but I never bothered to find out.'

'Do they still exist?'

'Indeed they do. That's to say the Pagani son lives in the family villa just outside Garda. A bit of a recluse. Rather a sad little man and I'm told that he's ailing. The del Duca family lives in a villa near Bardolino. General del Duca – the man Churchill would have met – is still alive. An old testament patriarch and a rabid Fascist.'

Peroni tried to think where he had heard the name before. Yes, the mayor, Bombarone, had mentioned him: the man who made the wine. 'One last thing,' he said, 'from your talk with the English girl did you get any idea, any hint of what specifically brought her to the lake?'

'Specifically no. She stuck to her story of a book right up to the end. But in general terms I've got no doubts. She had some sort of lead on to the Mussolini gold.'

CHAPTER 6

The house was surrounded by what appeared to be an impenetrable jungle, but on inspection Peroni found a path where the vegetation had not yet taken over. He walked up this to the Pagani family home, a late-nineteenth-century building with an air of respectability which seemed somehow offended by the reigning desolation. It should have been surrounded by nature, trimmed and tamed, and instead it had to put up with riotous flora clawing disrespectfully at its walls. The windows looked as though they had been brought up to expect polish and order and now they gaped offence at dust and broken shutters. The place had all the air of being deserted except for a small, tumbledown Fiat parked in front.

There being no bell Peroni knocked at the door and waited, but got no answer. He tried knocking again a couple of times and then finally set out to explore his way round the house. He went nervously. The word 'recluse' had disquieting connotations and he had no wish to be suddenly jumped upon by some hirsute wild man of the lake. But he encountered only silence.

What had once been garden on the other side of the house ran down to the lake and a ramshackle boat-house, but this side of the house was as overrun and deserted as the other. And still no sign of the recluse.

Through the vegetation Peroni was able to make out a stretch of pebbly shore, gently lapped by the tamest of wavelets and commanding an ample view over the lake to the Napoleonically profiled mountain on the opposite shore. It looked so inviting that Peroni walked down to it and, sitting on a rock, lit a cigarette.

'*Buon giorno.*'

The melancholy voice took him completely by surprise. He whipped round and saw, only a couple of metres from him a man entirely concealed in the shade of a tree, seated in a wicker armchair and wearing an off-white cotton suit which was too big for him.

40

'*Buon giorno,*' said Peroni. 'Signor Pagani?'

'The same. What can I do to help you?'

Peroni moved to shake hands with him, at the same time observing him more closely. He must have been about sixty, nondescript in appearance with a tame expression and empty, slightly watery eyes. He made Peroni think of certain long-term prisoners he had known who had got so accustomed to captivity that they ceased even to think of liberty, but then he remembered that the count had said that the man was ailing, so perhaps it was due to that.

'I'm making enquiries into the death of an English girl named Cordelia Hope who was drowned in the lake the night before last. Perhaps you heard of it?'

'Oh yes, indeed. I read about it in this morning's newspaper. Tragic indeed.' He blinked and touched his eyes with a handkerchief.

'My visit is quite unofficial,' Peroni went on. 'I'm acting on behalf of the family. They have asked me to find out what I can about the last days of her life and I understand that she visited you some days ago.'

'Yes. Oh yes. Quite so. A charming girl. I was really very pleased to see her. I lead a somewhat monotonous life, you see. I do my shopping in the village and sit for an hour or two in the bar, reading the newspaper and playing draughts.' His hands played restlessly on the arms of his chair and for a moment he seemed to have forgotten what they were talking about. 'Yes, yes,' he went on, picking up the thread again, 'a simple life and somewhat dull, so a visit from an attractive young creature like her was really quite an occasion.'

'I wonder if you would be so kind as to tell me about her visit?'

'Oh yes, of course . . .' Peroni had the impression that he had to make a mental stretch for the memory of it. 'She came in search of material for a book she was writing. Something about – yes, Winston Churchill in Italy. She had been given to understand that he paid a visit to this house in nineteen forty-nine and she was anxious for information about this.'

'Were you able to give her any?'

'A little, but not, I fear, what she was hoping for. You see, she was under the impression – as indeed Churchill had been before her – that the Duce, at the time of the fall of the Republic of Salò,

41

had entrusted something, documents, a map, something of that nature, into the keeping of my family. But I told her as I told Churchill all those years ago that any such possibility was quite out of the question.'

'May I ask why?'

'Because, you see, when the Republic of Salò fell my family had already been in Switzerland for some little while. I did not return until nineteen forty-seven by which time my parents had been killed in a car accident. There seemed to be no further point then in my staying abroad so I came back here and opened up this house.'

'Where two years later you received the visit from Churchill?'

'That is so.'

'And you were able to tell the English girl nothing else?'

'Unfortunately, no.'

'What was her reaction?'

'She seemed somewhat – er – disappointed, but then she cheered up and said – I remember her very words – "Oh, well, there's one more possibility."'

The del Duca family, thought Peroni, with its wine-making, Fascist patriarch.

She was lying on a deck chair in the shade of a giant yew surrounded by a regiment of children all with various forms of juvenile troubles including unchanged nappies, nose bleeds, hunger, thirst and violent disagreements with their peers, and all giving tongue to their feelings uninhibitedly. Their mother, if indeed she was the mother of so monstrous a brood, was finding solace in a large carafe of wine on a table at her side and one of the more outrageous Italian scandal magazines in which she was happily absorbed.

Peroni observed her from a distance. She was a mature, but still attractive woman dressed untidily in ragged jeans shorts, which allowed him to slaver over long and handsome legs, and a torn and grubby shirt. Her hair was as unruly as her children. Every so often, without interrupting her other activities, she dabbed vaguely at a nose or a mouth or uttered a reproof which had no effect whatsoever.

Peroni coughed to attract her attention, but then, realising that in the reigning bedlam a cough was about as much good as a

42

phony five lire piece in the Save Venice appeal fund, he called out, '*Mi scusi*, Signora . . .'

She looked up and apparently liked what she saw for she smiled, revealing good teeth with an attractive gap between the front two. '*Si?*' she said in a tone which suggested she was open to suggestions.

'Signora del Duca?'

'No,' she said, 'I'm only the daughter. But come in just the same. Sit down and help yourself to a glass of wine. Roberto, stop pulling Christina's hair. Haven't I seen you somewhere before?' Peroni opened his mouth, but she interrupted him. 'No, let me guess. Lie on the ground in the shade and keep still.' It took him a second to realise that these instructions were not for him, but for a little boy with a nosebleed. 'Lake society?' she went on. 'No, too intelligent. On telly? No, ditto. You weren't married to me once by any chance, were you? No, ditto again and I should have remembered you. Put that fish back in the pond at once, Alberto. I give up. No, I don't. Chin chin.'

Peroni had just lifted his glass to drink when she called out, '*Stop!*' with such violence that he spilled most of the wine down his front. 'That's where I've seen you before!' she went on triumphantly, regardless, '*Stop!* – the magazine.' She held up the scandal sheet she'd been reading to prove her point. 'You're the Rudolph Valentino of the Italian police.' Peroni winced. 'Whatever brings you here?' she continued. 'Don't do pi-pi on the azaleas, Marco! Murder?'

'I'm just making some routine enquiries,' Peroni tried feebly.

'Oh, don't be so dull!'

This time Peroni had to adjust to realise that the negative imperative was addressed to him and not to a child. 'I'm afraid I don't—' he began.

'The most glamorous detective in Italy walks through the gate and then announces that all he's doing is making some routine enquiries! You really must think up something more interesting than that!'

'I can't invent circumstances!'

'I'm sure you can if you try . . .'

'If I could there's nobody I'd sooner do it for than you.'

'Try then . . .'

As she leaned invitingly towards him, Peroni realised to his horror that, in response to her, he had slipped unwittingly into the very role suggested by his abhorred nickname. He tried unsuccessfully to switch to the impassive northern police functionary. 'I'm making enquiries about an English girl who I understand paid a visit here.'

'The red-head?' She winked at him knowingly and he pretended not to see. 'What's she been up to?'

'She'd dead.'

'What?' The news was obviously a complete shock to her. 'Oh no – poor kid!' To Peroni's surprise enormous tears started to well out of her eyes.

'You knew her well?' he said.

'No, no.' She dabbed at the tears with a grubby handkerchief that had already served various purposes in the children's hygiene. 'I scarcely met her, but I always find it unbearably sad when I hear of a death.' The tears continued to flow freely. 'Roberto,' she went on absently, 'stop hitting Martina with that spade . . .' She stopped short as a thought struck her. 'How did she die?'

'She was drowned in the lake the night before last while she was out with her yacht.'

Suddenly she stared as though she had seen a ghost. 'Murdered?'

'The official theory is that she died accidentally.'

'Then why are you—?'

'I'm just acting for her family,' he trotted out the soothing excuse. Gradually the fear drained out of her eyes, but it had been there and Peroni was very curious to know why. 'Signora—'

'Don't call me Signora,' she said, apparently quite herself again. 'Call me Nausicaa and I shall call you Achille.' She gave him her hand to seal the agreement.

'Nausicaa,' said Peroni, fighting to get the situation under control, 'all I'm trying to do is find out the background.'

'So you want to know what she was doing here?' Sensibly.

'That's right.' He realised that his attempt to get things under control was not being helped by the fact that his hand was still in hers. Regretfully but firmly he took it away.

'Well, she came here to see Papa. I was sitting here – just like I am now – and she came in through the gate and asked if she

44

could speak to General del Duca. One of the children took her to his study.'

'Did she tell you why she wanted to see him?'

'She just said she was researching for some sort of book and I wished her the best of luck.'

'For the book?'

'No, for Papa. He's not the easiest man at the best of times and if there's one class of people he likes less than another it's journalists.'

'And that's all you know?'

'I'm afraid so.'

'Perhaps then I might have a word with your father?'

'He's not very fond of policemen either.'

Peroni suddenly felt an invasion of chilly darts on the back of his neck and it took him a second to realise that he was being sprayed with a hose.

'Antonio, put down that hose at once!' shouted Nausicaa and, stirred at last from the comfort of her deck chair, she gave chase to the careless gardener. 'I do hope you didn't get too wet,' she went on, returning a moment later, and then without waiting for an answer, 'Well, if you're really bent on braving Papa, we'd better go and see Aristotle. Follow me.'

'Aristotle?' said Peroni, attempting to dry himself as he went after her towards the house.

'Papa's secretary. I call him Aristotle because he's always reading philosophy. He may be able to tell you something, too, because she talked to him after she'd seen Papa and I saw them together again in the village the next day. If you ask me he was a bit soft on her.'

They passed from the shimmering heat of the garden into a large *salotto*, cool and dark after the sunlight with all its shutters closed. This room was dominated by a large, illuminated portrait of a strikingly good looking young man in Fascist uniform with a little black beard and burning eyes.

'My elder brother, Gervaso,' said Nausicaa, noticing that Peroni's attention had been caught by the picture. 'He was killed by the partisans just after the war. Papa still idolises him. This way.'

They left the *salotto* and walked down a corridor to a small office where a neat looking young man was seated at a desk typing with an expression of deep grief.

'*Ciao*, Aristotle,' said Nausicaa. 'This gentleman's from the police. He wants to see Papa about the English girl. Did you know, by the way, that the poor girl is dead?'

'*Si*, Signora.' Aristotle's head hung limp in mourning. 'It's in this morning's paper. I've just seen it.'

'I said you might be able to help him, too,' went on Nausicaa. 'She spoke to you after she'd seen Papa, didn't she? And I saw you with her in the village the day after.'

Aristotle's grief gave way to some less easily definable emotion which made him flush a sunset red. 'Oh, that was quite f-fortuitous, Signora,' he said hastily and Peroni couldn't tell whether the stammer was habitual or the result of agitation. 'We happened to m-meet when I was doing some shopping for the general and I offered her a c-coffee.'

That the stammer was habitual was now clear. Less clear was the truth or otherwise of Aristotle's statement. 'How did you come to meet her?' asked Peroni.

'It was as she was leaving the house,' said Aristotle warily. 'We just chanced to m-meet and she asked me about the buses to Garda. I told her the timetable. That was all.'

'And the day after?'

'As I say, that was quite f-fortuitous. We just had coffee together.'

'Did she tell you what she was doing here on the lake?'

'She said she was on holiday.'

'Did you see her again?'

'No.' But Peroni caught the unmistakable smell of a lie.

Nausicaa had been following their exchanges with absorption, her head moving tennis-public style from one to other. Now she intervened to say, 'Well, Aristotle, I'll leave you to take the gentleman to Papa. And as for you,' she went on to Peroni, 'I'll be waiting for you in the garden to patch you up.' Then with a flame-throwing look of tenderness she left them.

'If you care to f-follow me,' said Aristotle, 'I believe the general is in the cellar.'

He led Peroni out through the back of the house and then in again by way of a small metal door which opened into a dark, downward-sloping tunnel. As soon as they had stepped inside he closed the door behind them saying, 'The general doesn't like the light to get in. It's bad for the wine.' He then led the way

46

down the tunnel, which seemed to go into the very bowels of the earth and in which the only light came from a dim, unshaded bulb.

Peroni was reminded of Dante's descent into Hell and indeed their destination when they reached it was less gruesome but every bit as unexpected. Having rounded a bend in the tunnel they came to three stone steps which led down to an enormous cave in the living rock, at all points equipped as a wine cellar. After the flaming July heat it was so cold that Peroni thought again of Dante and his lake of solid ice at the bottom of Hell. Stalactites spiked down from the heaving roof and the craggy walls were beaded with moisture. In the pale light of an oil-lamp huge barrels loomed against the walls like the fossilised remains of prehistoric monsters while other oenological equipment scattered here and there seemed in the weird surroundings to take on independent existence.

At first sight the cave seemed to be deserted of human presence. But then there came an ominous rumble which made Peroni think uneasily of the volcanic origins of the mountains around Garda. The rumble crescendoed to a roar which emanated not, as it seemed, from the rock itself, but from a figure bent in the shadow near one of the barrels, decanting wine. And being interpreted the roar amounted to 'What the hell do you want?' At the same time the figure straightened and was revealed to be that of a lean, gnarled ancient with monstrous white moustaches, a jagged hook of a nose and eyes of fire.

'Excuse me, General,' said Aristotle, 'but this gentleman is from the police and—'

'Police!' There was a marked increase in the volcanic nature of utterance. 'Learn, boy, that the words "police" and "gentleman" are incompatible. I am not at home.'

Peroni was in a fix. He could not impose himself on the general, who nevertheless represented his only remaining hope of finding out about Cordelia's death. Desperate cases call for desperate remedies. He sniffed at the air like a hunting dog trying to work out a smell.

'What the hell's the matter with the man?' the general flared when it became impossible to ignore Peroni's performance.

'There's a wine in torment here,' said Peroni.

'What do you know about wine?' said the general suspiciously.

'Compared to a true oenologist like yourself, nothing, but I have nose enough to tell when a wine is suffering.'

'Are you referring to my eighty-three reciotto?' said the general, still belligerently, but with a gleam of pure interest in the deadly eyes.

'I couldn't have told the year,' said Peroni modestly.

'The fellow's a wizard,' said the general to nobody in particular. 'The only other man I've ever met with a nose like that was an old peasant in Brianza before the war – and the locals thought he'd made a pact with the devil.'

Peroni felt an inner surge of self-satisfaction. Once again his native brilliance had not let him down and the gamble that in a cellar as large as that at least one wine was likely to be ailing had paid off.

'And a policeman, too, by the thunder of Mars!' the general went on, thrusting his hand at Peroni as though it were a bayonet. 'I am rarely wrong, sir,' he said, 'but I learned as a soldier to admit it when I am.' The grip was terrible and Peroni had to mask a wince with a smile. 'I am at your disposal,' the general continued.

'Very kind of you, sir,' said Peroni, falling into the role of a respectful junior officer. 'I understand that a young English-woman visited you recently—'

'Damned journalist! Can't stand the race!'

'She was subsequently drowned—'

'That's what comes of sticking your nose into other people's business!'

'It might be of great assistance if I were to know what passed between you.'

'Nothing passed between us, sir. The woman came out with some cock and bull story about the Duce entrusting some form of document to me which Churchill also enquired about when he came here later, but I quickly sent her about her business and that was the sum of it.'

'So there was no document?'

'No – as I told Churchill.'

'Can you suggest, sir,' said Peroni, almost saluting, 'how this rumour of a document or documents started?'

'How does any damn silly rumour start? Some damn silly fool starts talking about things he doesn't understand! I was in contact with the Duce at the time of the Republic of Salò and

48

indeed on one occasion he did me the honour of visiting me at the house we then lived in at Costermano. That would be more than enough to start tongues wagging among a bunch of idiots with more time than sense.'

'But nothing was entrusted to you?'

'Nothing whatsoever.'

So that was that. Cordelia had been directed to two paths, both of which had turned out to be dead ends. And as he thought this Peroni became aware of Aristotle, whose eyes were fixed on the general with an expression which it was difficult to interpret. The general was aware of this, too.

'What the hell are you staring at, man?' he roared.

'N-nothing, sir,' said Aristotle.

The general looked as though he would have taken the matter further if he hadn't been interrupted by the sound of the metal door being opened at the end of the tunnel and a voice that Peroni recognised calling out, 'Generale? *Permesso?*'

'*Avanti – avanti!*' called out the general, who had also recognised the voice. Footsteps echoed in the tunnel and then the country gentleman figure of the mayor, Bombarone, came down the steps into the cave.

'*Buon giorno, buon giorno, buon giorno!*' he said, going to shake hands with the general and then stopping short. 'Dottor Peroni! What brings you here?' He raised his right hand oratorically. 'No need to tell me. You've come to acquire some of the general's wine.'

'Wrong,' said the general, 'he's come to enquire about some damn fool of a woman who drowned herself in the lake.'

Inwardly Peroni cursed the ancient soldier; the last thing he wanted was for it to be known in official circles that he was still interested in Cordelia's death.

'Indeed?' said Bombarone. 'I thought that was all settled.'

'I have been asked to make enquiries by her family,' Peroni lied smoothly.

'I see, I see, I see. Well, just so long as you don't go digging up suspicions of foul play. As I said when last we met, that could have disastrous effects on our tourism. And now let us pass to the serious business of wine . . .'

'Ah, Dottore . . .'

Peroni looked up from the front page of *The Times* that he

was trying without much success to unravel and saw the brigadiere who had been in charge of the enquiry halted before the lakeside *caffé* table at which Peroni was having a last drink before his departure for Venice, where he was due to take up duty the next morning. '*Buon giorno*,' he said without much cordiality.

'*Buon giorno* to you,' said the brigadiere. 'I have some news that might interest you – about the Englishwoman.'

'You have?' Peroni couldn't repress a lift of renewed hope. His interviews with Pagani and del Duca had left him with the numb sensation that the odds against finding out the truth (if truth there were to find out) were just too heavy. 'What will you drink?' Hope made him cordial.

'Well, in this heat I wouldn't say no to a beer, Dottore.'

Peroni signalled a waiter and ordered a large beer.

'Yes,' the brigadiere went on when the beer had arrived, 'about your English friend. A woman came into the office this morning – makes ceramics in Peschiera, hand paints them and flogs them to the tourists at inflated rates, calls herself a zodiacal ceramist whatever that may be. Anyway, it seems that she'd only just heard of the death and she had some information she thought might be useful to us.'

Get to the point, Peroni urged mentally.

'She and the dead woman – what was her name? Hope—' (he pronounced it Oppay) '—They'd been friends. Pizzas together and long intimate chats over the wine into the small hours. Well, apparently the Oppay woman had told the ceramics woman that she was looking for something here on the lake, never said what it was, but gave the impression it was something big. Then the morning before she was drowned they met for the last time and the Oppay woman said that whatever it was, it had all fallen through and she had nothing to live for any longer. At the time she didn't realise just how serious it was, but when she heard that Oppay was dead she realised that it must have been suicide. Very upset about it she was, too.'

Peroni observed the brigadiere's face – red, mottled and indifferent to grief – detachedly as though it were on a television screen and at the same time he mournfully resigned himself to the fact that the whole thing was, after all, a literally dead end.

Part Two

THE DEPTHS

CHAPTER 1

Peroni sat in his office at the *Questura* or police headquarters on the Fondamenta San Lorenzo in Venice staring at the dismal looking geriatric hospital across the sluggish canal beneath his window. Something he could not define stirred restlessly in his mind.

Three days had passed since he had left the lake and during that time he had done his best to smother all thoughts of Cordelia in an orgy of work. But the work that fell to him had not lent itself to the purpose and when he went back, late at night, to the crumbling, damp *palazzo* near the Rialto where he rented a room, Cordelia's ghost was always there waiting for him, her red hair stirring on the musty air as it had in the water of the lake that tragic morning and her blue eyes pleading with him.

For what? he asked her as he slumped on the de-gutted sofa with a nightcap of Chivas Regal. And the answer invariably came back in a whisper on the silence: for her ghost to be laid. And that could only be done by finding out the truth about her death.

But if there were no truth beyond the brutal fact that she had committed suicide? blustered the down-to-earth police functionary who had become an integral part of Peroni over the years. And what if she hadn't? came back the Neapolitan gutter-snipe who, over the same years, had never been entirely suppressed. And so on, inconclusively backwards and forwards, went the argument between the two sides of Peroni's nature.

But now as he looked out over the canal it occurred to him irrationally that whatever it was that had just shifted in his mind might finally settle the argument one way or the other. But just as he was on the point of hooking it up out of his subconscious the internal telephone on his desk rang.

'*Pronto?*'

'*Mi scusi*, Dottore, there's a lady here whose daughter's run away from home.'

Peroni didn't suppress a sigh. 'Send her up.' That was life all over. Just as you were on the point of revelation somebody always had to go and throw a fiddling chore at you.

The lady turned out to be faded, tear-stained and defeated and Peroni felt guilty at having considered her little drama as a fiddling chore. 'Sit down, Signora,' he said, giving her his hand. 'Tell me what happened.'

'It's Lidia,' she said nervously. 'She's run away from home.'

'When was this?'

'The day before yesterday. I waited before coming just in case ...' She choked on a sob, broke down altogether, then tried to pull herself together. 'I'm sorry ...'

'Don't mention it, Signora. Now,' he drew a sheet of paper toward him, 'there are one or two things I shall need to know ...'

The story that emerged over the next quarter of an hour was as familiar to Peroni as the stairs at the *Questura*, but new in its pathetic humanity every time he met it. The girl's name was Lidia Martelli and she was fifteen and an only child. Her father had died when she was ten and ever since there had been a sort of war of attrition between her and her mother. It was not so much that they didn't love each other in their way, but rather that everything about each of them aroused the instinctive and violent hostility of the other. Lidia was feckless, generous, dreamy, untidy and wild. The mother believed in order, economy, discipline and punctuality. Lidia made scenes, the mother nagged.

Over the last two months the conflict had escalated as a result of Lidia's involvement with an itinerant break-dance team – an art form that she apparently considered to be her Heaven-sent vocation.

'Lot of layabouts with nothing else to do,' said the mother. 'They dance in the streets wherever they happen to be, throwing themselves about on the ground like a lot of maniacs. And then they go round begging for money – I ask you! Half of them are on drugs and I'm worried out of my mind that she'll start, too.'

It had been her mother's refusal to allow her to go off on a break-dance tour that had been the immediate cause of the girl's escape.

'Is this group run by anybody in particular?' asked Peroni.

'Yes, and that's another thing that worries me. It's run by a young man called Maurizio. She says she's in love with him, but I don't like the sound of him at all. He bosses her about no end and she, silly little fool, does everything he tells her. I'm afraid that he may – well, take advantage of her.'

'How old is he?'

'Nineteen.'

'That could get him five years,' said Peroni. 'Have you got a photograph of her?'

Sobbing, the mother took a passport photograph from her bag. 'It's not very good of her,' she said, passing it to Peroni.

He studied it carefully. The young eyes stared at him in defiance. The hair fell about her shoulders in exactly the stringy disarray that her mother had complained of. The make-up was garish and inept. And yet . . .

Every so often in a policeman's life some detail turns up to transform a routine job into a personal crusade. This happened now with the photograph. For along with everything negative and cheap that it showed he sensed rather than saw a pathetic vulnerability and an innocence, and he trembled at the thought of what the fringe world of exploitation, drugs and amateur prostitution could do to a child like that. He picked up his questioning again with a concentrated intensity which took the mother aback even in her state of alarm and grief. Finally he stood up and gave her his hand. 'I'll put this out immediately,' he said, 'and launch a full–scale search. Let me know immediately if she gets in touch with you. And try not to worry – we'll find her in no time.'

He wished he could feel as confident as he sounded. Hundreds of girls like Lidia vanished in Italy every year never to return or, what was perhaps worse, to return as irremediably broken wrecks.

And when the mother had gone Peroni found to his surprise that the thing which had shifted elusively in his subconscious had now surfaced of its own accord and there it was, sharp, clear and decisive: across the canal a geriatric hospital; across the waters of the lake a villa standing in its own park.

'I wonder who owns it.' He couldn't tell whether he had pronounced the words or merely heard them echoing at him out of the past.

'I know that, too.' Cordelia's voice was no longer a ghostly whisper, but seemed to vibrate with living energy. 'It's one of those ultra-expensive geriatric clinics – the sort where the nurses all glide and have built-in smiles and the guests are treated as reverently as though they were priceless pieces of porcelain.'

How had she known that? The place was too far for her to have come across it by chance. Besides, the description indicated that she must have been there. And that surely meant that it represented a stage in her search.

Just the time to put out a general report about Lidia and Peroni was on his way back to the lake.

A throbbing orange of a sun was tyrannising in a cloudless sky when Peroni, having left his car outside, walked through the gates into the large park surrounding the clinic. It was shady and pleasant there with fountains playing delicately on pools of stately fish, immaculately tended beds of flowers and statues of the gambolling, touchy company of Olympus. And everywhere you looked, almost less mobile than the statues themselves, were guests of the clinic, some being promenaded in wheel chairs, some seated on benches staring into an unimaginable past, all giving that awkward impression of having been dressed like dolls. Peroni remembered Cordelia's phrase, ' . . . the guests are treated as reverently as though they were priceless pieces of porcelain' and shuddered at the prospect of his own old age.

He walked through the front door into a white, elegant hall with marble columns, two enormous pictures of naval battles and a carefully organised, indefinable smell which gave the impression that it was expensively holding at bay a host of the more sinister odours of human decay. At a desk in this hall was seated a carefully lacquered middle-aged woman with a professional smile.

'Can I help you?'

Peroni said 'Police' and showed his card, which somewhat nonplussed the smile. 'I'm making enquiries into circumstances surrounding the death of a young Englishwoman who was drowned in the lake last week. I have reason to believe she came here.'

The smile was back in business. 'If you care to take a seat I will ask the signora.'

She used an internal telephone with satisfactory results and then led Peroni up a broad, winding stairway to the first floor where she knocked at a door and showed him into the presence of the signora.

The lacquered woman, Peroni saw at once, had been mere window display while the signora was the real business end of the clinic. She it was, he guessed, who sorted out the guests' tantrums, dealt with relatives and, when the Reaper called, arranged for the coffin to be smuggled discreetly in and out so as not to upset the remaining residents. She was a tall, bony woman in her fifties.

'What can I do for you?' she asked, having gestured for Peroni to sit down.

He told her, all northern police functionary without a flicker of the Neapolitan streak which he had immediately spotted would only put her back up.

'Yes,' she said, 'the young woman you describe did come here.'

He felt a jerk of excitement. 'May I ask why she came?'

The signora hesitated slightly. 'She wished to speak to one of the residents. She said she was gathering material for a book and she believed he might be of assistance to her. The request was unusual, but the gentleman in question, although ... ' she paused, looking for the right words '... although a trifle vague in his mind at times, enjoys any opportunity of speaking about the past, so I felt that the meeting would do no harm.'

'Who is this gentleman?'

'His name is Volpi.' This meant nothing to Peroni, but then she went on, 'He was a member of Mussolini's staff towards the end of the war.'

The *scugnizzo* within leapt with exhilaration, but the northern functionary kept an impassive exterior. 'And the young lady did, in fact, speak to him?'

'That is so.'

'Can you give me some idea of what passed between them?'

'I'm afraid not. I took her to his room and introduced her, but then I left them. You will understand that I have a great deal to do.'

'Of course. So there were no witnesses to their conversation?'

'None.'

So that left only one possibility. Peroni would have to see Volpi himself, but when asked if he might do so the signora looked doubtful. 'He's been a little off colour these last few days. He's ninety-one, you know, and I'm afraid he does tend to get a little muddled.'

'It would be of great assistance to us,' said Peroni, loading the pronoun to make it sound as though it referred to the entire Italian home office.

'Well,' she said, 'we'll go and see how he is.'

She stood up and led him out of the office and back to the ground floor where they made their way along a devious maze of corridors. As they went Peroni did his best to keep his eyes off the numerous testimonies of senility which strewed their path, but he couldn't control his ears, which were besieged with moaning, whimpering, hawking and howling, to all of which the signora was quite impervious. Finally she stopped before a door to which was affixed a card saying 'Col. Massimiliano Volpi' and, without knocking, she went in. Peroni followed her.

The room was dark and it took several seconds for his eyes to get used to it. When they had done so, he saw that a very old man was propped up on cushions in a cot-like bed obviously intended to stop him falling out. His mouth hung open; his head – bald except for a few feathery wisps of hair – lolled to one side, and his eyes were closed. Peroni thought he must be dead, but the signora knew better.

'Colonnello,' she roared in stentorian tones, 'there's a gentleman come to see you.'

After a long moment the eyes flickered and the toothless mouth twitched slightly, emitting a sound which Peroni could not interpret. But the signora presumably did for she bawled back as though in answer to a question, 'He wants to have a little chat with you.' There were more unintelligible sounds at this and Peroni wondered in desperation how, assuming the colonel was willing to talk at all, a single word of what he said was to be made out.

'I'll leave you two boys together,' the signora loud-speakered playfully and then, lowering her voice to a normal tone, she added superfluously, 'You'll have to speak up – he's a little hard of hearing. And whatever you do, don't upset him. If you want me I'll be in my office.'

She went out leaving Peroni in a swamp of gloom. Apart from the problem of understanding what the colonel said, there was the prior problem of how to get him to say anything at all.

He concentrated. 'I believe,' he shouted, 'that an English girl came to see you the other day. She wanted to ask you questions for a book she was writing.'

Something stirred in the old face. The filmy eyes shifted towards Peroni's, then fell back towards the sheets as though the effort were too great. More sounds emerged from the colonel's mouth and Peroni realised that he was beginning to understand them, but this was little consolation, for the colonel was saying, apparently half choked with tears, 'I don't remember. I don't remember anything. I don't remember . . .'

'Churchill,' tried Peroni. 'She asked you about Churchill.'

'Churchill,' the colonel echoed in desolation. 'I don't remember . . .'

'Winston Churchill – the English leader in the war!'

'I don't remember . . .'

It was hopeless. He would get nowhere with the colonel. Was it possible that Cordelia had managed to fish information from his hopeless sea of forgetfulness? And then, as though the mere thought of her were a source of inspiration, he realised that he was on the wrong track.

'The Mussolini gold,' he said. 'Tell me about the Mussolini gold.'

Again the eyes shifted towards Peroni's face, but this time they made the hard climb all the way. 'The Mussolini gold,' he said, 'I remember. It was early in 1945 . . .'

Colonel Volpi stood on the quay supervising the unloading from the lorries. It was already March, but it might well have been the depths of winter. The night was bitterly cold and an icy wind buffeted and spat at them across the lake from the mountains where there had been a heavy fall of snow the previous day. In his heavy military greatcoat Volpi trembled involuntarily and then, because a good Fascist should not display even such a natural weakness as that, he shouted at the men who were bent double under the weight of one of the two huge steel-bound cases, 'Be careful, idiots! If you drop it I'll have the lot of you court martialled!'

And indeed the responsibility he bore was heavy. Three days previously he had been summoned by the Duce in person – an honour that had only fallen to him twice before, and on both those occasions he had been called in company with other

59

officers. This time he was alone: face to face with the greatest Man of Destiny since Julius Caesar.

Mussolini was looking tired. He was unshaven, the flesh around his jowls sagged and his eyes were heavy and strained with lack of sleep.

'Volpi,' he said, 'I have a mission for you. It is a mission of extreme importance and I have considered with great care before deciding which particular officer to entrust it to.'

Standing rigidly at attention, Volpi glowed with stern joy. 'Sit down,' said Mussolini and Volpi sat, but still at attention. 'Things are going badly,' went on the Duce. 'It may soon be necessary for me to withdraw to the mountains and there with a nucleus of my finest men – men like yourself, Volpi, purified of the cowards, fools and traitors who have dragged us down to our present depths – there to continue the fight which is destined to end in the re-establishment of Italy's ancient glory!'

Volpi thrilled. Years before in Piazza Venezia in Rome he had heard Mussolini speaking before a huge, enraptured crowd and he had felt himself caught up to the Empyrean by the sheer power of his words. He would never have dreamed then that the Duce would one day speak in such a way for him alone, and the fact that the words were being uttered at a moment when all seemed to be lost made them the more moving.

'Withdrawal to the mountains is near, perhaps imminent, and when the moment comes we must travel light. We must take no more with us than that which is indispensable to enable us to live and die as heroes. And this is where your mission comes in, Volpi. I have here a quantity of bullion which constitutes the treasury of this Republic. In this supreme moment of destiny we have no need of such dross – and anyway the Germans would almost certainly get their hands on it if we tried to take it with us – but the day will come with the establishment of the new empire when it will be necessary again. In the meantime it is our duty to see that it is kept safe from the grasping hands of criminals and traitors. I have reflected long on this and I have decided that there is only one place where it can be entirely safe. Do you know where that is, Volpi?'

'No, Excellency.'

The Duce lifted fateful, tired eyes to the high windows by his desk and waved majestically towards the waters below. 'The lake,' he said. He paused, then continued, 'But it must be done

60

in secret – the Germans are everywhere. As you know, however, a lorry leaves this villa every night to collect supplies. When you have located a suitable position for depositing the bullion – a position where it can easily be salvaged when the moment comes – I will have it loaded in cases on that lorry. You will travel with it together with sufficient men to carry out the operation. The Germans are accustomed to seeing the lorry at that hour and will not stop it. You understand?'

'Yes, Excellency.'

Mussolini stood up. 'I am putting the future of Italy in your hands,' he said.

Volpi raised his right arm in the Fascist salute. '*Saluto* al Duce!' he said.

The next three days had been gruelling. In that time Volpi had had to acquire a large amount of the vast store of knowledge which men had amassed over the centuries about the bed of Lake Garda. Parts of it were shallow, others unfathomably deep; in the one the bullion could be too easily salvaged by marauders; in the other it could never be recovered by the Duce himself when the day of his triumph came.

The right depth was about twenty metres and indeed many parts of the lake were approximately that deep, but time and again those points had to be rejected for a variety of reasons: too near the shore, too far out, reputed to have a bottom unsuitable for the depositing of heavy weights or with currents unsuitable for a salvage operation.

Volpi went backwards and forwards across the lake surface in a motor-boat sounding, calculating, assessing. And finally he came upon what he considered to be exactly the right spot. It was about a kilometre from the shore, in a calm, sheltered part of the lake without particular currents and with a small harbour – the Furnaces at San Benedetto di Lugana – near enough to be of practical use when it came to salvaging the bullion. Moreover, it had the added advantage of not being readily overlooked from the shore.

This settled, Volpi reported to the Duce and handed over to him a map showing the exact point at which the bullion was to be lowered into the lake – a point Volpi had marked with a temporary buoy. When this buoy was removed nobody, not even Volpi himself, would be able to locate the exact spot without the map.

Mussolini personally supervised the crating of the bullion and in the small hours of the next morning a military supply lorry with Volpi, his men and the two great cases left Gargnano. They passed two German check-points, but no attempt was made to stop them and they reached the Furnaces unhindered.

The transfer of the cases from the lorry to the waiting boat provided a tense twenty minutes because Volpi knew that they could at any minute be interrupted by a German patrol, but this, too, was completed successfully and the boat was cast off and headed, chugging gently, into the night. The captain was a nervous little man who knew no more than that he was involved in something considerably bigger than himself and he steered obediently in silence as Volpi, standing beside him, directed him towards the area where the temporary buoy awaited them.

In the almost total darkness, illuminated only by the boat's own pale lights, it took longer than he had expected to locate the buoy, and dawn was not far off when the engines were switched off, the anchor lowered and the group of men gathered by the side to start the work of consigning the Mussolini gold to the depths of Lake Garda.

They worked in silence broken only by grunts and mono-syllabic orders. This last phase of the operation was carried out briefly and without hitches and ten minutes later the waters of the lake had added yet another secret to the considerable host they already stored.

Volpi wondered when it would be given up again, and a sense of pre-dawn despair smuggled in after the word 'when' the woeful clause 'if ever'.

'. . . I heard the splash as the second crate broke the surface of the water and in the darkness I was just able to make out the first ripples. Then it disappeared from sight. The men lowered the chains as far as they would go, then disengaged them and drew them up again. I remember them dripping on the deck. We then removed the temporary buoy, started the engines and headed back for the harbour. The mission was accomplished.'

The colonel came to a halt. The telling of the story put Peroni in mind of a very old film being played through. Once it had been located in the archives and put on the spool, it started to go, scratchily, jerkily, at times incomprehensibly, but with sufficient clarity to enable the viewer to follow what was going on.

Then, with the close-up of the chains dripping on the deck and the long shot of the boat chugging back in the night towards harbour, the reel came to an end, the sound-track cut off, the screen was filled for an instant with the flickering of meaningless lines and then went dead.

But without reel two, reel one was useless. How to find it and start it playing?

'The map,' said Peroni. 'What became of the map?'

The old man's eyes were lost; his mouth hung open again; his fingers plucked spasmodically at the sheet. 'I don't remember . . .'

'When Mussolini was captured by the partisans no map was found on him,' said Peroni. 'The night before that he spent in Como and all the most exhaustive enquiries there have failed to come up with anything. So where *could* he have left the map?'

'I don't remember . . .'

'It must have been here at Lake Garda! Try to think, Colonel Volpi – before he left Garda did Mussolini contact anyone with whom he might have left the map?'

The fingers continued to twitch at the sheet, but the eyes were dead and the face void of all understanding.

'Did you hear of him consigning anything to anybody?'

'I don't . . .' And then, with almost frightening unexpectedness, the facial muscles jerked as though the old man had been given an electric shock and the eyes seemed to flicker at returning memory. 'The night before the Duce left for Como . . .'

Another reel had started to play. It remained to see whether it was the right one.

'Volpi . . .'

'Excellency?'

'A car, Volpi, procure a car at once. A small car, something that will not attract the attention of the Germans. A Balilla, Volpi, and a driver. Tomorrow we leave for – Never mind that now. Get the car. I have a visit to make tonight. Immediately. You will accompany me as my aide. Is that understood?'

'Yes, Excellency.'

'I shall join you in the courtyard immediately.'

'At your orders, Excellency.'

That meeting with the Duce in the corridor had been like an

63

encounter with a ghost and, at the same time, it was almost as though it were Mussolini who had seen the ghost, for he started and stared at Volpi for a moment before stammering out the order for a car.

His appearance had deteriorated dramatically since the day when he had supervised the crating of the bullion. He now seemed physically ill. His features looked as though they were disintegrating and his eyes were wild and haunted.

And the general situation had deteriorated no less. The most outrageous rumours were flying about like bullets in a battle: he was going to fly to South America; he intended to commit suicide; he had concluded a secret pact with the English. He himself continued to insist spasmodically that he was going to take refuge in the mountains and conduct a resistance campaign to the death.

Volpi hoped that this was so, for he preferred the prospect of a heroic death to that of being captured and shot by the partisans, which was the most likely alternative facing the officers who had surrounded Mussolini in these last weeks. And now the order to get a car had nourished his hopes of a last stand in the mountains; maybe the Duce intended to visit somebody in order to organise their departure from Gargnano.

Car and driver were quickly organised and, as he waited beside it in the courtyard, Volpi wondered uneasily whether the Duce would come. Either out of forgetfulness or because he had changed his mind, he had been increasingly erratic lately in his planned attendances.

But not this time. Stumbling slightly, he emerged from the building carrying a portfolio only a few minutes after the arrival of the car. He came down the steps and gave rapid instructions to the driver in such a low tone that Volpi was unable to hear anything, though whether this was deliberate he could not tell. This done, he climbed into the back of the car and signed for Volpi to get in beside him.

Again it was well after midnight and there was little traffic about. The car drove fast, heading in the direction of Peschiera. The regulation blue-dimmed headlights picked out no more than blurred hints of the road.

Although he had asked for Volpi's company Mussolini didn't seem eager to take advantage of it. He shifted impatiently in his seat, occasionally mumbled incoherently to himself, opened and shut the lock of his portfolio, stared morosely out of the window.

Before they had gone very far the driver turned off the main lake road and they started to travel along smaller roads, some of which were not much more than tracks. Volpi presumed this was to avoid check-points. But soon, what with the unknown route and the dimmed headlights, he had lost all track of where they were beyond a general realisation that they were more or less on the opposite side of the lake from where they had started off.

After about an hour they reached their destination. The car turned into a drive leading up to a villa standing in its own grounds. It was in complete darkness with no sign of life, but there was nothing strange about that for everybody did their best, in those days when danger was omnipresent, to give the impression that nobody was at home.

When the car halted before the front door Mussolini seemed to hesitate for a moment. He started to say something to Volpi, then changed his mind. 'You wait here,' he said after another moment's indecision. 'Keep guard – make sure nobody comes. Nobody! Shoot if necessary.'

'*Eccellenza, si!*' Volpi got out of the car and went round it to open the door for Mussolini, who climbed out heavily with obvious effort and then started to walk, half shuffling, towards the front door, where he paused for a moment, apparently in concentration, before knocking. This done, he stood waiting and his powerful back, looming in the darkness, seemed to be hunched in defeat.

From the road came the sound of approaching engines and Volpi eased his gun out of its holster, ready to obey the Duce's order. The sound grew louder and louder, climaxed and then began to diminish. After a minute silence was restored. Probably a military convoy of escaping Germans.

He looked back to the front door where Mussolini was still waiting, motionless as a rock. Maybe the place really was deserted. Or more likely the inhabitants just weren't answering.

Mussolini knocked again and this time, after a few seconds, the door was opened. Briefly the person within shone a torch on himself, almost as though he wished to reassure Mussolini. And indeed he must have recognised him, for he then gave the Fascist salute. He was a young man with a short, black beard and

65

wearing a military greatcoat. There were two or three brief exchanges and then he stepped aside to let Mussolini enter before closing the door behind them.

Time goose-stepped in slow motion. Sparse traffic on the road, stirrings of the foliage, the driver's suppressed throat-clearing. Then when Volpi's emotional time-stream had flowed for at least an hour while his watch merely said ten minutes, the door was opened again and Mussolini emerged. Volpi could just make out the same young man raising his hand once again in the Fascist salute. Mussolini responded absently, then started to walk heavily towards the car. Volpi got out and went round to open the door for him and the Duce, muttering 'Gargnano' to the driver, climbed back inside.

It was as Volpi was walking back to his side of the car that he noticed the sun.

Carved in the stone-work beside the front door, it was a bit like a child's drawing of the sun. It had a human face, jovially benign, and rays of stone shone wavily from it. For some reason this detail stuck in Volpi's mind and came to symbolise for him that strange journey with Mussolini during the last night of the Republic of Salò.

CHAPTER 2

'Virgin, I declare!' said the woman with the heavily caked make-up who wore violet denims to match her finger- and toenails.

'I beg your pardon?' said Peroni, startled.

'I meant your zodiacal sign, of course.'

'Oh. No, I'm not.'

The woman smiled at him winsomely. 'You're not being strictly astrological, I believe,' she said. 'No, but seriously, let me guess. I'm quite infallible when I set my mind to it.'

'You'd be wasting your time,' said Peroni. 'The fact is I don't know the date of my birthday.' This wasn't true, but he had a belief – hungover from his Neapolitan childhood, but ineradicable – that, like your name, your zodiacal sign somehow mysteriously represents you and should not be lightly given away. Particularly to a witch. And something inside Peroni that the commissario would have disavowed said that this woman was a witch.

'Oh, but we must find out,' she said playfully. 'All my pieces are designed for particular signs of the zodiac and it would be most inadvisable to take one that was not intended for you. I am,' she went on more seriously, 'the first zodiacal ceramist in Europe.'

'I haven't come here to buy ceramics.'

'Oh?' A wary look came into her eyes. 'What have you come for then?'

When the second reel of Colonel Volpi's story had jerked to a blank halt, Peroni realised that he had come to a point of no return in the affair of Cordelia Hope. Up till then, whatever his opinions, the accidental death theory had been bound to have the upper hand, but now he was convinced that she had been on a path where murder lay in wait and he did not intend to abandon the enquiry until he had learnt what had befallen her.

Assuming she had evinced the same two reels from Colonel Volpi, then she, like Peroni, would have identified the young man at the villa who had received Mussolini with General del Duca's dead son whose portrait she, too, would certainly have seen. And she would also probably have drawn the conclusion that Mussolini's portfolio that night contained the map, which he had entrusted into the safe keeping of the del Duca family who had then been living at Costermano.

But her visit to Colonel Volpi had been made *after* she had seen the general and heard his brusque denial that any map had been delivered into the family keeping. So who would she have gone to after she had seen Volpi? Peroni thought he could guess and intended to go to the same person. Another question mark concerned how Cordelia had got on to the old colonel at the geriatric clinic. And that might be important, too.

When he had emerged from the clinic the tyrannical sun was in the process of being deposed, and he had to be back in Venice that evening. If he was lucky, he reckoned, there was just time to make the planned call and, on the way, to call in on the lady ceramist at Peschiera who had told the brigadiere of Cordelia's presumed suicide and whose libidinous cordiality had been cut so abruptly short when Peroni had announced that he had not come to buy ceramics.

'What have you come for then?'

'Police,' said Peroni, showing his card.

The wary look became icy calculation. 'In that case you'd better come into my office.'

She turned and led the way to a small office at the back of the gallery-cum-shop and, as he followed her, Peroni eyed the ceramics on display, all dramatically painted with animals and plants and other less readily definable and probably less pleasant objects. They were cleverly done, but he felt that he would have mistrusted them even if he had been less certain that the hand that had formed them was that of a witch.

'Drink?' When she turned to face him in the office, having carefully closed the door, all calculation had vanished, giving way to a sort of lubricious playfulness.

'No, thank you.'

'I will, if you don't mind.' She concocted herself a brew from a miniature bar in the corner and then lit a cigarette in a long, thirties-style holder, blowing smoke slowly in Peroni's direction. The whole performance had a disconcertingly ritualistic air about it. 'Well?' she said when it was done.

'I understand you were on friendly terms with a young Englishwoman who was drowned in the lake last week and that you told the carabinieri you believed she had committed suicide?'

She had wound so powerful a spell about herself that it was impossible to tell her reaction. 'That's right,' she said. 'Poor *tesoro*! How my heart bled when I heard the news!'

'It took rather a long while to reach you, didn't it?'

'I never read newspapers – the horoscopes they give are dangerously misleading. And how else would I have heard?'

Peroni decided to let that pass. 'How did you meet her?'

'She came into the gallery and admired my ceramics. The friendship that arose between us was immediate, spontaneous and as deep as the waters of the lake.'

It seemed improbable; the Cordelia that Peroni had known would never have formed a friendship with this theatrical witch. 'Go on.'

'After that she would often visit me and we would sit up together into the small hours of the morning laying bare our souls.'

Less and less probable. 'She told you that she was searching for something here on the lake?'

'That's right.'

'Did she give you any idea what it was?'

'None whatsoever. It was the only secret she kept from me. But I understood from the way she talked that it must be something of great importance.'

'What made you so certain that she committed suicide?'

'The last time I saw her – only the morning before she died as I later discovered – she told me she no longer had any hope of finding whatever it was and that consequently she had nothing left to live for. "I would like to sail my yacht into the middle of the lake," she said, "and then just let myself go into the water and swim and swim and swim until I could swim no more, and the lake would wrap me peacefully in its breast." Of course it never occurred to me then that she actually meant to do it.'

'No, of course not,' said Peroni with sudden gleaming cordiality, giving her his hand. 'You've been most helpful in finally clearing up the matter.'

'Oh?' she said, taken off balance by his new mood. 'Well, of course I'm delighted to be of assistance to the police.'

'As an artist you must have found her fascinating.' Quite unexpectedly Peroni was a warlock.

'Oh, I did.'

'Her appearance was so striking, don't you think? Particularly her long black hair.'

'That's right,' said the witch, 'as black as the heart of the night.'

The gleaming stereo on the pavement, almost as long as a car, blared hard rock as Lidia danced with Maurizio. A fairish crowd had gathered to watch and indeed the couple presented quite a spectacle. They both wore black leather jackets hand painted with whorls and constellations and flowers. At shoulder level his jacket said PANTHER and hers KESTREL. He had a punk hair-cut dyed purple, green and yellow and wore on his wrist a heavy bracelet covered with metal studs which gleamed and flashed as he danced. She had long, fair, dishevelled hair and a flaunting bead necklace, and her face was slashed with scarlet, green and black.

Maurizio searched the air with the palms of his hands as

69

though he were trying to escape from an invisible glass cage. Lidia jerked non-existent threads attached to various parts of her face making them twitch alarmingly. Then they started to dance more and more frenetically, jerking and rolling about on the ground with demented energy.

Lidia was in Paradise. This was real life at last. A pity about Mamma, but then she'd asked for it, and anyway things were too exciting to worry about her for long. More and more frequently Maurizio was choosing her as a partner instead of that little cow Susanna, who, she observed, was standing on the opposite side of the road with the other two boys in the group observing her vindictively. Well, let her be as jealous as she liked. Whose fault was it if Maurizio preferred Lidia as his girl?

The music moved towards a crashing, thudding climax and the couple whirled so fast that it was no longer possible to distinguish their flailing limbs singly. Then finally it and they came to a halt and there was a scattering of applause from the spectators.

'Quick!' Maurizio hissed at her from the corner of his mouth. 'Church collection before the bastards have time to slink off. You go for the pricks and I'll take the cunts.' Saying which, with a charming little boyish smile on his face, he started to move among the crowd with one of the tin plates they used for collecting money. Lidia followed him with the other.

Then she halted in sudden terror. A young carabiniere was moving towards them in a purposeful looking way. Had Mamma told the police about her escape? It was just the sort of ridiculous, old-fashioned thing she would do. Couldn't she get it into her silly head that Lidia was a fully responsible, mature adult and not a baby any longer? Still, it was no good going on about that now. The immediate danger was that if Mamma *had* gone and sneaked to the police they would be keeping a look-out and maybe the carabiniere had recognised her. If he tried to arrest her she would make a run for it, but in the meantime she must try and bluff it out. She resumed the collection, trying to look indifferent.

'Pack it up, you two,' said the carabiniere. 'Begging in the streets is illegal.'

Lidia felt a rush of relief. It wasn't her he wanted after all.

'OK,' said Maurizio, meek as a lamb. 'I'm very sorry about that, Officer. We wouldn't have dreamed of doing it if we'd known it was illegal. We'll be on our way at once.' The carabiniere nodded, turned and started to move off, mollified by the respectful tone. Then when he was a short way off Maurizio mouthed a soft 'Fuck you!' with an expression that was quite venomous enough to make up for the lack of volume.

Lidia giggled. He was so brilliantly clever and witty.

A couple of hours later the young carabiniere, having finished his turn of duty, went back to headquarters where practically the first thing he saw was a photograph of a girl among the missing persons, and in spite of the comparative absence of make-up he was certain it was the same girl he had seen dancing in the street before.

'Pity,' said the lieutenant to whom he reported this. 'It only came in this afternoon. We'll have a look round, but they might be anywhere by now. And we'd better report straight through to Venice, too. The silly little cow's under age.'

CHAPTER 3

As he drove towards Bardolino, Peroni pondered the implications of what he had just learned. Somebody must have primed the witch to go to the carabinieri with a false suicide story. Why? To stop Peroni from continuing his enquiries. Again why? Because he was the only person who even suspected that Cordelia had been killed.

And who would have primed the witch? Whoever it was that had killed Cordelia. Or somebody who wanted to protect that person. Peroni let his mind range over some of the people he had met over his enquiries. The mayor, Bombarone, genial, bibulous, the wily politician who enjoyed playing the role of peasant; the cavalry twill gentleman at San Vigilio, a long shot perhaps, but the field was still wide open; Count Attilio up at the Villa Mimosa, cynically aware of his own failure in life and cocking snooks at it with whisky and invisible orchestras; Pagani, the ailing hermit; General del Duca, the barking Fascist maker of fine wines; or, come to that, his daughter, Nausicaa, with the terrifying brood and the appealing gap between her front teeth; or the philosophical secretary, Aristotle. Anyone.

And what line to take now? If it had been an official homicide enquiry the obvious thing would have been to take in the witch for questioning and find out who had set her on, even though Peroni suspected that squeezing the truth out of her would have presented a problem, witchcraft lending its practitioners strange immunity. But there were two objections to this course. For one thing he didn't have the authority. And for another any further action against her would put whoever-it-was behind her in a state of alarm which might well destroy for good and all his chances of getting at the truth.

No, better to coddle secretly the certainty she had given him that the suicide story was a lie and continue the enquiries for the moment as if he had not spoken to the witch. Then later, when and if he found out who Cordelia's killer was, return and dismantle her.

The village of Bardolino was just beginning to twinkle in the gloaming when he arrived there. A deftly selected old lady, knitting outside her front door, provided him with the information he needed and he made his way to the bungalow on the outskirts of the village which she indicated.

His ring was answered by Aristotle himself, whose reaction on seeing Peroni was even more violent than that on the previous occasion. He started and went corpse-white.

'Just one or two little questions,' said Peroni amiably as though he had noticed nothing.

'C-come in,' said Aristotle. 'If you'll excuse me for just one m-minute . . .' He went into the front room, and such was his agitation that it occurred to Peroni that he was going to do violence to himself. But instead he spoke to two elderly people, presumably his parents, who could just be made out on the sofa watching television. 'A gentleman to s-see me,' he said. 'Business from the villa.' The old people nodded like dolls without taking their eyes off the screen. 'If you don't mind c-coming in the garden,' said Aristotle to Peroni, and led the way out to a tiny rectangle of grass with some seven flowers behind the bungalow.

There were two inappropriate upright chairs beneath an umbrella and on these they sat. 'What can I do for you?' asked Aristotle, the tremble in his voice belying the routine formality of the phrase.

72

Peroni took his time. 'Information,' he said at last, studying the word as though it were a doubtful museum piece, 'has reached me to the effect that your dealings with Signorina Hope were not quite as superficial as you gave me to understand.'

'I don't follow—'

'I think you do.' Peroni realised with irritation that he had fallen into a smoothy movie detective act and was unable to shake it off. 'Listen,' he went on, 'if you tell me just what happened, I may be able to ensure that nothing more is said outside this . . .' he looked about him ' . . . this garden. But if you don't I shall have to treat you as a hostile witness which will mean that everybody will get to know about it. You choose.'

It was a phony performance, but it worked. 'Very well!' said Aristotle, something like defiance taking the place of terror. 'I know what I did was wrong, but I loved her! I've never loved a w–woman as much as I loved her and if she'd asked me to do something a m–million times worse I'd still have done it!'

'I understand,' said Peroni, this time completely sincerely; he had been there himself. 'Go on.'

Somewhere surprisingly near came the sound of a guitar and a silky male voice singing a love song.

'After she'd spoken to the g–general – when I was showing her out – I asked her if I could meet her again and she looked at me in a s–sort of assessing way and said, "If you really want to." Then she thought for a m–moment and went on, "Maybe there's something you can do for me, too." I told her I would do anything and she said she wanted to get hold of the n–names of Mussolini's staff at the Villa Feltrinelli at Gargnano towards the end of the war. For a book she was writing. Well, it so happened that I'd s–seen a list of personnel there not long before among the general's papers. He wasn't actually there himself, but he had something to do with s–security. I said I'd copy it for her. Well,' defensively, 'there was nothing really wrong with that – after all, it's history. So I did copy the names and I gave them to her the next day.'

'Was one of the people on that list a Colonel Volpi?'

Aristotle looked very surprised. 'Yes,' he said, 'as a matter of fact it was. It was the only n–name I knew because the general has been to visit him several times at a clinic near Sirmione.'

So that explained how Cordelia had got on to Volpi. 'And the other names?'

'They meant n–nothing to me. I told her they were probably all d–dead by now, but she said she'd try to trace them just the s–same.'

'Did she do so as far as you know?'

'Not that she told me.'

'Could you get hold of those names again?'

'They're at the villa. I can copy them tomorrow. If you telephone me here at lunchtime I'll let you have them.' He gave Peroni the number.

There was an awkward silence. It was evident not only that Aristotle's story was unfinished, but also that the most compromising part was yet to come.

'Go on,' said Peroni.

'I saw her again a couple of days later and she asked me—' He gulped. 'She asked me if I would help her look for s–something which she had good reason to believe was at the villa.'

'Did she say what?'

'A d–document.' So that was it: Peroni's guess had been right. ('Why shouldn't I be involved in something illegal?' Cordelia's voice chimed at him out of the past.) 'She didn't want to s–steal it,' Aristotle went on, 'only photograph it to get information for this book she was writing. All she wanted it for was historical research.' ('Though in fact I'm not quite sure about the ethics of it myself. Legally wrong, morally OK might just about sum it up.') 'Nobody would be the worse for it and the general would never know. But how could she search the villa without being seen, I said. "Don't they ever s–sleep?" she asked me. And, in fact, the general goes to bed early. The signora, his daughter, when she's there, and the children are all in their part of the house and the servants watch television. I often go up there to work in the evening – I've got my own k–key – and I have the lower part of the house completely to myself. By midnight everybody's asleep. "We could go up tomorrow night," she said. I was a bit s–scared, but she said "Don't worry – we shan't be caught." And she had a way of making you believe that what she said would come true.'

I know she had, thought Peroni, I know.

'Well, we did go up the next night and I showed her to the general's study which is where she said the document would probably be. Then I k–kept watch while she searched and after about twenty minutes I heard her whisper "G–got it!" and the sound of her camera clicking several times. That was it. We left the house and walked back to the village together—'

'Did you ask her what the document was?'

'Yes, I did. She said it was some sort of old map.'

Right. The map showing the whereabouts of the Mussolini gold had been entrusted to General del Duca and Cordelia had photographed it. So much was clear. But what would she have done next? Without some means of salvaging the gold the map was no more than a piece of paper. She would have needed help and anybody who could provide the sort of help she wanted might well have been a very tough person indeed. The sort of person who would have been ready to murder so as to ensure exclusive rights on what was reputed to have been a quite considerable treasure.

Who? The answer was still anybody except, presumably, General del Duca, who was more concerned to keep faith with the Duce's memory. Or was he?

At this stage Peroni would have needed a great deal of time and a small flock of assistants to continue the enquiry. But he had neither. And his commitments in Venice could not be side-stepped altogether. So finding out the truth about Cordelia would have to remain a spare-time occupation. And, even so, where to go next? Now that the dazzling flash of revelation provided by Colonel Volpi and Aristotle had somewhat faded, the path ahead seemed as dark as it had done before.

Red and green neon winked invitingly on the road ahead and Peroni pulled into the courtyard of a bar, and went in for a drink. It was empty except for a group of men playing cards and a woman behind the bar.

'Campari soda, *per piacere.*'

He sat down with his drink at a table with the *Arena*, Verona's local paper. The deaths page – each *caro defunto* in his own coffin-like box of print, often plus photograph – was always rich in material for meditation. He started to turn to it, but was halted by the word 'Garda' in a page three headline.

'SETTLEMENTS ON STILTS FOR GARDA'S EARLIEST INHABITANTS,' it announced enigmatically. But a proliferation of sub-heads made matters clearer. 'Congress on the lake's prehistoric platform dwellers at San Benedetto di Lugana,' they announced. 'To open tomorrow evening. Delegations from

75

many European countries. Exhibition of photographs and artefacts. Lectures by authorities of international reputation.' But it was the last of these sub-heads that stabbed Peroni's attention quivering to the page. 'Underwater exploration team headed by Prof. Daniele Bellini,' it said.

Peroni read on with drilling concentration, letting his Campari get warm at his elbow. First there was a fair wodge of semi-academic information about the platform dwellers, whose existence he had never even heard of. To protect themselves from wild animals and marauders they had built their homes on rafts resting on poles which, in their turn, were embedded in the lake bottom. Remains of these settlements were to be found in lakes all over Europe, in Switzerland, Austria, north Germany, the Baltic, Holland and England, but the most notable were in Italy, particularly at Lake Garda. The dwellers themselves, small farmers and fishermen, had kept all kinds of domestic animals – except the horse, which would have been a little cumbersome on a lake platform. And they continued their peaceful aquatic existence from the Aeneolithic age to the Bronze age.

Peroni's interest flagged a bit, but revived towards the end of the article when Professor Bellini and his team of four re-appeared. They had carried out underwater explorations all over the world, and in fact Peroni remembered having seen a television programme about them. Bellini, the newspaper announced with pride, had been born locally. He was famous for his daring and originality and had invented and built a remarkable craft which combined the functions of a bathyscaphe with those of an ultra-sophisticated tug, so that while it could submerge to explore at mind-boggling depths it also served as a base for aqualung diving and could be used for loading and transporting submarine finds.

But the final and most telling kick to the piece was in the last paragraph, which said that Bellini and his team had arrived some ten days previously at the lake, where they had been engaged in underwater research concerning certain forms of mollusc which were to be found on its bed. So they had already been there several days before Cordelia was drowned.

A million lire to a packet of spaghetti, thought Peroni, that Professor Bellini had been her next call after she had got the map into her hands.

* * *

The news that Lidia had been seen at the lake was doubly satisfactory. For one thing, it made the chances of tracing her quickly that much higher. And for another, it gave Peroni the excuse to get back to the lake and make at least one enquiry before the opening of the prehistoric platform dwellers congress which was at six o'clock that evening.

He put out a special call regarding Lidia to all police and carabinieri stations on the lake and then spent the rest of the morning dealing with some of the back-log of work which had accumulated in Venice. At lunchtime he had a beer and a couple of toasted sandwiches sent in to him and telephoned Aristotle for the promised list of Mussolini's staff at the Villa Feltrinelli at Gargnano. It contained twenty-eight names ranging from chiefs-of-staff to cooks and drivers, but the only name which meant anything to Peroni was that of Colonel Volpi. Obviously most of the others would be dead or otherwise untraceable, but even the remotest possibility that Cordelia had been in touch with one or more of them could not be ignored, so he passed the list to a junior colleague with the request that it be checked as quickly as possible. By two o'clock he was on his way to the lake.

First of all he made a deviation to the village of Garda. Here there turned out to be three photographer's shops, but at the second he was lucky.

'Yes, I do remember her,' said the scatty looking woman with erratically dyed hair and pink butterfly-wing glasses who ran it. 'Poor thing – I heard she was drowned. People really should be more careful, don't you think? Yes, she brought in photographs to be developed once or twice. I offer a twenty-four-hour service if you ever should ... I don't know if you're a photographer yourself ... No, I'm afraid I can't remember when she came in for the last time. I'm rushed off my feet at this time of year. But yes, now you come to mention it there should be some prints for her. Oh well, I suppose since she's dead, poor dear, and you are the police it can't do any harm ...'

She pulled out a drawer under the counter and started to finger through envelopes of prints. She went through them all once, then frowned and went back to the beginning again, checking this time more carefully.

'That's strange,' she said when she'd finished. 'I could have sworn there were some for her.'

'Could somebody have taken them without your knowing?'

'Well, they *could*, I suppose. It would have to be somebody who knew the shop, of course. There are moments when I'm out at the back on the telephone or in the darkroom, but never for very long.'.

'You've no idea, I suppose, what the photographs might have been of?'

She shook her streaky head. 'I'm afraid I'm far too busy to look at customers' pictures. Besides, I don't do the developing myself. I have a man who calls in twice a day during the season to deliver prints and collect negatives. I could call him if you like.'

'Please.' It was a long shot and predictably failed to hit anything. So Peroni set off for the congress opening with the disquieting knowledge that somebody had stolen a group of Cordelia's photographs, of unknown subject matter.

CHAPTER 4

Peroni had the impression that he was being followed. He had reached San Benedetto with time in hand before the opening of the congress and so, after parking his car, he had set out on a prowl of inspection round the village. And almost immediately he had felt that unmistakable sensation of someone behind him.

What with the holiday-makers whose numbers were swollen by delegates and visitors to the congress it was impossible to check on this. He did everything he could to take counter-action: he used shop windows as mirrors, dodged into doorways and even once doubled suddenly back on his tracks, but all in vain. Whoever it was remained doggedly on his heels.

Finally he came to a church, which gave him an idea. He nipped inside and looked quickly about while hastily genuflecting and crossing himself. The place was deserted and there, conveniently to hand in the shadows, was an old-fashioned confessional. He scuttled into it, pulled the curtains and waited.

Sure enough about ten seconds later the main door of the church was edged open and a female head looked cautiously in.

It was followed by a female body and, putting the two together as he peeped through the curtains, he had no difficulty in recognising Nausicaa, the gap-toothed mother of a teeming brood.

She, too, bobbed in the direction of the altar, looking about her as she did so. Then, seeing nobody, she made her way with sleuth-like mien towards a lateral door through which, presumably, she imagined Peroni had gone. He let her reach it and then boomed as sepulchrally as he was able, 'Nausicaa!'

She span round with much the same expression that Eve must have had when God called to them in the Garden of Eden after the eating of the apple. 'Achille?' she said a little nervously.

Peroni emerged from his hiding place like – or so he chose to think – some mythical hero rising from the waves.

'Oh, Achille,' she said with relief, 'you did give me a turn! Not but what,' she went on, relief shading into reproof, 'I can say I consider hiding in a confessional in accordance with the rules. If it's not downright sacrilege.'

'What rules?' said Peroni.

'However,' she went on, ignoring the question, 'you must admit I did pretty well. A good quarter of an hour I kept you on your toes and I'm the rawest of amateurs.'

'Amateur whats?'

'Detectives of course!' she said in the tone she must have used with the more backward of her children.

'Nausicaa, do you mind telling me what this is all about?'

'Not at all, but first of all I think you should buy me a drink.'

Peroni found this prospect pleasing and, leaving the church, they went to sit at a *caffe* table near the water's edge. 'What will you have?'

'A bottle of San Benedetto di Lugana, please,' she said as though it were the most normal thing in the world, and then, seeing his slightly startled expression, she went on in an explanatory tone, 'For both of us, I mean. It's always cheaper to order by the bottle.'

Peroni conveyed the order to a waiter and then repeated his question about her unusual behaviour.

'I was following you, of course,' she said. 'I thought that would be obvious.'

'Yes, but why?'

'Well, why not?' Irritating she might be, but there was no

denying she had a mysterious charm. Peroni observed her with pleasure, which she seemed to enjoy. She was no tidier than on their previous meeting. She wore rather grubby pale-coloured slacks, espadrilles and a man's shirt sufficiently wide at the neck to reveal the straps of her bra – a spectacle Peroni would have found indelicate in most women, but which, in her, had a disturbingly aphrodisiacal effect. In the same way the nest-like confusion of her hair and the little beads of sweat on her neck aroused him rather than put him off.

'I happened to see you getting out of your car,' she was going on, 'looking like Hamlet – that was the one who was always thinking, wasn't it? So I thought I'd see how long I could follow you without you noticing. I mean it was a bit like playing chess with a master. And I'd have won, too, if you hadn't made that sacrilegious move into the confessional.'

'But why should I suspect that someone would be following me?'

'Ah, but you did, didn't you? I could almost see your mind churning over the problem through the back of your neck. Not to mention all that jumping into doorways and looking in shop windows.'

She was a strange woman, no doubt about it. And then, when the wine came and the waiter was opening it, he wondered whether she might not be a dangerous one as well. The story about following him as a game was in character all right, but was it true? She was certainly on the fringe of the Mussolini gold labyrinth; who was to say she was not at the heart of it?

With a little phut the cork came out of the bottle and the waiter poured for them, leaving the remainder of the wine on the table. 'Chin chin!' she said. 'You're wondering whether I'm telling the truth, aren't you?'

'Certainly not,' Peroni lied stoutly. 'Whatever makes you think that?'

'I can read men upside down like one of my children's comics.'

'Apropos,' said Peroni, snatching at the chance to change the subject, 'what have you done with your children?'

'Left them with Papa. I do that every so often. It gives us all a marvellous treat. I get a rest. Papa becomes an active general again with his own private army to roar at. And the children do just exactly whatever they feel like.'

80

'I thought they did that anyway.'

'You should see them with Papa.'

'And what brings you to this part of the lake?'

'Oh,' she said vaguely, 'I know some people at this congress they're holding. What about you?'

As she spoke the last three words there was an almost imperceptible increase of tension in her manner which told Peroni that the question was not spontaneous, and he remembered the fear that had come into her eyes at their first meeting, when he had mentioned Cordelia's death. 'I'm interested in underwater exploration.' The lie was bland this time.

'Really?' she said suspiciously.

'Why not? It's an enthralling subject.'

'Yes, it is, isn't it?' She took a gulp of her San Benedetto and it looked to Peroni like a gulp of relief. 'Well, in that case,' she went on, quite herself again, 'I expect you'd like to meet the Hero of the Depths, the King of the Underwater World.'

'Daniele Bellini?' She nodded. 'You know him?'

'Oh yes, I know him.'

Something in her manner made him look at her more closely. 'He wasn't by any chance a husband of yours, was he?'

'Oh no, nothing like that – I would never marry Daniele. I knew him when he was a little boy – he was born in these parts. I'll introduce you if you like. You two really ought to meet.' For some reason the idea seemed to amuse her, then she looked at her watch and started dramatically. '*Santo cielo*! The opening ceremony must have already started.' She tipped the last of the wine into Peroni's glass. 'Drink up quick' – making it sound as though she were telling one of her brood to finish its milk – 'and we'll be off.'

'. . . local lad makes good. The sort of story that is perennially dear to the human heart. And in Professor Bellini – Daniele if he will permit me – we have that story personified.'

As Peroni and Nausicaa entered the large, high-ceilinged chamber the mayor, Bombarone, was orating genially to a large audience which seemed to have occupied all the chairs. The walls were lined with large photographs of huts or groups of huts on platforms raised above the water on poles. There were also portraits of partially clad men and women with primitive agricultural or fishing gear who were presumably settlement

81

dwellers. And beneath these were lines of brilliantly lit glass cases containing artefacts and bones, one imagined, of all the domestic animals except the horse which the settlement dwellers kept.

'There're a couple of chairs there at the front!' Nausicaa hissed loudly. 'Come on!' And taking his hand she led him up one of the side aisles. Their progress attracted some attention and Peroni felt that everyone was assessing his southern appearance, but Nausicaa was not in the least put out.

'. . . his earliest years on the lake where he acquired his lifelong passion for the depths. As a boy—' There was an almost imperceptible check in Bombarone's oratory as he recognised Peroni, but then the genial flow of words was resumed, as rollingly musical as before.

The chairs Nausicaa had so unluckily spotted were in the centre of the third row and their progress as they made their way along it, with Nausicaa breathily whispering '*Permesso*' at each person they passed, had rather the effect of a couple of drunks erupting in church and, indeed, Peroni realised with dismay, their breaths after a bottle of San Benedetto must have been fairly fruity. The ecclesiastical simile was fortified by a fully attired bishop in the front row who finally gave way to the temptation to look round and see what all the confusion was about.

'. . . many hours spent in a yacht learning the tricks and rhythms of great waters . . .'

'*Permesso, permesso* . . .' Following shame-facedly in Nausicaa's chaotic wake Peroni suddenly found himself unexpectedly knee to knee with the zodiacal ceramist witch whose eyes, as they looked straight into his, seemed to be full of spells. Then as Nausicaa pulled him implacably on to the next pair of knees the witch gave him a slow Circean smile.

Mercifully the two empty chairs were only five places further along the row, so that a few seconds later Peroni was able to sink down into relative anonymity, though he continued for a while to feel the ping of outraged glances.

He gave his attention to the platform where Bombarone was by no means the only speaker. Ten people were sitting at a long, carved table (excluding Bombarone, who was standing in the centre). Of the five on his left Peroni recognised two from the days when he had been stationed in Verona. They were top regional brass. But it was the five on Bombarone's right who aroused his interest. The first of these was outstandingly good looking with Greek features and a mass of black hair just tinged at the temples with grey, and there was a classical elegance about his clothes which matched the rest of him.

'Daniele,' Nausicaa hissed loudly indicating this one and confirming Peroni's guess that he was indeed the Hero of the Depths.

Beside him was a man with a pleasantly ugly, skew-whiff face, prematurely creased, and wise monkey eyes. The next two were, respectively, vulpine and feline. But it was the one at the end of the row who was most spectacular in appearance. He was a squinnying giant with a black beard and a monstrous cowboy hat. Peroni decided he would not like to meet this one down a dark or any other sort of alley.

Bombarone's speech changed key with smooth skill into introduction as he presented Daniele Bellini, who then rose from his chair with a quick glance of thanks and a modest smile at the audience. 'Your Excellency,' he began with a respectful bow towards the bishop, 'Mr Prefect, Honourable Perandini, Mr Mayor . . .' And so on, one after the other, he bowed at all the congregated VIPs before launching into his speech proper.

'This is his polite little boy act,' Nausicaa whispered loudly. 'He's like Father Christmas – there's not one he hasn't got in his sack.' But she sounded quite admiring just the same, Peroni thought.

Bellini talked briefly about his childhood on the lake, his feelings on returning to it after so many years, and then went on to give a quick, non-technical and even amusing review of the research they had been doing over the last few days into the mollusc life on the bed. And finally, having outlined some of the activities that would be taking place over the four days the congress was due to last, he went on, 'In underwater exploration, particularly at any depth, a very particular relationship is formed among the divers. Each one is dependent upon the others for his safety, which means that this relationship must be composed not only of deep friendship, but also of total mutual trust. That is why in presenting this enterprise to you it would be gravely misleading if I were to introduce myself without at the same time presenting my four colleagues. We are five men, but when we dive we are a single heart and a single mind.'

'Oh, very nicely put!' said Nausicaa, starting a round of applause.

'Next to me,' went on Bellini when the clapping had died down, 'is Willi Meyer.' The man with the skew-whiff face stood up embarrassedly and sat down again with relief. 'Teo and Leo Mantovani – the only professional underwater explorers who are also twins!' Leo and Teo stood up to more applause looking smug. 'And finally Max Schleier ...' the giant '... or, as he is known in the team, little Max.'

'Oh, very funny,' said Nausicaa. 'Still, it always goes over well with the plebs.' Then shortly afterwards when the ceremony was done she announced, 'Drinks! Though only for the nobs. This way.' And taking his hand she led him off in the opposite direction, he was relieved to notice, from the witch. She dodged and bulldozed a way for them through the crowd and eventually into a smaller chamber where the nobs had already started clustering fairly densely. Here she halted a startled looking waiter whom she relieved of four glasses of champagne which she lined up on a marble ledge near one of the windows. 'That should keep us going for a few minutes,' she said, downing one of them. 'Now if you stay here I'll try and organise a summit meeting between you and Daniele. Don't move now!' Saying which she plunged back into the crowd.

Peroni wondered suspiciously why she had to organise the meeting without him, and then immediately postponed the problem: Nausicaa was beyond explanation. He picked up one of the remaining glasses of champagne and followed her example.

'*Buona sera* . . .'

Peroni choked slightly and turned to meet the speaker, who was Pagani, the hermit. '*Buona sera.*' He took the proffered hand, which was as chill and limp as a dead fish.

'So interesting, didn't you find?' Pagani went on. 'Yes, indeed, yes ...'

Peroni only half listened, being more taken up with the man's appearance. Scarcely a week had passed since they met and yet it might have been a year to judge by the changes that had taken place in Pagani. Before, he had been ailing in some unspecified way. Now he seemed to be gravely ill. The off-white cotton suit looked as though it had not been taken off since then and the eyes were filmy. But worst of all he gave off a sort of dank smell of putrefaction so that Peroni had to make an effort not to retreat.

'. . . a certain relief in the monotony of one's daily existence. Yes . . . Well, I must be moving on. So nice to have seen you again.' And, after another graveyard handshake, much to Peroni's relief he tottered off into the crowd.

To get the taste off his mental and physical palate Peroni disposed of another glass of champagne and was just wishing Nausicaa would come back when he was greeted once again, this time very much from the land of the living.

'So we meet again. By chance or design? And in the latter case, whose?' Count Attilio Remigi must have had a hip-flask with him if he had sat through the previous ceremony, for it would have taken more than a couple of glasses of champagne to get him into his present state of swaying geniality.

'Now whatever brings you of all people to a congress concerning the mysterious depths of Lake Garda? Depths which, if we are to believe all we hear, contain a great deal more than molluscs. However,' he went on, raising a slightly trembling finger to his lips, 'I am dumb. And indeed, if I go on for much longer the way I am, I probably soon will be literally as well as figuratively. What news of your lovely cousin?'

Before Peroni had time to answer, the two of them were swept irresistibly aside by the passage of Max Schleier who for some reason had changed headgear and was now wearing a sort of baseball cap.

'Bellini must know what he's talking about,' said the count when he had gone by, 'but I should find a relationship of deep friendship and mutual trust a bit of a strain with a natural force like that.'

'He's changed hats,' said Peroni, picking on the incongruity.

'He's famous for it. Headwear is his peculiar eccentricity.'

'You know them?'

'No, no,' said the count, taking out the guessed-at hip-flask and tipping it into two of the empty champagne glasses, 'I know *of* them. I attract gossip like a magnet attracts filings.'

'And Daniele Bellini?' said Peroni haphazardly. 'What does gossip say of him?'

'Gossip says he has protection.'

'Any idea what sort? Or who?'

'Achille, come along at once!' said Nausicaa, emerging out of the crowd like Botticelli's Venus from the sea. 'Oh, you're busy. Do you mind very much,' she went on to the count, 'if I take this man away from you?'

'I shall miss his company,' said the count with tipsy courtesy.

'People are flocking round Daniele like wasps round a jam-pot,' said Nausicaa, dragging Peroni through the crowd, 'which, of course, is what he likes best. But I think I can just about get at him now.'

As they went Peroni wondered whether she and the count knew each other. From their brief exchange it was impossible to say one way or the other. All these people, he thought, seemed to be pullulating with unknown factors.

They came to the fringe of a group of people centred round Bellini and, standing on tiptoe, Nausicaa started to make gestures to attract the attention of the Hero of the Depths. If they hadn't been so absorbed, the people about him might have been somewhat alarmed at this performance of hers. She contorted her mouth with voiceless words, at the same time hooking her left index finger downwards in the air and then whirling it round and round its opposite number as though she were trying to give the impression of a merry-go-round.

Bellini seemed to be accustomed to this sort of summons for, excusing himself from the group with bird-from-tree charm, he came over to her.

'*Ciao*,' he said. 'Something gave me the impression you wanted to speak to me.'

'That's right,' said Nausicaa, either unaware of the irony or ignoring it. 'I want you to meet a friend of mine.' She introduced them and they shook hands, bowing slightly and exchanging smiles which, had they but realised it, were surprisingly similar. 'If either of you were anybody else,' she went on, 'you would certainly have heard of each other, but as it is I am sure that each of you has only ever heard of himself.' With a scratch of irritation Peroni wondered whether that was what she had meant when, at the *caffe* earlier, she had smiled at the prospect of their meeting. 'Daniele,' she said to Peroni, 'is King of the Underwater, while Achille,' she turned to the other man, 'is King of the Underworld. That's to say a very famous policeman. And I think that if you want to talk in peace you should show Achille your favourite toy.'

Bellini had shown no surprise at the word 'policeman' and this mention of a toy had all the air of prearrangement. Just what was going on?

'I shall be delighted to show you what Nausicaa is pleased to call my toy,' said Bellini, turning to Peroni, 'that is, if you're interested in a descent to the depths?'

Peroni felt a nudge of uneasiness at the prospect, but he put a bold face on it and said he would be enthralled.

'In that case let's go.'

'See you later,' said Nausicaa, caressing them both with a look.

CHAPTER 5

The bathyscaphe lay in the waters of the harbour looking as though it had newly arrived from outer space. It was a large, rounded surreality of steel, gleaming in the still bright sun and attended by a crowd of admirers.

'The *Proserpina*,' said Bellini, halting dazed with admiration either for the craft or his own skill in designing it. 'If you remember, she went into the depths of the earth among the dead. And in a sense that's what underwater exploration is about.'

The comparison was an eerie one and Peroni's nudge of uneasiness became a muffled, drum-like thud. But there was no going back now. They walked along the quay to where the *Proserpina* was moored. 'After you,' said Bellini, indicating a steel ladder built into the side. Peroni climbed up it on to the deck, which was as bare as any submarine. Bellini followed him and then opened a hatch in the deck, politely waving his guest to enter it. Peroni started to climb down another steel ladder and Bellini followed, closing the hatch with a clang and battening it down.

A neon strip illuminated the surprisingly ample interior of the bathyscaphe, which was filled with engines, miscellaneous equipment and diving gear. 'The engine room,' said Bellini and then, patting one of the curved, gleaming walls, 'On this side there's an airlock compartment for underwater loading and over here there are two decompression chambers. And now we go into the actual bathyscaphe section of the craft.'

Saying this he opened a small door in the forward part of the engine room and, stooping slightly, went through it followed by Peroni. The effect was dramatic, for the entire front part of this ample cockpit was a single window of reinforced Perspex, curved so as to permit maximum vision but at the same time lying as low in the water as though it were a partly submerged canoe. There was a control panel as complicated as that of a jet, but designed so skilfully that it hardly obstructed the view of the surrounding waterscape at all.

'Quite something, isn't it?' said Bellini, gesturing for Peroni to sit beside him at the panel. 'Right then,' he went on, starting to turn on switches and press buttons, 'off we go!' The *Proserpina* began to hum gently and then to edge her way slowly through the glistening water. Their progress was so smooth and the nearness of the water so restful that Peroni's apprehensions were calmed and he began to enjoy himself. They went on like this in silence for about five minutes, after which Bellini pressed a button which stopped the *Proserpina* and said, 'Now we'll make a preliminary dive.'

His fingers moved deftly over the panel and slowly the waters of the lake began to rise about them. The drum inside Peroni resumed its muffled beating. Gently and silently the water closed over their heads and he found himself in a green, submarine world in which the light of the sun was doused but not extinguished.

Just ahead of them a large school of the tiny, sardine-type fish often seen near the surface of the lake swarmed into view. They seemed quite indifferent to the huge steel whale and swam right up to the Perspex window, only at the last moment veering off obliquely and out of sight.

'Who gives the order to change direction?' said Bellini. 'Have they got a leader or is it a collective decision? As far as research into the behaviour of fish is concerned what we've done so far is about the equivalent of the tip of an iceberg.'

It was all so pleasant and reassuring in the half light, like being in a huge, very peaceful aquarium, that Peroni began to feel that given time he might become quite a dab hand at this underwater exploration business. But as the light grew dimmer and dimmer and he felt the physical motion of the descent in his stomach like a lift this optimism wavered somewhat.

A group of larger fish swam lazily into their ken. 'Tench,' said Bellini. 'Beautiful to watch and delicious to eat. Particularly with risotto.'

With a lurch Peroni remembered his dinner with Cordelia at Lazise and the memory conjured up a vision of her so vivid that it seemed more real for an instant than all the waters and fish of the lake and it chided him for letting himself be dominated by his surroundings when there were questions to ask. He opened his mouth to ask one, but in spite of himself he was suddenly overwhelmed by the sheer sense of increasing depth and he shut it again. Better to let Bellini concentrate on the driving.

The shade of green about them grew deeper and deeper and Peroni was just able to make out what looked like the slender trunks of two underwater trees appear indistinctly before them.

'Those are the remains of two supporting poles of a platform dwelling,' said Bellini. 'They're thousands and thousands of years old and the effect of the water on the wood has been to make it as hard as rock. Of course the level of the lake has changed since they were sunk in place – they were nearer the surface then.'

Three ghostly forms drifted between the poles. 'Trout,' went on Bellini, 'and more of a rarity nowadays than you might imagine. When you order lake trout in a restaurant they give you fish raised in artificial ponds. The taste is quite different. With the vast distances of the lake these fellows build up powerful muscles that are entirely atrophied in the pond fish. You have to know somebody to get one of these. There we are – we've reached the bottom. But this is still shallow. Now we'll go back up and try something a bit more ambitious.'

Peroni didn't like the sound of this at all. 'How do you and your colleagues divide up the work between you?' he asked as the bathyscaphe started to rise again, more to keep his mind off the prospect of something a bit more ambitious than because he wanted to know. 'I mean, who does what?'

'Whenever possible I do the actual aqualung diving out in the water with one of the others. Apart from the fact that I like to be in direct contact with the material we're researching or salvaging, it still remains the greatest thrill that life has to offer and the only one that never palls with time. Then two more of the team are always in here: one where I am now, in charge of

89

the lights and this panel here, and one at the back supervising the engines and the decompression and any loading that the two of us in the water need to do.'

The water about them started to grow brighter and greener and Peroni felt a sense of lifting oppression marred only by the prospect of another and yet deeper submersion. Then when they broke through the surface into the sunlight again the bathyscaphe started to cruise once more on the smooth water. After a few minutes it halted again.

'Now we're over one of the really deep parts of the lake,' said Bellini, 'unfathomable to all intents and purposes. There are a lot of these vast underwater chasms in the lake and anything that finishes down one of them is never going to see the light of day again.'

Once again the bathyscaphe started to dive and Peroni relived the alarming experience of leaving the sunlight world behind.

'And the fifth?' he said after some time had passed.

'The fifth? Ah yes – the fifth man. He monitors the entire operation from headquarters on shore. We have automatic closed-circuit television feed-back of all that goes on here. And he also keeps in constant radio contact with the bathyscaphe and that's all recorded on tape.'

'Nothing left to chance.'

'With this sort of work you can't afford to leave anything to chance. A minimum error can mean death.'

Peroni didn't like the sound of this. 'For the aqualung divers you mean?' he said to reassure himself.

'Even in the bathyscaphe it's far from being a planetarium trip,' said Bellini. 'Look at that gauge,' he went on, pointing to the control panel. 'The needle shows the distance between us and the surface. Think of all that water over our heads. A jet pilot on the other side of the sound barrier has got far more chance of saving his skin if something goes wrong than the crew of a bathyscaphe.'

Peroni watched the needle in horrid fascination. It was just quivering on the five hundred metre mark and still going up. His sense of oppression mounted with it. And then with dagger swiftness the idea stabbed at him that the whole thing had been deliberately planned to get rid of him. Nausicaa had handed him over to Bellini like a trussed goose for the slaughter. An expert like Bellini, after all, would have no trouble in consigning a body to the lake in such a way that it would never be given back. Some awkward questions, but nobody except Nausicaa and Bellini knew that he had gone out in the *Proserpina* so nothing could be proved. And the only other person who knew of Cordelia's search for the Mussolini gold would be silenced for ever.

The water about them had got darker and darker until now all shade of colour had left it and they were in a murky, limbo–like world where all normal terms of reference had to be abandoned. Peroni could not remember when he had felt such a sense of impotent dread, but Bellini appeared to be half intoxicated. 'This is where diving begins to get really interesting,' he said, 'when you reach the confines of the known world. And beyond them the point of no return. D'you know I often dream of going to meet death one day somewhere beyond that point.'

Peroni could think of few less pleasant deaths and even in his state of nightmare claustrophobia he suspected that Bellini wouldn't be so keen on it either if the prospect were imminent. The man was a showman.

Suddenly light flared into the surrounding darkness and the effect was that of car headlights in dense fog: it made a bit of difference, but not much. Sufficient, however, to reveal a huge fish almost on top of them. 'The king of the lake,' said Bellini, 'a giant carp. You can get them almost as long as a motor-cycle.'

The bathyscaphe sank below the carp, the needle on the gauge pushed remorselessly towards the thousand metre mark and Peroni had to fight a wild urge to implore for an immediate return to the surface. 'Gets you, doesn't it?' said Bellini, grinning. And still they continued to descend. Then after a long, long time the bathyscaphe tilted sickeningly forward as though it were being crushed by the incalculable mass of water over it. Peroni sweated with terror. Either something had gone wrong ('A jet pilot on the other side of the sound barrier has got far more chance ...') or this was the attempt upon his life, and never had he been more powerless to face such an attempt.

By the lights, which no longer shone horizontally, but almost vertically downwards, he was able to sense rather than see a vast, narrow abyss gaping beneath them. It was as though, having come to the bottom of the world, there opened up at your feet a well of incalculably greater depths than you had already travelled. Peroni stared in horrified awe.

'Even I can't go down there,' Bellini almost whispered.

Finally, after a time that had nothing to do with watches, the *Proserpina* righted herself and started to move slowly upwards. The needle on the gauge began to fall and Peroni felt like a condemned man who has been given a new lease of life.

They made the ascent in silence, but as they went he felt a growing impression that Bellini was waiting for him to say something; that the trip had indeed been planned, not, as he had thought before, with murder in mind, but rather that whatever it was might be said. He waited until the world started to tinge with light again and then said, 'There was something I wanted to ask you, by the way.' Immediately he felt a heightening of tension as though Bellini had been waiting for this moment and yet at the same time dreaded it. 'I'm making enquiries,' he went on, 'about an English girl who was drowned in the lake. Cordelia Hope. She had – very striking red hair. Did she by any chance get in touch with you?'

'Yes,' said Bellini. 'How ever did you find out? She did in fact come to see me – it must have been about two weeks ago. I heard by chance the other day that she'd been drowned. Appalling! Such an attractive girl and so full of life and interest.'

'What did she come to see you about?'

'Oh, she had some wild idea about some sort of treasure on the lake bed and she wanted me to help her get hold of it.'

'What did you say?'

'That without a great deal stronger evidence I couldn't possibly commit my team and equipment to a wild goose chase. We are, after all, a scientific équipe.'

'She didn't show you, by any chance, a map locating this treasure?'

'No, no – no map.'

They broke the surface of the water, now burning golden-red in the late sun.

'And then?' said Peroni, trying not to show his relief.

'And then nothing. I said that if she came across anything more concrete I would be glad to give it my consideration. She thanked me and went, and that was the last I saw of her. But,' he went on showing, or feigning to show, sudden alarm, 'you're not suggesting there was something – deliberate about her death?'

This time it was Peroni who held the other man over a

92

metaphorical abyss and he paused deliberately, letting him hang there. He believed now that he knew why the meeting had been arranged. Bellini wanted to let him know of Cordelia's visit before Peroni found it out for himself. He also wanted to make it clear that the meeting had been innocent, mapless and without sequel – something which Peroni strongly doubted. And finally he wanted to know what else Peroni had found out.

The realisation of this instilled in Peroni a firm confidence that he was heading in the right direction. A great deal more would have to be found out about Bellini and his underwater activities. And in the meantime, on balance, it would probably be most profitable if he could be tricked into a sense of false security.

'No, no, nothing like that,' said Peroni reassuringly, 'I'm just enquiring on behalf of her family who want to find out all they can about her last days.'

'Oh, I see – well, I'm sorry I can't be more helpful.'

'No need to apologise,' said Peroni innocently, 'you've been very helpful.' And he noticed with satisfaction that it was Bellini's turn to try and conceal relief. The trick had worked.

The *Proserpina* nosed her way delicately back into harbour.

'Well, that's it,' said Bellini, glowing with self-satisfaction. 'Now you know what there is beneath the pretty postcard scenes of Lake Garda.'

CHAPTER 6

The British Vice-Consulate in Venice is housed in a palace on the Grand Canal, but Italian though this may sound the place has come to acquire a subtle, but quite unmistakable English flavour. There is one corner of a Venetian *campo*, in fact, which is forever England. And the dividing line is as sharp as if an invisible frontier post had been set up. One moment you are in the heart of Venice with the Accademia Gallery, usually closed, staring at you forbiddingly, gondolas and *vaporetti* busily plying on the water, tourists milling touristically and a tempting smell of cooking coming from a restaurant somewhere round the corner. And the next moment, having stepped through a door in a high wall into a little garden, the atmosphere about you could not be more English if you were surrounded with bobbies and beefeaters.

Peroni recognised and enjoyed the transition. His memories of an earlier six month special attachment to New Scotland Yard had become vague and ridiculously over-glamorised, but his attachment to the idea of England was as powerful as ever.

He crossed the garden, went into the building and climbed the stairs to the first floor offices of the Consulate, admiring the elegant eighteenth-century frescoes as he went. He told the young man who met him in the reception hall that he wished to speak to the British vice-consul and was asked to fill in a slip stating his name and the purpose of his visit.

What was the purpose of the visit? Vague, to say the least. Being detained in Venice by work that morning and therefore unable to pursue the Bellini line of enquiry, it had occurred to him that it might be useful if he could find out something more about Cordelia's background in England. He hovered uncertainly over the purpose of the visit for a second, tempted by the idea of writing in block capitals 'MURDER'. But sobriety prevailed and he wrote 'Death of Cordelia Hope'.

Three minutes later he was fished out of the waiting room, where he had started grappling unsuccessfully with a copy of *Country Life*, and shown into the consul's office.

'Do sit down,' said the Consul, having shaken hands. 'I'm sorry that we're meeting for the first time over such a sad affair. How can I help you?'

Peroni had been contemplating the somewhat Baroque approach he would have employed with an Italian authority, but the consul's frank, simple and amiable manner disarmed him and he strained various long-unused mental muscles by coming straight to the point.

'I don't believe her death was accidental,' he said.

'Oh dear.' The consul looked grave. 'May I ask why?'

'There are various reasons. The first is that I went sailing with her shortly before she died. We ran into a very nasty storm indeed and she coped with it single-handedly. I can't believe that a woman capable of that could have fallen into the lake during a much less serious storm.'

'I see.' He thought for a moment. 'But maybe she didn't

94

exactly fall. Maybe she . . .' He completed the sentence with a sparse but expressive English gesture.

'Suicide,' Peroni interpreted it, taking the consul somewhat aback with the bluntness of the word. 'I might just have accepted that theory – out of character though it certainly is – if it hadn't been put to me by a woman who said that Cordelia told her of her intention to kill herself and who, I then discovered, had never even met Cordelia.'

The consul put his fingertips together and studied them. 'That does alter the situation,' he said, adding after a pause, 'I am completely at your disposal.'

'It might be helpful,' said Peroni, 'if I could find out something about her English background – family, friends, life at Oxford and so on. I realise that this would normally be a job for Interpol, but that tends to be a top-heavy operation, particularly when the official verdict is still one of accidental death. So I thought that you, having been in touch with the affair, might be able to help me a little more informally.'

'I think I see exactly what you mean,' said the consul, plainly meaning just that, 'and indeed formally there is little I can do for you in view of the fact that the official verdict is still one of accidental death. However, what you have just told me – not to mention the authority conferred on you by your own consider-able reputation—' Peroni tried unsuccessfully to look modest —'arouse considerable doubts in me in, let us say, my private capacity. And I think I may be able to give you a piece of informal advice. I was visited three days ago by a lady by the name of Miss Kathleen Porter, an aunt of Miss Hope's and the nearest surviving relative. She came out here to clear up her niece's affairs, which was why she came to see me, and I think I may say she was even more firmly convinced than you, though with less evidence, that Miss Hope did not die accidentally or take her own life. She announced her intention of staying on for another week in Venice and she asked me if anything further came to my knowledge to inform her at once. I think you may represent all and indeed more than she intended by that. If you hang on just a minute I'll give you the name of her hotel.'

The consul's words had provided a slight, indirect hint as to the sort of person Miss Kathleen Porter might be, but this was nothing compared to the reality which now came out of the hotel lift, spotted Peroni at once and made purposefully towards him. She was a small, forceful woman in her fifties who looked like and indeed was a headmistress. 'We are a family of academics,' she explained when she informed Peroni of the fact later.

'You are the policeman of whom the British consul spoke to me on the telephone,' she now stated rather than asked, at the same time giving him a firm, male handshake. Peroni had the oddest impression that she already knew him. 'Good,' she said, her grey eyes assessing him as though he were a new boy. 'I have been expecting you for some days.'

'Expecting me?' said Peroni, completely taken off balance.

'That sounds strange to you. The fact is I was altogether unconvinced by this idiotic talk of accidental death – an expert yachtswoman like Cordelia indeed! – and still less by the wicked insinuation of suicide.' She spoke a precise, grammatical Italian and Peroni remembered that Cordelia had said in the restaurant that languages were a family thing. 'However,' Miss Porter went on, 'to judge by what the consul told me, there was little I could do about it. So I decided to leave matters in the hands of the Almighty, which is an infallible way of ensuring that they work out for the best. And here you are. Now please let me order you a drink and I will then endeavour to answer any questions you care to put to me.'

After a brief Neapolitan flurry of protest at letting her buy the drinks, Peroni (falling effortlessly into the role of head of the class) submitted to her position as headmistress and obediently did what he was told. He was mildly shocked to see that she, like him, ordered a Chivas Regal whisky.

'Now then,' she said.

'Perhaps you could tell me something about Cordelia's life at Oxford?'

'If you are referring to her social life I'm afraid I know little or nothing. Cordelia was an independent person – it is a family characteristic – and I did not feel that as an aunt I was called upon to enquire into her private affairs – even as an aunt *in loco parentis*. She could, as they say, very well look after herself.'

Remembering the matter-of-fact way she had announced her intention of not going to bed with him, Peroni was ruefully compelled to recognise that Miss Porter was right. 'She didn't mention that she was living with you.'

'Why should she? She gave me no trouble and a great deal of pleasure.'

'Can you tell me something about her family?'

'Her father died when she was only ten years old ...' For an instant she seemed uncertain as to whether she should add something else, but the instant passed and she continued with her previous assurance. 'Her mother – my sister – died five years later and that was when Cordelia came under my care. She was only fifteen, but her own nature and my sister's upbringing were such that her behaviour was already that of a fully responsible and highly intelligent adult. As I say, she gave me no trouble. She was already at boarding school and she came to stay with me in the holidays.'

'She was good at school, I imagine?'

'Brilliant.' The word was spoken drily, but Peroni was able to catch the satisfaction gleaming behind it. 'She got a scholarship to Lady Margaret Hall – my old college.' Again that little flash of satisfaction.

'She was studying history, she said.'

'Reading,' Miss Porter corrected without presumptuousness.

'You knew she was coming out to Italy?'

'Well, of course. She always spent the long vac abroad. To acquire a new language or improve an old one. It was a sort of family hobby.'

'And that was why she came out to Italy?'

'To improve her Italian – yes.'

'It was the only reason?'

She looked at him oddly. 'So far as I know, yes.' She put a just perceptible accent on the 'know'.

'She gave you no idea that she might have had some other purpose?'

She thought for a moment. 'Commissario,' she said eventually, 'Cordelia was an extremely adventurous sort of girl. Oh,' she went on impatiently as though winkling a thought in his mind, 'I don't mean where love affairs were concerned. Unlike so many of her contemporaries she was not promiscuous. But she was adventurous in the broadest sense of the word. She liked adventurous sports.'

'I know,' said Peroni. 'I went sailing with her in a storm.'

'And not only sailing – mountaineering as well. And she

97

belonged to a gliding society at Oxford. She sought adventure and she believed that life itself should be an adventure.'

'Adventures can be dangerous.'

'I am aware of that. And so was she.'

'Has it occurred to you that it might have been an adventure which caused her death?'

'Yes, it has.' She paused an instant and then went on in the tone of a headmistress announcing an important decision. 'When she said goodbye to me before setting off . . .' the memory was almost too much for her and she had to make a visible effort to continue '. . . I did have the impression that she was, let us say, in search of something even more important than the improvement of her Italian.'

'Did she give you any hint as to what it might have been?'

'No, but she has a mischievous expression which, when she was a little girl, was always a sign that she was up to something.' She paused once again in thought. 'There is, perhaps, one thing I should tell you, Commissario,' she went on. 'I did not mention this to the consul, nor have I spoken of it to anyone else, because under the circumstances it seemed pointless to bandy about family matters which could serve no purpose. But I think you should know of it. It concerns Cordelia's father.' Peroni remembered again that brief hesitation. 'He was an adventurer and, although that is not quite the same thing as having an adventurous spirit as his daughter did, I am nevertheless bound to recognise that she got it from him. He was already nearly fifty when he married my sister in nineteen sixty-four. It was his second marriage.' She took a generous sip of whisky as though to fortify herself against the thought of her brother-in-law. 'I did not approve of it. And if my sister had not been the sort of person who obstinately refuses to abandon anything they have undertaken the marriage would certainly have broken up long before he died. However, it is his career before either of his marriages which concerns me now. He must have been a young man of considerable potential abilities, however little he chose to develop them later, and he did extremely well during the war.' She paused. 'So well that he was selected to be aide to Winston Churchill.'

It was Peroni's turn to lean on the whisky. 'Do you know during what period this was?'

'I do indeed,' said Miss Porter drily. 'On the occasions when I dined with my sister and brother-in-law he would invariably after the first two or three glasses regale us with his autobiography. He only joined Churchill's staff in the last months of the war, but he remained on it afterwards. He accompanied Churchill on both his Italian holidays: to Como in nineteen forty-five and to Garda in nineteen forty-nine.'

(... something that felt like a pouncing eagle landed on his shoulders and he felt himself being pulled up to look into two remorseless grey eyes.

'What are you up to, young man?' said Churchill's escort.

'I was playing!' said Attilio, trying to sound indignant. 'I always play here!'

'We'll see about that!'

And Attilio was carried in an implacable grasp round the clump of trees to the lakeside where his father and Churchill were sitting on the bench.)

'And Cordelia learned of those visits from him?' said Peroni.

'She did. Understandably, as a little girl she did not see her father in the same light as a sister-in-law. For her he was a hero and even his alcoholic ramblings were invested with magic.'

'What did he tell her?'

'A great deal. Of course, even he could not pretend that he had been privy to Churchill's secrets, but he said that nobody on the staff was in any doubt that some sort of a search was being carried out and that this search involved Mussolini, both at Como and at Garda four years later.'

'Did he know the reason for the gap?'

'Apparently the Como search was fruitless and Churchill had reluctantly decided to give the whole thing up. But then in nineteen forty-nine an intelligence officer uncovered a rumour concerning a visit of Mussolini's to a house on Lake Garda towards the end of the war during which he handed over some sort of document or documents for safe keeping. It seemed that the story had emanated from a Fascist bully who had been in some way employed at the house. When the war ended this man had been captured by the partisans to whom he told the story in an unsuccessful attempt to bargain for his life. He was shot, but the story was passed on until it reached the ears of Churchill himself, via the intelligence officer. It seems that it was fairly vague, with no clue as to which the house was, but it was enough to send Churchill off on a second painting holiday.'

'Which was no more successful than the first one?'

'According to my brother-in-law, no. He was convinced that there was still, as he put it, unfinished business to be done at Lake Garda. And he insisted that he would go back there one day and trace what Churchill had failed to discover. What exactly that was he didn't know. There was talk of a correspondence between Churchill and Mussolini and also of some kind of actual treasure—'

'The Mussolini gold.'

'Yes, that would be it. But predictably where my brother-in-law was concerned it was no more than a sort of football pools fantasy.'

'But not with Cordelia?'

'Perhaps not. She certainly took it seriously enough as a child. She was an avid reader and all the adventures she read about in books were embodied for her in this quest of her father's. Consequently when she told me she was going to Lake Garda I couldn't help wondering whether there was any connection. And when I heard of her death, it did occur to me that the quest might have been in some way responsible for it.'

'I believe it was.'

'Then I was right,' she whispered after staring at him for a second. 'But in that case,' she went on in her normal voice, 'for Heaven's sake why is her death still officially considered accidental?'

'It's not as simple as it may sound,' said Peroni. 'For one thing I am the only person – or more exactly the only policeman – to be aware of this quest. The whole thing started like this ...' Peroni told her enough of the story to persuade her of the ambiguity of his position. 'So you see,' he concluded, 'there's nothing substantial enough yet to reverse an official verdict or persuade an examining magistrate to open a murder enquiry.'

'So what do you intend to do?'

'Go on looking until there *is* something substantial enough.'

'And how can I help you?'

'You've already been of inestimable help. But I'm beginning to feel that I need to know much more about what Cordelia did when she was at the lake and all the people she was in touch with. At the moment there are far too many gaps.'

'In that case there may be something more I can do.' But she seemed to be curiously hesitant. Waiting, Peroni signed for their glasses to be refilled. 'She wrote to me only the day before she . . . was killed.' The last two words conveyed the salutary pain of surgery. 'I have the letter with me now. If I appeared reluctant to show it to you it was only because – well, because there are numerous references in it to somebody who I now see is yourself. But I think I know you well enough to be confident that you will take it in the same spirit in which it was written.'

Now Peroni understood why he had the impression that she already knew him, and when Miss Porter took an envelope from her bag and handed it to him he accepted it with some apprehension. The handwriting on the envelope gave him a shock; it was so much a self-portrait of Cordelia that she almost seemed to have risen from the dead before his eyes. He took out the letter and unfolded it.

The date, he calculated quickly, was that of their last but one day together. The day they sailed to Malcesine and the day of their first and only kiss.

'Dearest Aunt K.,' he read, 'I'm sorry not to have written sooner, but I've been fairly hectic what with one thing and another. And maybe, just maybe, I shall come back to England with something rather interesting. There seems to be nothing on Lake Garda that I haven't explored. In fact today I've come up to the village of Costermano which is on the way to Verona. It's relatively cool up here and it's very pleasant to get away from the tourists or, if that sounds snobbish, the other tourists.

'I'm quite pleased with my Italian: I manage to speak it a fair amount and I try to find time to do a canto of the *Divine Comedy* per day, though more often than not that means per night as I rarely manage to read before midnight.

'Believe it or not, I've already collected two proposals of marriage! It's amazing, I find, how quickly and uncomplainingly most men return to the old rules of the game if you let them know unequivocally that you have no intention of playing by the new ones. (Not, I hasten to add, that this is a calculation. It's just the way things fall out. And I sometimes seriously doubt whether I shall ever get married.) Anyway, proposal number one came from a philosopher, a very nice, desperately sincere and woefully shy boy who works for an elderly gentleman I went to visit at Bardolino. I tried to let him down as gently as I could, but I'm afraid he was hurt just the same. Proposal

101

number two was made by a chap called Willi – a professional aqualung diver of all things!' Peroni's mind went taut. That was the one with the pleasantly ugly, skew-whiff face. Another thread to be followed. He read on. 'He was very nice, too, but fortunately a bit less vulnerable. Attractively ugly sums *him* up and I liked him very much. Anyway, that's all over now as well.

'But with some diffidence I have to tell you that there is yet *another* man on the scene, though this one hasn't yet proposed marriage. He's in quite a different category from the other two. Bottom-pinching Latin lover you would say if you saw him in the street.' Peroni drained his whisky in one go. 'Exceptionally handsome, very southern appearance with that slightly swarthy colouring they do have. Black hair, very good teeth, marvellous features and fire-coal black eyes which he can make glow at you in a professional sort of way when he wants. Quite a bit older than me ...' Peroni felt a lurch of desolation '... though that, of course, is neither here nor there and indeed some women would consider it very much here. You must think I'm going soft at the edges rambling on at such length about a mere man, but there is more to this one that you would imagine. Oh, there is no doubt he had every intention of starting the old, old story with me and would have done if I hadn't insisted upon a firm no-mucking-about clause in the contract – and even then his mental reservations were about as subtle as a flock of angry crows. But after that just the same I began to appreciate more and more what an interesting person he really is.' Sun began to filter through the fog of desolation. 'For one thing he's a mass of contradictions. He sees himself as a sort of sexual butterfly, but it's one woman he's looking for and, just for a moment, he thought that I was that woman, which I don't mind admitting made me feel enormous delight and tenderness. Then again he has a quite exceptional mind (a marvellous balance of male reasoning and female intuition), but he mixes this with quite astonishing obtuseness over some things. He is capable of great courage, but when I took him out in the yacht last night and we ran into a bit of a storm he was absolutely gibbering with terror.' Peroni's ego felt groggy from this battering of rights and lefts. 'I'm very curious to know what he does. When I asked him he said he worked for the Ministry of Home Affairs, but I'm quite certain that this is either a whopper or a half truth to cover up his real activity. I wouldn't be surprised if he were a sort of

James Bond. One thing I do know: when the visit comes to an end – and I think the next day will see the end of it one way or another – I shall leave him with real regret. But I shall leave him.

'Fond love, Cordelia.'

As he finished the letter Peroni noticed with surprise that his glass was being refilled. 'I thought you might need it,' said Miss Porter as he looked up in bewilderment.

'I do,' said Peroni. '*Salute!*'

'If it's any consolation, I don't remember her ever taking another man quite so seriously as she took you.'

'It's more than consolation,' said Peroni.

'I don't know whether the letter is much good to you from the point of view of your enquiries. There are those two references: when she says she may bring something rather interesting back to England and then at the end when she says that the next day will probably see the end of it one way or another. She could be referring to the Churchill business. Or she could be referring to something else. But it's certainly not the letter of somebody who's contemplating suicide.'

With difficulty Peroni thought back through the heart-swamping second half of the letter to the revelation in the first half about Willi. 'The letter is very helpful indeed,' he said, handing it back to her.

But, even as he said this, Peroni had the impression that it was telling him something of even greater importance. But concentrate though he might he couldn't understand what it was.

CHAPTER 7

Concealing himself as best he could behind a bush, Peroni focused his binoculars on the *Proserpina*. He was hiding not so much from the crew, who couldn't possibly have seen him from that distance, as from stray passers by. He had once been engaged on a job concerning a sort of club of *guardoni* or peeping Toms. These gentlemen used to repair regularly at certain hours to an area much frequented by courting couples. Here they would dispose themselves in strategically sheltered vantage

103

points which were not only pre-selected but, like boxes in Italian theatres, were reserved for the season by each particular peeping Tom. And once ensconced they would train their binoculars – opera glasses for connoisseurs of lust – on the amorous activities that offered themselves. Ever since then Peroni had associated binoculars with voyeurism and he was convinced that anybody, seeing him use them, would automatically categorise him as a Tom.

The bathyscaphe was lying peacefully on the evening-gilded waters of the lake about a kilometre off-shore. Bellini, still in his rubber diving-suit, but without helmet, was kneeling on deck checking something on his wrist and speaking into a walkie-talkie. Then the hatch was pushed open and the head of Max the giant appeared, now crowned with a vast sombrero. The rest of him followed and he and Bellini started talking together.

Peroni had lain awake into the small hours the previous night in the high-ceilinged, flaking, decadently aristocratic room in which he slept and which his landlord had crowded with the most improbable and inappropriate pieces of furniture that he had acquired in his devious and shady dealings in the city of Venice.

Cordelia and Willi. In view of the map she had photographed at the del Duca villa it seemed probable that the romantic relationship (on his part) had grown out of a more practical relationship with the team as a whole. And the implications of that were sharp and grim.

Assume Bellini was lying and Cordelia had shown him the map, how could things have evolved? They couldn't have salvaged the gold immediately. For one thing, they would have needed a certain amount of time to locate it and prepare the expedition. For another, it would have been impossible to carry out a major dive, with all the secrecy which the removal of the gold would make indispensable, in the full publicity glare of the congress.

On the whole it seemed certain that the Mussolini gold was still safe on the lake bed. And if Bellini had Cordelia's photograph of the map he would be most likely to try a salvage operation after the end of the congress in three days' time.

And it was beginning to look as though it was only by uncovering the search for the Mussolini gold that Peroni would get at the truth about Cordelia's death and demonstrate to the

104

most hidebound of his colleagues that it hadn't been accidental.

But how to uncover it?

Willi. If he had been in love with Cordelia that could make him the vulnerable spot in the underwater team. Somehow, without Bellini's knowledge, Willi must be got by himself. So the following afternoon Peroni had driven over to Garda again.

What looked through the binoculars like a rubber ball bobbed up to the surface beside the *Proserpina*. The rubber ball then revealed itself to be a diver whom Bellini and Max helped out of the water and on to the deck. The three of them went below and shortly afterwards the *Proserpina* started to move towards the shore.

Back at the harbour a now fairly large crowd offered Peroni ample cover and when the bathyscaphe had docked and its crew had landed he followed them at a safe distance, mixed up with the gogglers as they made their way along the lake front behind the team. They came to a single-storey building which looked like the headquarters of a yachting club-cum-boat-house. It stood some little way outside the village, and parked outside it was a magnificent, gleaming, custom-built car which could only be Bellini's. Here, after a brief astronauts-return-from-space performance by Bellini for the benefit of the crowd, during which Peroni hid behind a monumental German matron, the team disappeared into the building.

Peroni walked back to the village centre wondering how to get hold of Willi by himself. The problem was not made simpler by the fact that, although he had no trouble in discovering the hotel at which they were staying, he didn't know their habits of an evening and was reluctant to ask questions for fear of making himself conspicuous. It was already dark and he was beginning to fear that the problem would have to be put off to another day when quite unexpectedly it solved itself.

He was prowling undecidedly about the village when he saw Willi seated at a table alone at the edge of a terrace-garden bar. Peroni started to climb the stone steps which led up to this bar, trying to work out a line of approach as he went.

'*Mi scusi . . .*'

Willi squinnied up at him belligerently. Willi was drunk. 'Go 'way,' he said.

'I was a friend of Cordelia Hope,' said Peroni.

Immediately the belligerence crumbled like a plaster mask

struck by a hammer and beneath it there appeared pain, eagerness and even, surprisingly, hope. The announcement seemed momentarily to sober him up, too. 'Sit down,' he said. 'But how . . .' Then as Peroni sat the expression changed again giving way this time to bewilderment. He peered at Peroni's face as though he were trying to read it. 'Are you the policeman who came to see Daniele?' he said.

Peroni had been hoping to postpone this. 'Yes,' he said, 'I am.'

Again the result was totally unexpected. Relief surged into Willi's wounded, ugly features as perceptibly as a blush. 'Thank God!' he said. 'Ever since he told us I've been trying to think how to get in touch with you.'

'He told you?'

'Tha'ss right.' Impatiently, still slightly slurred. 'He said a southern cop was going round asking questions about Cordelia and to say she'd only been here once for a short visit and never came back.'

'And that's not true?'

'Course it's not true!' Willi swallowed a large grappa he had before him and his expression became warped by a driving necessity for revenge. 'Three days running she came here,' he said, 'right up until just before she was drowned. And I'll tell you something else,' he went on, the desire for revenge wrenching itself painfully into pure grief while large, maudlin tears started to pour down his cheeks. 'She was murdered.'

Peroni breathed in deeply. It was the first time somebody involved in the events had said this and there was an element of catharsis about it. 'How do you know?' he said very softly.

'Because she put them on to something of great value that's lying at the bottom of the lake—'

'The Mussolini gold – yes, I know about that.'

'She got hold of the map that shows where it is and they wanted her out of the way when we salvage it. They didn't want her to have any share in it.'

'Who are they?'

'Daniele for a start. But not only Daniele. Whoever sent her to him.'

Peroni looked quickly at Willi. 'Somebody sent her?'

'That's right. It was early afternoon and we were all of us in the shore base. Somebody called Daniele on the telephone. This person talked for a long time and when he'd finished Daniele

106

said to us, "There's a girl coming round who might put us on to something of more practical value than platform settlement artefacts or molluscs. She's got hold of a map that's meant to show the location of the Mussolini gold. When this congress is over we're going to look for it." Not long after that she arrived and Daniele took her into his office where they talked for about an hour.'

'When was this?'

Willi thought with difficulty through grappa fumes. 'Yes,' he said after a second, 'it was two days after we arrived on the lake, so it must have been the tenth of July.'

That was the same day Peroni had first met her, when she had said that she had an appointment. So, if the meeting with Bellini was in the afternoon, it sounded as though her appointment would have been with whoever sent her to Bellini. Something was moving at last. 'When did you see her again?'

'The next day. She arrived about ten o'clock in the morning.'

And that would have been after Peroni's first sailing lesson. She had said that she was likely to be busy for the next couple of days. It fitted. 'What happened that day?'

'We spent a lot of time out on the lake.'

'With the bathyscaphe?'

'No, an ordinary motor-boat. Daniele was working out the exact location of the cases and he wanted to arouse as little attention as possible.'

'And you were out all day?'

'On and off until evening.'

'And then?'

Willi looked about him for a waiter and signed for two more grappas. Then he stared wretched into his empty glass and said, so softly that Peroni could hardly hear him, 'She came out to dinner with me.' To judge by his tone that must have been when he proposed to her.

'And then?'

'She came back the next day and went out again on the lake. But some time towards late afternoon she went off to make a telephone call and when she came back she said she had to go to Verona. I offered to take her, but she said she preferred to go by bus.'

'She gave you no idea where in Verona she wanted to go?'

'No.'

That was the day when she had arrived late for their

appointment looking depressed – the night of the storm. So something must have happened in Verona to upset her. 'When did you see her next?'

'I never saw her again.' Peroni thought he had never heard anyone sound quite so desolate.

The two of them drank grappa in silence for a moment. Then Peroni said, 'Can you think of anything that might indicate who it was sent her to Bellini?'

Willi shook his head. 'But from the way he talked on the telephone,' he said, 'it was somebody he knew. I never heard him use a name, but it was somebody he knew well.'

And it just might be the same person, thought Peroni, who had told the zodiacal ceramist witch to put out a false story about Cordelia's intention to kill herself. Something like a pattern was beginning to form. 'The salvaging of the Mussolini gold,' he said, 'when is it to be? Bellini said after the congress. When after the congress?'

'I don't know.'

'Can you find out?'

Willi looked doubtful. 'I don't see how I can,' he said. 'I still belong to the team. I owe it my loyalty. And it can't do any good to her.'

'But it can!' Peroni tried to smash through the reluctance with urgency. 'Maybe it's only by knowing about the salvage that I can get at whoever killed her!'

Willi scratched his head. 'I don't know,' he said. 'No. No, I can't.'

'You're worried about your share of the haul,' said Peroni with nicely calculated contempt. 'When it comes to the point that's more important than finding out who killed Cordelia.'

For a moment he thought he'd overdone it. Willi's face became very ugly indeed and it looked as though he were going to start a fight, but then the aggressiveness crumpled into sheer misery. 'All right,' he said, 'I'll try and find out tomorrow and let you know in the evening. Out on the main road, just by the bus stop, there's a little bar. I'll meet you there tomorrow at seven. OK?'

'OK,' said Peroni, standing up and offering his hand.

'You were wrong,' said Willi, taking it, 'when you said that about my share being more important than finding out who killed Cordelia. You shouldn't have said that.'

'No,' said Peroni, 'I'm sorry.'

It was dark now and when Peroni reached the head of the steps he saw a street light throwing back a gleaming, jewel-like reflection from a large, completely bald pate below, and for some reason the sight of the pate seemed to sum up for him the atmosphere of that strangely intense dialogue with Willi. By the time Peroni had got to the bottom of the steps the pate was gone.

CHAPTER 8

Lidia lay in her sleeping-bag under a tree, unable to sleep, sounds reaching out at her from the night blown up and distorted.

They had camped in this small public garden a couple of hours before and sat round for a long time smoking and arguing. Then one by one they had wriggled into their sleeping-bags and by now they were presumably all asleep. Except Lidia.

From quite near there came a sort of creaking, groaning sound as though a very old person were lamenting pain. She stared wide-eyed into the darkness trying to identify it, but she could make out nothing. Then as suddenly as it had started, it stopped. A branch, she told herself, it must have been a branch, go to sleep. But her mind refused to obey.

During these last three days they had picked up much less money than usual from their improvised break-dance shows and as a result they were all short tempered. It was her fault. After their encounter with the carabiniere, Maurizio had said that if a description of her had gone back and if a search were concentrated on the lake she would be found at once. Susanna, the bitch, would have been only too glad if she had been found, but for the moment she didn't dare say so and they had moved away from the lake. But the lake was where the holiday-makers were and when they left it behind them they left the money with it. Takings had dropped from nearly two hundred thousand lire a day to less than fifty thousand and that wasn't enough for them to keep going in cigarettes, much less food.

A car headlight swept over her like a quick, bright snake and left her blinking, dazzled, in the darkness again. The car stopped on an abandoned, newspaper strewn patch of ground just the other side of a wire fence near which Lidia was lying. A man and a woman got out of the front seats and then immediately got in again at the back. Just for a moment Lidia wondered the reason, but then it was made all too plain. She watched in horrified fascination as the quick, brutal act was played out. Then the couple climbed back into the front and drove off again.

Lidia forced her concentration back on to her own circumstances. Three days ago when Maurizio had said they must get away from the lake he had sounded quite convinced about it. But now he no longer seemed so sure. He liked money; she had never been in any doubt about that. So how much longer would he put up with her when she continued to put a brake on his earnings?

Her thoughts went on dismally see-sawing and she had almost fallen into a vexed, shallow sleep when she became aware of movement again and started into full wakefulness. Somebody else had arrived on the other side of the wire fence, not a couple this time, but a single man who was half sitting, half squatting with his back to her. He was doing something with his hands on the ground in front of him and again, briefly, she was uncertain what was going on. Then this, too, became horribly obvious as he lifted his bare left arm and she saw the glint of the needle as the hypodermic syringe moved down towards the waiting flesh. Lidia was an expert on the hard-drug scene. She knew it all and held her mother's ignorant, prejudiced remarks on the subject in high contempt. But when you actually saw it like this the whole thing somehow acquired a new dimension.

And if, she canalised her thought again, if Maurizio was getting fed up with the situation, how much longer before he got rid of her? And when he did what was the next step? In her mind's eye she saw again the heaving hump in the back of the car and the dull glint of the descending needle. Where would she go from here?

Movement again. Nearer this time and inside the fence. She turned to face it and saw a crouched figure moving purposefully towards her. Her mouth was already open to scream when she recognised Maurizio.

'Oh, it's you,' she said. 'I thought . . .'

He curled himself on the grass beside her and put his arm

110

round her, his mouth searching for hers. She liked that. Her fingers moved to a bristling, purple chunk of his hair. He kissed divinely.

His hand moved to the zip of her sleeping-bag and opened it, then purposefully to the top button of her jeans. Suddenly she felt scared. Not now. Not yet. 'No, Maurizio,' she said. 'Please—'

'Shut up!' he said. 'Just lie still and keep quiet!' Both his hands were tearing at her clothes.

'Maurizio—'

'I said shut up!'

'Please . . . Leave me alone . . .'

'Leave you alone, you silly cow? We've hardly been earning a fucking lira these last three days thanks to you! The least you can do is give me something in exchange!'

Suddenly, unexpectedly her alarm was swamped in indignation. Who did he think he was? 'Get away from me!'

'Stay still, you little bitch!'

In the darkness she lifted her right hand and with a glancing blow planted her nails in his cheek. The pain of it halted him for a second and he blasphemed horribly. Lidia took advantage to pull herself away and up to her feet.

For the second time she opened her mouth to scream, but this time she let it rip.

'She's been gone a week now. D'you think she'll ever be found?'

Lidia's mother looked as though she hadn't slept since her daughter had disappeared and she asked the question with a flat, lifeless tone that Peroni recognised only too well. It was despair.

'You mustn't lose hope, Signora. Everything possible is being done.'

This was true and yet Peroni himself felt hope draining away. It was three days since the report of Lidia being seen on the lake and a pitiless world could do a lot to a teenage girl on the run in three days.

The mother attempted a smile and he showed her gently out. When he got back the intercom phone was ringing. '*Pronto?*' he said picking up the receiver.

'*Buon giorno*, Dottore.' It was the colleague to whom Peroni had entrusted the list of Mussolini's staff at the Villa Feltrinelli.

'Those names you gave me – I've managed to trace one man, a private soldier who was on general duties at the villa. Name of Toffali.'

'Where is he now?'

'He runs an antique shop in Verona.' Peroni tingled; that sounded very like Cordelia's visit to Verona mentioned by Willi. He got the address of the antique shop, checked that the Lidia search mechanism was functioning efficiently, did some smooth delegation and set off once again.

From the days when he had been stationed in Verona, Peroni knew well the street where the antique shop was situated. It was called Sottoriva and it lay behind and beneath the Austrian-built river embankment. Its appearance was misleading. It looked like and, indeed, once had been a poor quarter and the eighteenth-century-style *osteria* and the dark, narrow pavement running beneath a stone arcade all still gave this impression. In fact, it was one of the costliest areas in an already costly city. You would need a computer to study the prices asked and paid for property there and the seemingly modest little shops and furniture restoration workshops – the biggest craft boom in the Veneto – were all run by local Pirellis and Agnellis in shirtsleeves.

Toffali's shop belonged perfectly to its surroundings. It looked humble, with junky bric-à-brac scattered apparently at random in the window, but the prices were of the sort that teach you to make a very careful count of the noughts.

As Peroni went in a little bell on the door tinkled with an appropriately antique sound. He was at once swallowed up in a chaotically jumbled world of things out of context, all coming from or purporting to come from different moments of the past: gilded *putti* and Madonnas that claimed once to have been part of the harmonious whole of some church; mirrors, candlesticks, furniture from the long since broken up contents of old *palazzi*; even things belonging to specific dead – lace handkerchiefs, spectacles, snuff boxes, fans and prayer-books. It was a world so exclusively of things that Peroni had the uncomfortable feeling of being an intruder.

Then his eye fell on a ring. It might have been episcopal; it was certainly magnificent. And although the commissario considered the wearing of jewellery tantamount to doing a striptease in St Mark's Square, the *scugnizzo* within had retained

112

a shameful itch for flaunting. And this ring was made for flaunting.

He picked it up and it glinted invitingly at him. It would, so to speak, reach those parts of him that other indulgences couldn't get to. One *scugnizzo* urge led to another. What was to stop him dropping it into his pocket? He looked furtively about. The shop was deserted except for a large, embalmed bear. It was a pushover. So why not?

'Can I help you?' said the bear.

Peroni repressed a guilty start, returned in a flash to his senses and put the ring back in its place. Closer observation revealed that the bear was concealing a desk at which was seated a portly, grizzled gentleman in his early sixties with several chins to spare and an enormous floppy bow-tie. This character now heaved himself out of his chair.

'Signor Toffali?'

'Si.' The bow-tie took on a wary air.

'*Questura*,' said Peroni and immediately got a reaction that he knew very well indeed. Fear. Quick to exploit the advantage he went on in what he hoped sounded like a dangerous voice, 'I should like to have a word with you.'

'Yes of course ... Er ...' Toffali nervously tinkled a little golden bell on his desk and a bookcase behind him opened to admit a faded woman with wispy grey hair, but expensively dressed and hung with diamonds. 'Excuse me disturbing you, *cara*,' went on Toffali, 'but I have to have a word in private with this gentleman. If you'll be so kind as to look after the shop ...'

She looked at Peroni disapprovingly, grunted and nodded. Toffali then led the way through the bookcase and closed it behind them. They were in a small office in which more antique pieces jostled improbably together with a vague air of actors waiting in the wings to go on stage. There was also one of the most expensive makes of safe. Paper-knifing his shirt collar with a plump forefinger, Toffali sat at a paper-covered desk and nervously with his other hand waved Peroni to be seated as well. Peroni sat and gave him a searing policeman-with-the-X-ray-eyes look. It worked splendidly and Tofalli displayed all the right symptoms of shifting uneasily in his chair, licking his lips, sweating and looking desperately everywhere but at Peroni's eyes.

'I understand,' said Peroni when he judged that the man had

seethed for long enough, 'that you were visited here a couple of weeks ago by a young Englishwoman named Cordelia Hope.'

At this Toffali's face underwent a sort of chain reaction series of expressions, all of which were disconcertingly other than what Peroni had been expecting. The first was surprise, which gave way in turn to disbelief, bewilderment, calculation, relief, amusement and geniality. He got out and offered a box of enormous cigars. 'No?' he said. 'Then I will if you don't mind.' Peroni reflected bitterly that he would probably never know what ripe plums of fraud had escaped his grasp. 'Cordelia Hope?' said Toffali. 'Yes, I remember the young woman.'

'Why did she come and see you?'

Amusement flickered again in Toffali's well-pouched, rodent eyes. 'My criminal past,' he said teasingly. 'I have not always been a respectable antique dealer. Once I was slim and eighteen with a head full of ideals. It was that alas long deceased self that the young lady came to see.'

'Please explain,' said Peroni icily, his dignity still smarting from the clown tumble it had taken.

'You see,' said Toffali, waving his cigar, 'like almost all my contemporaries in those days I was a Fascist, but I went further than many in that I was also a Blackshirt and in that capacity I was stationed at Gargnano during the last days of the Republic of Salò . . .' He halted, apparently uncertain.

'Go on.'

'It's just that – I prefer not to remember those days. Life has changed so completely and I with it. When the English girl came I at first refused to discuss the subject, but she was very persuasive.' Lazy lust trickled into his eyes as he looked back on the scene.

'I can be persuasive, too,' said Peroni nastily.

Fear paid a brief return visit. 'All right,' said Toffali, 'I told her so why shouldn't I tell you? It's all dead history . . .'

The atmosphere was dispiriting. The usual lassitude induced by winter on the lake was made unbearable by the general situation. The SS were everywhere, the Allies were approaching rapidly and in the total absence of all reliable information they all had to feed their famished appetites for news with reports provided by the only journalist on the staff, Rumour.

For Toffali all this had been off-set on his arrival by the fact that he would be near the Duce, a verification of all the dreams that had been more real than reality for him for the past three years. His first glimpse of Mussolini from afar – wandering aimlessly with a book in his hand and lack-lustre eyes in the grounds of the villa where he had set up his office – had checked but not halted this enthusiasm. With the passing of the days, however, its pace had become more and more laboured. In February people were quoting his German doctor, Zachariae, as saying that his eminent patient had undergone 'a serious physical and moral collapse' and was 'totally lacking in energy and intelligence'.

But then towards the end of the month Mussolini had had a sudden renewed upsurge of optimism and confidence which had given a new, intoxicating lease of hope to those around him, including Toffali. This had followed a three-day absence of the Duce in Germany. Rumour said he had met Hitler near Munich and the two leaders had gone by car to an unknown destination, returning from which Mussolini, transformed, had said to his personal escort, 'I have seen things that will change the entire course of the war in a few days.'

Naturally everybody had to be their own judge as to how true that might be, but on his return to the lake the Duce's car had slowed down near a group of Blackshirts including Toffali and the leader had poked his head out of the window and shouted, 'Hold on, lads, we've already won the war!'

Two days later the summons came. Toffali and one of the others had been on call in the improvised guard room when Giovanni Dolfin, Mussolini's secretary, arrived and brusquely convoked them. 'There's a job to be done.'

They had followed him along the corridors and up the stairs to the so-called drawing room in which Mussolini liked to receive his visitors. It was a mean little room which put you in mind of the waiting room of some provincial government offices and all its furniture consisted of a threadbare leather sofa, an armchair covered with a flowered fabric, a radio and a low table. On the table, almost as though it had been put there deliberately to catch the attention of visitors and excite their curiosity, was a small pistol decorated with golden arabesques of the type, thought Toffali, carried by ladies in their handbags when they call to threaten erring lovers.

With a jerk of his head Dolfin directed Toffali and his

companion towards a door which led from this room into Mussolini's study and this they now entered. It was a sad come-down after the magnificence of Palazzo Venezia from which Mussolini had reigned in his hey-day. But the first thing Toffali noticed about it was the suffocating heat which emanated from a green majolica stove in extreme contrast to the cold which reigned everywhere else – the temperature, indeed, had an almost more deleterious effect on morale than the war situation.

The Duce was seated at a desk in the corner apparently totally absorbed in the composition of some document, but Toffali, who had curious eyes, saw that the paper before him was covered with labyrinthine doodling. Piled along the walls of this room were a large number of sacks which at a quick glance looked as though they might contain mail and, emerging after a moment from his trance of concentration, Mussolini lifted his right hand and pointed fatefully towards them.

'Downstairs,' said Dolfin, interpreting the gesture.

Toffali and his companion went over to the sacks and tried to hump one on their backs. They certainly didn't contain mail, more like bricks, and unusually heavy bricks at that. It took their combined strength to lift one sack.

'Follow me,' said the secretary.

They went downstairs again and along more corridors to the back of the villa, where they had never been before, and there beside a door leading out into the grounds were two large cases. Dolfin lifted the lid of one of these and they put the sack inside.

The work of loading took them over two hours and they were never for an instant left alone, but as they were putting one of the sacks into the crate the fabric at the neck ripped slightly. It wasn't much, but it was enough for Toffali's already expert eye (his father was a jeweller) to recognise that the bricks they were carrying were bricks of pure gold.

When they finally came to the last sack the Duce himself accompanied them and watched in silence as it was put into the crate and the lids were clamped down. Then unexpectedly he thrust his hand at the two Blackshirts and Toffali noticed that his eyes were watering slightly.

'Lads,' he said, 'what you have carried today is the future of Italy.'

CHAPTER 9

Peroni went into the bar where he was to meet Willi and ordered a glass of San Benedetto di Lugana, the local wine Nausicaa had introduced him to. Somehow its clear, dry taste seemed to evoke the flavour of Cordelia and her unfinished story.

Willi hadn't arrived yet, but it was only quarter to seven so Peroni lingered over the wine. He stared at Cordelia's face in the bottom of the glass, but then when it started getting mixed up with Nausicaa's he got irritated and started thinking instead about the interview with Toffali.

There was something about it which didn't fit. If Toffali had told the truth, she had learned from him that the crates were loaded with gold bullion. Surely that must have been good news and yet she had been depressed when she met Peroni that evening. Why? Had something else happened that day in Verona? Without having the remotest idea of the answer to those questions he had the impression that much depended on it.

The wine count had gone up to four glasses when Peroni next looked at his watch and was surprised to see it was already twenty past seven. Either Willi was unpunctual or he had been delayed. But after another half hour it began to look as though he had changed his mind. Loyalty to the team had prevailed, which created a serious hindrance as Willi was the only person from whom he was even remotely likely to learn the details of the salvage operation.

Peroni had a final glass of Lugana before walking into the village. He stopped for a while looking up at the terrace-garden bar where he had sat with Willi the previous evening and he was so immersed in the problem of how to handle this new situation that he almost failed to notice Nausicaa crossing the street. Just a flash of bird's-nest hair and a brightly coloured man's shirt

117

alerted him in time to her presence. He ran to catch her up. 'Nausicaa . . .'

To his astonishment the face she turned towards him was awash with tears.

'What's the matter?'

'You don't know?' He shook his head. 'It's Willi – poor Willi's dead.'

The news was a hammer blow and the still fresh encounter of the previous evening, Willi's painful love for Cordelia, his maudlin wretchedness, his desire for revenge conflicting with stubborn loyalty to the team, all made it the more dreadful.

And then suddenly, like an illuminated balloon appearing against a night sky, Peroni had a mental image of a large bald pate seen from above, from the head of the steps leading down from the terrace-garden bar. At the time he had stupidly overlooked the possibility that their conversation might be overheard. Now he realised with painful clarity that somebody standing immediately beneath the terrace could have followed everything they said. Who? The answer now seemed obvious. What was more likely to go with total baldness than flaunting headgear like a cowboy hat or a sombrero? 'They killed him!'

'Oh no! Achille, what are you saying? Why ever should they kill poor Willi?'

Peroni was on the point of telling her, but then he changed his mind. For all her riotous femininity, for all the aching desire he felt to cushion his head upon her breasts, he still had no idea what part she played in events. 'I don't know,' he said, 'but when you said he was dead I just assumed—'

'Oh no, you were quite wrong. He died accidentally!'

'Like Cordelia?' Peroni couldn't help saying.

'I hadn't thought . . .' She paused, considering the idea, then rejected it. 'But no, this was quite different. Here, let's go and have a drink – I need it – and I'll tell you what happened.'

They went to the same *caffè* they had stopped at before and she took it upon herself this time to order a bottle of Lugana.

'Why do you say this was different?' said Peroni.

'Because he was diving. Aqualung diving can be very dangerous, you know, and people do die.'

'Even professionals like Willi?'

'Even professionals like Willi. Apparently he was fairly deep –

118

and in the depths things can easily go wrong.'

'What did go wrong?'

'I don't understand the details – you'll have to ask Daniele. But, oh, poor Willi!' She broke off for tears and wine.

'Presumably the police have been over?'

'Well, of course.' She looked slightly shocked. 'From Brescia – they come under Brescia here. I saw him. A nice little man who looks like a very conscientious chemist. Nothing like you, of course, but I'm sure he does his job very well.'

'And does he say Willi's death was accidental?'

'Well, the enquiry hasn't closed yet, so I suppose he hasn't actually said, but as far as I can make out there's no doubt about it.'

On the contrary, thought Peroni, there was a great deal of doubt. So much doubt that it began to look as though Peroni would be able to stop doing an awkward and inefficient solo act at last. Willi's death would convince the police that Cordelia's had not been accidental after all, that the two were connected and then, with the resources of officialdom brought into play, it should not be long before the whole thing was cleared up and Cordelia's ghost could rest in peace. It was time to go and see the Conscientious Chemist. Peroni drained his glass. 'I must go,' he said.

'Must you?' said Nausicaa, fondling him with large eyes that were now filled with a different kind of sadness. 'Must you?'

Her breasts, swelling with tenderness in the man's shirt, summoned as irresistibly as sirens. What else mattered except laying his head upon them? 'I must.' Averting his eyes from their mute invitation, he wrenched himself away.

To avoid the temptation of looking back, he turned immediately up a small, dark alley leading in the general direction of the main road. He walked fast to shake off the coils of desire and clear his head.

Music sounded somewhere ahead of him, getting louder as he walked. It was the thud-thud-thwack-thwack sort of music that always sent him heading straight in the opposite direction, but now the opposite direction meant the siren breasts and half a bottle of unfinished Lugana wine. Determinedly he walked towards the music.

He came into a square where a small crowd of people were

119

watching a group engaged in some sort of frenzied mime.

Break-dancing.

The realisation crashed into his mind like a ball into a formation of skittles. He studied the group more closely. As they hurled, tweaked, arched, pounced and span about like dervishes their faces were almost unrecognisably contorted, but there was a girl with long, grubby, fair hair falling in a hundred rat's tails down her back – surely that was Lidia? Like Chinese, all neo-beats looked exactly the same, but height, weight, age, colour of eyes, even last-seen-wearing all fitted. And to make it more certain the young man who seemed to lead the group corresponded exactly with the carabiniere's description of the man with Lidia: punk hair-style, stud bracelet, good looking, arrogant expression.

The music came to an end and the girl and the group leader started going round the crowd collecting money. Peroni waited until the girl came to him. The face, now that it was in repose, was right, too: the same puffy sullenness he had observed on the pathetic passport photograph her mother had given him. 'Lidia?' he said, the thought that this pursuit at least had reached its end giving him a lift of excitement.

She looked at him with hostility. 'Who the fuck are you?'

He gave her a snake-charming smile. 'Police,' he said. 'And you are Lidia?'

Hostility still, but now tinged with fear. 'Like hell I am!'

Peroni smiled again, fatherly now. 'Have you got a document?'

Without taking her eyes off him she got an identity card out of the back pocket of her jeans and pushed it at him. It said that her name was Susanna Locatelli and that she was resident in Milan, and the date of birth made her over the legal age of consent.

He felt both stupid and disappointed. Then he noticed that the other three male members of the group had placed themselves in formation round him. He could have dealt with all three, but had no desire to try.

'*Sbirro*,' said Susanna and their looks changed from generically hostile to specifically menacing.

'You,' said Peroni to the leader, getting in first, 'abducted from home an under-age girl named Lidia Martelli.'

'I didn't abduct her!' said Maurizio, confirming Peroni's

guess. 'She wanted to come with me!'

It had worked, though. There was an edge of fear in his voice and the other three, sensing this, had fallen backwards like wolves round a camp when something aflame is thrown at them.

'What she wanted or not makes no difference,' Peroni pressed home his advantage. 'She's under age.'

'I never touched her!' Fear expanding.

'That'll be for the judge to decide.'

'It's true!'

'It could cost you five years.'

'I said I never touched her!' Fear rampant. 'She wouldn't let me!'

Peroni noticed three parallel scratches on Maurizio's cheek. 'Did she do that to you?'

Maurizio looked about him uncertainly and his thought was transparent. He didn't like to admit a defeat before the other three, but there seemed to be no alternative if he was to get off the hook on which Peroni had skewered him. His tongue darted snake-like in and out of his lips and he nodded. One of the other boys snickered and Maurizio flushed with rage and humiliation.

'You tried and she stopped you?'

Maurizio nodded again even more reluctantly. Peroni felt a glow of satisfaction, almost as though it were a personal triumph for himself.

'Where is she now?'

'She went off by herself during the night.'

'Where?'

'She didn't say – she just went. In the morning she'd gone with all her things.'

'After you had tried to rape her?'

The multi-coloured head hung in confusion. 'Did she hint to any of you,' Peroni went on to the others, 'where she might be going?'

They shook their heads. He then, having given a last twist to the screw of fear concerning under-age girls, left them. At least he had the satisfaction that he had learned the truth about Lidia until the previous night. And that up till then she had been unharmed.

* * *

'My enquiry isn't officially closed, of course, but there are too many indications that his death was accidental to leave me in any doubt about it.'

Nausicaa's description of the man as a conscientious chemist was extraordinarily accurate. He had thick horn-rimmed spectacles, a lean, serious, anxious face, hair fast receding and wrinkles deepening. He was a shade wary, but at the same time he had obviously heard of the Peroni legend and was impressed by it.

Driving to the *Questura* at Brescia, Peroni had prepared his story carefully. He had decided to avoid mention of the Mussolini gold for the moment on the grounds that he didn't have enough evidence for it. He stuck to his story about having been asked by Cordelia's immediate next-of-kin to enquire privately into her actions during the last days of her life, adding that as a result of this he had discovered her connections with Bellini's team and that he now believed she may have been in search of something which had been responsible for her death and Willi's. The Conscientious Chemist was cordial and eager to help, but obviously sceptical.

'Would it be incorrect,' said Peroni, 'if I asked what the indications are that Willi Meyer's death was accidental?'

His Brescian colleague looked rather as if he had been asked for drugs without a prescription, but he mustered a smile. 'Of course not,' he said.

The indications turned out to be four, of which the first concerned Willi's character. Although a highly professional diver he had retained a fascination for the depths and a tendency always to go two or three metres further down and, in fact, he had been in trouble once before when the team had been diving at Lake Ledro. Bellini, who had been in the water with him, Teo who had been monitoring the dive from the shore and Leo and Max who had been on board the *Proserpina* all confirmed that on the occasion of his death Willi had gone below the established depth and beyond the immediate range of the bathyscaphe which had meant that precious time had been wasted when they realised that he needed help.

Secondly, he shouldn't have been on the dive at all. 'Enquiries revealed that he was extremely drunk last night,' said the Conscientious Chemist and Peroni looked as though this were a complete surprise, 'and the first requisite for aqualung diving is one hundred per cent physical fitness. An orgy of alcohol less than twenty-four hours before is asking for trouble.'

The third indication was technical. The breathing equipment was naturally checked before each dive and Willi's had been in perfect working order, but minute examination afterwards had revealed slight wear in the rubber membrane of the air distributor which transmits hydrostatic pressure to the small lever which, in turn, opens the valve that allows the air to pass. This membrane was normally changed every year.

'It shouldn't have been even slightly worn,' said Peroni's colleague, 'but I've gone into the point with experts and it does sometimes happen that a membrane will begin to wear before its time. In itself this wouldn't have been a determinant factor. Spare breathing equipment is routine, but he had gone too far for them to get it to him.'

'All this depends on the word of the other members of the team. What if they're lying? After all, the membrane could presumably have been substituted.'

'That had occurred to me, too, but there is a fourth indication which, taken in conjunction with the others, is practically conclusive. The whole thing was recorded.' For the first time Peroni felt his confidence shaken. 'Apparently, apart from the television monitoring, all the communications that pass between the divers, the men in the bathyscaphe and the man on shore are automatically recorded. And every detail of the accident is confirmed by that recording.'

'May I hear it?'

'I'll play it for you immediately.' He got out a tape and inserted it into a machine on his desk. 'The recording starts when Bellini and Meyer went into the water. They dived from the surface and the bathyscaphe submerged with them. They can dive directly from it at small depths, but not if they intend going any way down because otherwise the pressure would be too great.'

He turned on the machine. At the beginning the recording consisted of no more than mechanical sounds, a low humming, metal on metal, occasional creaks, with the tersest human interventions from two male voices. 'OK . . . Fifteen metres . . . Starboard . . . Lights . . . Twenty . . . Steady . . .' This went on for some while. Then there was a voice which sounded as though it came from the bottom of a deep cave and was largely unintelligible. Peroni could just make out the words 'Stop' and 'Lights'.

'That's Bellini,' said the Conscientious Chemist. 'I had to play the whole thing through several times before I could understand exactly what they're saying. He's telling the men in the bathyscaphe to halt where they are. He's reached the bed. Then he asks for light as he thinks he's found something.'

This was followed by more mechanical noises and a change in the timbre of the humming, which became slightly acuter.

'What is it?' After the muffled distortions of sound which Peroni's ear had grown accustomed to, these three words spoken by a male voice were so loud and clear that the effect was startling.

'Teo,' said Peroni's colleague. 'He's the one who's monitoring the dive on shore.'

'Don't know yet. What is it, Daniele?' Peroni had never heard Max speak, but this was obviously his voice, deep and grinding.

The reply that came from Bellini was almost entirely incomprehensible.

'He says he's not sure,' the policeman interpreted. 'He thinks it may be an axe-head, but it could just be a stone. They'll take it up for examination.'

This was followed by a loud exclamation from Bellini and more speech in which Peroni made out quite clearly the words 'something else'.

'Now what?' Teo on shore.

'Something something skull.' Bellini. 'Something something.'

'Part of a skull,' interpreted the policeman. 'Probably a dog's.'

'Seems to confirm the axe.' Leo from the bathyscaphe.

'We've never found at this depth before.' Max.

There was a pause with more indefinable noises of movement and machinery interrupted suddenly by a staccato bark and several urgent, but unintelligible words.

Peroni's colleague halted the tape. 'That's Willi Meyer,' he said. 'I'll play it back.' On the second hearing Peroni was able to interpret the bark as the single word 'Help!' and on the third and fourth he pieced together the words that followed. 'Air supply cut off!' After a fifth play through the tape continued.

'Willi!' Max. 'Daniele, can you see him?'

Even on tape the sense of danger was almost tangible.

'No, something something after him something light.' Bellini.

Another change in the timbre of the humming suggested that the *Proserpina* had started to move.

'I can't see him!' Leo from the bathyscaphe.

'Where the hell has the idiot got to?' Max.

'Help!' Willi. This was followed by an agonised choking sound which continued as an uninterrupted background.

'There's a dip in the bed over there – he must have gone exploring that!' Max again.

'Hell, it's more than a dip – it's a bloody great hole!' Bellini. 'Something something down. Stay with me. Something decompression chamber . . .'

For what seemed a long time there was no sound except for the bathyscaphe engines and Willi's desperate fight against suffocation.

'There he is!' Leo.

For a good while none of them spoke and gradually the ghastly mechanical saw noise from Willi's lungs got weaker and weaker and finally stopped altogether.

'Too late . . .' Leo.

'We'll try artificial respiration.' Max.

'OK, I've got him!' Daniele, almost unrecognisable with fatigue.

Long pause filled with grunts and monosyllables.

'Here they come . . .' Max.

'Open outer door.' Leo.

'Check. Outer door open.' Max.

'As soon as they're inside open the inner door.' Leo. 'We'll have to risk skipping decompression.'

Grinding mechanical noises. Bangs. Gasping.

'Got him in . . .' Bellini choking hard.

'Close outer door.' Leo.

'Check. Outer door closed.' Max.

'Open inner door.' Leo.

The sound of this was easily recognisable and it was followed by other sounds which suggested the movement of feet on the metal floor and the dumping of a heavy weight.

'Get his helmet off!' Max. 'I'll do respiration. Start to surface – quick!'

The thumping urgency of artificial respiration accompanied by a deepening of the engine hum went on for a long time.

'How is he?' Teo from the shore.

For a good ten seconds nobody answered. Then Max said in a low voice, 'He's dead.'

'Go on with the respiration!' Bellini. Tired, compressed fury.

'It won't do any good – he's dead.'

The policeman stopped the tape and started to wind it back. 'That's all that's relevant,' he said. 'They went on with the respiration, but he *was* dead.'

CHAPTER 10

Peroni eyed the expanse of golden thigh on display just inside the half open car door. Then, doing his inadequate best to concentrate on business, he parked his own car behind hers and went round to inspect. She was a large blonde with a bright yellow skirt, a screaming red blouse and shoes that were the footwear industry equivalent of skyscrapers. She gave him a professional smile and the muscular movement involved seemed to make the dried caking of paint on her face creak audibly.

'Seventy thousand lire,' she said, 'but I make a ten per cent discount for Neapolitans.'

The nearest that voice had ever got to feminine softness was before its owner had started shaving. Amazing, thought Peroni as he showed his police identity card, how they still managed to fool you.

'My papers are all in order,' said the transvestite huffily.

'It's not your papers that interest me,' said Peroni and then, realising from a renewed flicker of interest on the painted face that the phrase had been wrongly interpreted, he hastily got out the photograph of Lidia and handed it over. 'Have you ever seen this girl?' he said.

'I'm not likely to recognise anybody round here. I've only been here a couple of days.'

'Look just the same.'

Having come against the apparently solid barrier of evidence that prevented him from crossing to a murder verdict on Willi's death, Peroni had returned reluctantly to Venice where another lead on to Lidia had been awaiting him. An aunt, visiting a relative in Verona, had spotted the girl 'hanging about' in the vicinity of the railway station. Lidia recognised her relative and made off rapidly in the opposite direction. The aunt then, having made what sounded like a very half-hearted attempt at pursuit, caught her train back to Venice where she informed Lidia's mother who, in turn, informed the police.

The Polfer (railway police) in Verona were not able to help. 'She certainly wasn't sleeping in the station,' a *maresciallo* told Peroni, 'or we'd have seen her. And if she was hooking for drug money outside she'd have been meat for the city police.'

But Peroni had already tried the city police, which meant that the only remaining chance lay with the hawkers of gutter sex around the station – and if she had fallen among them, dreams of rescue were slim indeed.

The all but hopeless search had taken him to the transvestite who was now studying the photograph with bored dislike. After a few seconds he looked up from it with empty eyes. 'Yes,' he said unexpectedly, 'I think it must be her. I saw her last night. I noticed her because she was picked up by a woman.'

'What?' said Peroni, startled. 'Tell me exactly what happened.'

'Well, the kid was hooking – shifting about looking for customers. And this woman went up to her and started talking to her. At first I thought she was a dike, but there was something about her which didn't fit that. So I decided she must be a brothel keeper on the look-out for talent. Anyway, she was in luck because after about ten minutes the girl went off with her.'

'Can you describe her?'

'Tall, thin, pale. Probably in her thirties. Wearing a grey coat and skirt.'

'What about the car?'

'There was no car. The woman arrived on foot and they went off together on foot.'

This was so improbable that it had to be true. The car was the all-purpose world for railway-station sex in Verona and Peroni knew from his days in the city each one of the condom-strewn empty spaces they parked in. And Lidia had gone off with a woman on foot. If the transvestite was right this could only mean that the brothel was in the immediate area. 'Which way did they go?'

'Down there.' The transvestite pointed to an anonymous looking street which led off the square and then, as Peroni turned to move off, he added quickly, 'Fifty per cent discount for the police.'

Peroni ignored him and made for the street. It was even more anonymous than it had seemed from a distance. Down one side ran a wall scrawled with half-hearted graffiti and along the other there loomed a succession of warehouse-like buildings, all of which seemed to be irrevocably closed. Nothing here to suggest Roman Verona, medieval Verona, tourist Verona or even red-light Verona; just a characterless straight line, and he walked it more out of curiosity than with any hope of actually finding a trace of Lidia.

And then abruptly the street debouched into a small square without any other issue. In its way the square was as anonymous as the street. The wall gave way on the right to a fenced-off no man's land of rubble and undergrowth. On the left was a large, boarded-up house and in the middle, opposite the street, was a building standing behind walls in its own grounds. Unless Lidia and the woman had scrambled over the fence into the waste-land or gone to ground in the closed-up house on the left, they must have finished up at the second building.

Peroni carefully inspected what the high wall and iron gate let him see beyond, which wasn't much. It might be a house of appointment or it might not. But there could be no harm in trying to find out. He went up to the gate and pressed the button of the small intercom built into it.

'*Si?*' A neutral, cautious, female voice. Surely the voice of a bawdy-house portress.

Peroni decided against saying he was police. If Lidia were being illegally held it would only raise the alarm and she could probably be got out and away through the back. Better play it as a potential customer as long as it held together; and be careful, intervened the commissario, that it didn't hold together for too long. 'I want some information,' he said, congratulating himself on the choice of phrase – just the sort of feeler that a first-time client would choose, and if the place were bona fide the woman certainly wouldn't be satisfied with it. But the iron gate clicked obligingly and, as he pushed it open, Peroni decided that his calculation had been confirmed.

He stepped into a gravelled courtyard and crossed it to the front door. This, he guessed, would open to allow him into a non-committal but respectable hall with perhaps an umbrella-stand and coat-hanger and, on one side, an equally no-give-away reception office where after discreet vetting by the portress he would be sent on to the delights within.

And the door did in fact open into a hall with umbrella-stand and coat-hanger on the left of which was a reception office. Peroni was just admiring the extraordinary accuracy of his foresight when the sight of the portress seated at a table confounded it on a single but significant point. For she was a nun.

An exceedingly nunnish sort of nun at that, as indisputably all black and white as an early movie, and formidable, too. The metal frame of her glasses glinted menacingly as she looked towards him with another quelling '*Si?*'

Ever since his childhood in Naples Peroni had gone in awe of nuns who, he firmly believed, could see straight through him, and even if evasion had now seemed expedient he would not have dared attempt it. With the air of a small boy caught spying in the girls' toilets he blurted out the whole story, only omitting his misunderstanding.

'You'll be wanting Sister Caterina,' said the nun, with a warm smile as unexpected as a crocus in winter. 'If you don't mind waiting a minute I'll call for her.'

She showed him into a dark little parlour and closed the door on him. It looked, thought Peroni, as though it had been furnished for a set piece in a waxwork museum. He picked up a missionary magazine and didn't read it. Five minutes tiptoed liturgically by and then at last the door opened to admit a tall, thin, pale woman, probably in her thirties, all just as the transvestite had said. Only she wasn't wearing a grey coat and skirt, but the habit of a nun. He stood up as she moved purposefully towards him. 'I understand,' she said, giving him a brief, matter-of-fact handshake, 'that you're looking for Lidia.'

'That's right,' said Peroni, completely taken off balance.

'She's upstairs having her supper. She'll come down when she's finished. Please sit down.' They both sat and the nun went on, 'I daresay I owe you an explanation, though I didn't of course know she was being sought by the police. I happened to find her yesterday and, realising that she was in serious danger, moral and physical, I brought her here.'

'How is she?'

She gave him a quick, shrewd look as though sensing his anxiety. 'Well enough under the circumstances,' she said.

'The circumstances presumably being heroin?'

'She has taken no form of drug.'

Peroni looked at her quickly. 'Are you sure?'

'I have some experience in these matters.'

She spoke with such authority that he had to accept it. 'And what about . . .' He stopped, unable to phrase the question.

'Nor has she lost her virginity, if that is what you want to ask. Fundamentally she is quite sound morally.'

'But she ran away from home,' Peroni observed irritably.

'That isn't necessarily a sign of moral depravity.'

'And she was hanging around in the station!'

'One has to remember one thing about the station other than the fact that it is a centre for vice, and that is that trains and buses arrive there. The poor child had got off a bus and was looking for a place, literally, to lay her head – not so easy when you are desolate and penniless. Wherever she turned she was met with some new form of attack. It says a lot for her that she continued to defend herself.'

Peroni was beginning to feel harassed. His anxiety about Lidia, and with it sympathy, had grown over the days, but this nun was taking it too far. At this rate they'd end up canonising the girl rather than giving the seat of her jeans the good dusting they so badly needed. 'And what about the poor child's mother?' he said. 'Have you been in touch with her?'

'Not yet.' Peroni opened his mouth to protest, but she quelled him with a look. 'I'm quite aware that I'm legally in the wrong, but my principal concern is to achieve a lasting solution to the problem. If I had aligned myself with the mother or sent her back before she was ready to go she would only have run away again, probably with tragic results. As things now stand she has admitted her own very considerable share of the blame; she has realised that running away solves nothing and she is prepared to go back and concentrate on her work at school.'

Peroni opened his mouth again and then shut it. If Sister Caterina had really achieved all that he was bound to concede that the work of the police would be greatly facilitated if there were a few more Sister Caterinas about. 'Do you do a lot of this sort of thing?' he asked.

'When the Lord gives me the opportunity.'

He eyed her quickly, but she remained tranquilly oblivious to his mute suspicion. 'The description I had of you said you were wearing a coat and skirt. I thought you weren't allowed to go out without uniform.'

'Habit,' she corrected him. 'I have a special dispensation from the bishop. If I were to go looking for girls like Lidia wearing our habit I'd never be able to get near them.'

'How many girls like Lidia have you – well, rescued?'

'I've never counted. Probably about five hundred.'

Peroni gaped. 'Whatever started you on this?'

An expression he could not identify – pain? sorrow? – leapt into her eyes. 'It's something I prefer not to talk about,' she said, 'but I suppose I owe it to you.' She looked at her watch. 'While we're waiting for Lidia.' She picked up the missionary magazine and rolled it nervously.

'Before I became a nun,' she began, 'I lived with my family in Bardolino on the lake.' In the street market anarchy of Peroni's mind something went taut. 'My parents and my younger sister, Beatrice. We were a very happy family. Then when Beatrice was fifteen she fell in love with a local boy. I didn't like it from the start. He was three years older than her and he had altogether too high an opinion of himself. It seemed to me that beneath his superficial charm there lay cruelty and ruthlessness. I tried to hint this to her, but she immediately flared up. She wouldn't hear a word against him and I couldn't insist because she would only think it was jealousy. My parents felt much the same as I did and were equally powerless to do anything about it.

'Then one day Beatrice told me she was pregnant. I don't need to tell you that in those days and in a small village community like Bardolino such an event was still charged with drama and potential tragedy, too. But she didn't seem to be aware of that. She was radiantly happy and convinced he would marry her. I asked her if he knew. She said no, but she was going to tell him immediately. She went out with him that evening on the lake in his yacht. She never came back. She was accidentally drowned.'

Peroni felt another jerk of sudden tension. 'Just what happened?'

'The weather was a little blowy that night, though not what you would call dangerous. Some people out in a motor-boat came upon a yacht and saw a male figure diving from the deck. He said later he was diving for a second time, that he had already been in the water for ten minutes searching for her and had only briefly climbed out because he had a violent cramp.

'He said she had been knocked off the yacht by the boom, which had struck her in a sudden gust of wind, and although he dived straight after her he had been unable to find her immediately. He thought she had lost consciousness because of the blow from the boom, gone under and been carried away by a current. When her body was recovered there was a mark on her neck which was said to be consistent with a blow from the boom.'

She paused, so obviously re-living the tragedy that Peroni hesitated to interrupt her memories. 'And the baby?' he said after a couple of seconds.

'Oh, yes, she was pregnant all right. That came out, of course, and the whole thing seemed to be fairly clear – to me at any rate. She had told him and he had realised that the alternative to marriage might well be a charge of illegal intercourse – he'd already been involved in one or two scandals and he knew his way about that sort of situation. Neither of the alternatives appealed to him so he took the only other course that seemed open to him. He knocked her unconscious and threw her into the water, standing there watching while she drowned. I wasn't the only one who thought like that and there was talk of an enquiry. But then suddenly everything went very quiet and when I asked I was told there wasn't evidence to justify an enquiry. Her death was accidental. And if I tried to insist I at once received the impression – though nothing was ever said – that there was a figure invisible behind the scenes organising the whole thing.'

'But somebody must have known that he was going about with her – that he was the father of the child?'

She winced. 'That was taken care of, too. Shortly afterwards we heard a rumour that another boy in the village had been sleeping with Beatrice, and the fact that she had always cordially disliked him didn't seem to make a great deal of difference. It was only a rumour, of course, but it was enough to establish the general belief that practically anybody might have been the father of the child.' She paused again. 'When I became a nun shortly after that,' she went on after a second, 'I determined that I would dedicate myself as far as possible to saving other girls in trouble in memory of Beatrice. Perhaps in reparation.'

There was a silence while Sister Caterina stared in the past. It was interrupted by a knock at the door. '*Avanti*,' the nun called, forcing herself into the present, and Lidia tumbled into the parlour.

Anatomically she was the same girl as the one in the photograph, but what Peroni had not been prepared for was the abundance of vitality which seemed to explode from her and prevent her keeping still for an instant. Wearing jeans and a shirt, she was prettier than he had expected and she didn't seem much the worse for her adventures. But the inescapable impression he received was that Sister Caterina, incredibly, was right: fundamentally the girl was quite sound morally. A glance was enough to see that she wasn't on drugs and her headlong personality was framed with innocence. She studied Peroni with open curiosity and then looked questioningly at Sister Caterina.

'This gentleman,' said the nun, with a severity which Lidia didn't seem to notice, 'is from the police. He has been wasting his valuable time looking for you.'

'*Buona sera*,' said Lidia to Peroni, looking downcast for about half a second. 'I know I've been an imbecile, but I shan't ever do it again. I promise. I've learned that you solve nothing by running away. And I'm sorry.'

She smiled at him and Peroni, not being as self-controlled as Sister Caterina, couldn't help smiling back; it was good to be involved in at least one story that had a happy ending. Unlike Beatrice's. Unlike Cordelia's.

The details of Lidia's return to her mother having been settled and she having enthusiastically accepted Peroni's invitation to visit him at the *Questura* in Venice, Sister Caterina showed him out. 'Just one thing,' said Peroni when they were at the iron gate of the convent grounds. 'What was the name of the man . . .' he hesitated for an instant, then committed himself '. . . who killed your sister?'

'Bellini,' she said. 'Daniele Bellini.'

CHAPTER 11

The single-storey boat-house loomed in the darkness as forbid-dingly as if it had been Everest. Huddled on a bench some way off, waiting for all activity to cease, Peroni experienced the queasiness that precedes danger. His plan was imprudent at best, suicidal at worst and not made any more advisable by the fact that, having come over that day in pursuit of Lidia, he had left his gun behind. Part of him would have given a great deal to convince the other part to get back into the car and drive back to Venice, whisky, bed and safety. But the ghosts of Beatrice and Cordelia wouldn't let him.

Distant footsteps diminuendoed into silence broken only by the gentlest possible stirring of wind in the trees. He waited for ten minutes more and then, after making quite sure that nobody was about, moved like a swift shadow to the doors of the boat-house and set to work on the two locks. They were surprisingly sophisticated for a boat-house, but Peroni's training in the days of anti-respectability made him more than a match for their manufacturers and within ten minutes he was inside with both of them re-locked just to be on the safe side.

By the slender beam of a pocket torch he surveyed the interior. This was dominated by a sort of huge operation centre with television screens, transmitting equipment and a panel of buttons and switches. Obviously where the dives were moni-tored from. To the left of this was a series of large racks containing diving equipment, masks, and underwater guns, and behind these a large motor-boat was propped upside down against the wall. The opposite side of this ample interior was dedicated to relaxation. Easy chairs ranged round a table with various more or less girly magazines, a cupboard with provi-sions and a large, portable cooking stove. There were two doors apart from the main entrance from the lake front. One at the back and one to the right. Peroni went first to the one at the back and was just about to open it when he checked in sudden alarm. Somebody was in there. He could hear whispering. It was a curiously insistent whispering as though a very old person were constantly repeating the same thing to an imaginary companion. Rigid with tension Peroni tried to catch something of what was being said.

Then gradually failure to understand even a word brought realisation and relief. It was water pipes that were whispering. Slowly he edged open the door and found that it led into a wash-house. He closed it again and went to the second door which he tried gently. It opened and he edged into a narrow, elongated office. On the desk at one end was a telephone, a note-pad and an office diary. He started to flip through this. There were many place names – Rome, Geneva, Mexico City, Auckland – and hotel names jumbled up with addresses, but for the most part it was dedicated to calculations and technical details which obviously concerned diving, but which Peroni was unable to make head or tail of.

Then a name jumped up at him. Willi. The entry was dated Sunday April 27th and said laconically 'Willi rescue Ledro' and Peroni remembered that the Conscientious Chemist had mentioned Willi being in trouble on a previous occasion at Lake Ledro. He was turning forward to the current week when he was halted by another sound.

This time there was nothing remotely equivocal about it: a key had been fitted into one of the outside locks. Peroni looked about him. There was not a scrap of cover in the office. Swiftly he left it. With two locks to be opened he had eight seconds at the outside in which to hide. His eyes took less than one of them to assess the possibilities. Operation centre. Diving equipment racks. Motor-boat. Peroni headed for the boat and dived across it into the narrow space between the craft and the wall. Only just in time. One of the two sides of the main doors was pushed open, a switch was clicked on and the boat-house was flooded with light.

For a moment he could make out nothing but breathing as whoever it was stood looking about him. Bellini? Leo? Teo? Or Max? Fervently, Peroni hoped it was one of the first three. With them he might just about stand a chance, even if they were armed. But with Max there would be no hope.

Then there was a curious noise which Peroni couldn't immediately identify. It sounded as though someone were meditatively cracking a whip. But after a couple of seconds he placed the source of this oddly menacing noise. Not a whip but bones. Somebody was standing there surveying the boat-house and thoughtfully cracking his finger-bones. And who but Max could make them snap like writhing thongs? This identification was confirmed almost immediately by a ponderous giant tread which seemed to make the floor shake.

The tread moved towards the operation centre and Peroni realised that, although the ordeal was certainly only beginning, he had at least been wise not to choose that as a hiding-place.

The wash-rooms next and the whispering of the pipes crescendoed as though in alarm at Max's approach. Peroni's mind churned: could this be just a routine check or had somebody somehow got wind of his breaking in?

The Goliath steps moved towards the office and Peroni realised he had left the diary open. Would Max notice that? He contemplated making a run for it, but, for better or worse, contemplated it too long and heard Max coming out of the office again.

Now the thunder of feet moved across towards Peroni in his narrow, horribly precarious concealment. The racks first. He could hear Max's heavy breathing as he prodded about among the diving equipment. And that done, only one more hiding place was left. The breathing and the steps came nearer and Max was standing practically on top of Peroni. Just the boat between them. If Max moved forward a few inches he would see his prey.

And move he did. The sound of it was clearly audible. Peroni expected to see the great face (surmounted by what new crowning eccentricity?) looming into horrid view above him. Instead he heard a grunt and felt his shelter heave over on top of him. It was unbelievable, but Max was actually lifting one bow of the motor-boat, presumably under the impression that everybody had his strength, and looking underneath and inside the craft.

The movement had the effect of hiding Peroni even more securely under the bow, but under the circumstances this cover had all the advantages of being crushed to death. The weight increased remorselessly, crushing him into the wooden floor like an insect being ground under the heel of a shoe. He seemed to hear the crack of his own bones breaking and feel a cry of torment breaking from him which would at least have the advantage of procuring a less painful death.

And then the weight started to diminish. The bow shifted off him and away. For the moment Max was satisfied. Peroni heard him cross the floor again, cracking his bones as he went, back to the office, where he picked up the telephone receiver and dialled a number.

'*Pronto*, Daniele?' Peroni heard the deep rumble of Max's voice. 'Nobody. Must be another flaw in the alarm system. This is the second time in a fortnight.' There was a pause and then he continued, 'Well, you'll just have to get it checked again, won't you. I'll be right back.'

So that was it: an alarm system linked with Bellini's room. The possibility of that had never occurred to him.

He listened while Max went out, switching off the lights and locking the door behind him. Then he lay there for ten minutes, partly as a precaution, partly to give his tormented limbs time to make some sort of recovery, and even after the pause he was surprised to find that he could stand at all. Then, after cautious observation from one of the windows, he hobbled dolorously back to the office and started to look through the diary again.

Apart from an entry to mark the opening of the congress, various official dates ('Lunch mayor', 'Press conference' etc.) and a mass of technical data there was nothing in the recent past to interest him. Then he turned the page to the next day and saw there three brief entries: '1941 443 Waning c.'. He studied these for a moment and finally, after making sure there was nothing else, closed the diary. He felt reasonably certain that he had found half of what he had hoped. Unfortunately a brief, but efficiently thorough going over of the place did not reveal the other half.

It was time to go. His exit, he realised, would probably sound off Bellini's alarm again, but this would now almost certainly be considered as another result of the flaw and anyway he would have plenty of time to get away clear. He opened the two locks, slipped out and closed them behind him: no point in letting them know they had had a visitor.

He was just setting off towards his car again when an idea occurred to him. He looked about quickly. Nobody. Then he started to manoeuvre his way cautiously round the building. At the back, just outside a door leading from the wash-room, was a dustbin. He lifted off the lid and with some distaste started to sort through the contents. He had a couple of unpleasant encounters with a dead mouse and a mass of still damp tea-leaves, but at the bottom he found what he was looking for.

When Peroni got to the *Questura* in Venice the next morning he passed on his dustbin find to a colleague, who said, 'But what order do you want them in?'

'The order doesn't matter.'

'The result'll be pretty odd then.'

'The important thing is that they should be put together.'

'OK – if you say so.'

Peroni then went to his office, where the first thing he saw was the letter on his desk. The handwriting was so incontestably English that he had to look at the stamp to see that it had been posted in Italy. Severe, orderly, with a discreetly restrained hint of originality, it was equally incontestably Miss Kathleen Porter's handwriting. He opened the envelope.

'*Caro* Commissario,' he read, 'I have tried to contact you, but you never seem to be in your office. An excellent thing, I hasten to add: a headmistress who is always in her office is not doing her job properly and I am sure the same thing can be said of a policeman. I am obliged to return to England today . . .' he looked at the date and saw that it was two days previously. '. . . so I will have to content myself with a written *addio* or rather *arrivederci* as I hope you will come and visit me in England before long.' She went on to give him her address and telephone number and invite him to stay at her house – an invitation he determined to take up if possible.

'I wonder if I might ask you a favour,' the letter went on. 'I am informed that a small remainder of Cordelia's personal effects are waiting to be collected at the carabiniere headquarters at Garda. Even if I had time this is something I should prefer to avoid. I wonder if you would be so very kind as to do it for me? There is no need to send these belongings on to me. Please keep them until we next meet.

'I greatly enjoyed meeting you and I have the fullest confidence that you will in due time find out the truth about my niece's tragic death. I much look forward to hearing from you when you do so.

'Yours very sincerely, Kathleen Porter.'

Peroni wished he could feel as confident as she did. Things, it was true, were assuming a shape and the double discovery of the previous evening promised well, but something was still escaping him. He had a curious feeling that he was doing the wrong jigsaw puzzle. He stared at the canal below his window and it stared back at him unhelpfully. Then a ray of sun speared it with dazzling suddenness and he saw, as though by the brightness of the wink it gave him, why the jigsaw puzzle was wrong. He grabbed a piece of paper, scribbled on it briefly and then sat back to view the result.

'Third July,' it read, 'C. arrives at Garda. Tenth, meets me and has appointment with somebody else, goes to Bellini for the first time that afternoon (pinpointed by Willi) and dines with me in the evening. Eleventh, first yachting lesson with me, rest of the day with Bellini. Twelfth, arrives late for evening meeting with me, dejected, storm on lake. Thirteenth, letter written to her aunt from Costermano, sails with me in the afternoon to Malcesine. Fourteenth, last day, C. alternately exhilarated and depressed, watched by someone (?), sails out alone in *Spaghetti Western.*'

That was the jigsaw puzzle he should be doing, the one that formed the picture of Cordelia's stay on the lake. And those few pieces that he knew for sure were the basic ones around which all the others should be fitted in. He picked up the telephone and about an hour later the general shape of the puzzle, with one or two pieces uncertain and one or two still missing, lay before him.

July 3   C. Arrives at Garda.
July 4   Goes to San Vigilio, the Capri bar at Garda and Count Attilio at Villa Mimosa.
July 5   Visits Pagani and del Duca.
July 7   Talks with Col. Volpi at clinic near Sirmione.
July 9   With Aristotle's connivance photographs map at del Duca villa.
July 10   Meets me, then somebody else with whom she has appointment, goes to Bellini in afternoon.
July 11   With Bellini.
July 12   Antiques man. Toffali, in Verona (?) Date unconfirmed, but logically must be today. Returns dejected. Why?

July 13 Morning at Costermano. "Maybe, just maybe, I shall come back to England with something rather interesting."

July 14 Exhilarated–depressed. Followed by someone (?) Drowned.

Apparently the most striking question mark resulting from this incomplete pattern concerned the identity of the anonymous figure she had had an appointment with on July 10th. And for the moment Peroni saw no way to give it an answer. But there were two other problems, less immediately obvious, but maybe no less vital.

The first concerned Cordelia's dejection of the evening of July 12th. It sounded as though something had gone wrong, but what? And then the next morning she had written to her aunt about coming back to England "with something rather interesting". It almost sounded as though she had lost the way and then found it again.

The second problem was related to the time between her visit to Costermano and her death. Peroni realised that apart from the hours she had spent with him he knew nothing whatsoever of her activities during this vital period. What had she been doing the morning before she was killed? Why the alternation of exhilaration and depression? Was she indeed being watched, and if so why and by whom? The way to the truth mentioned by Miss Porter in her letter lay through those three doubt-swathed fields.

The intercom phone on his desk rang and he picked up the receiver.

'*Pronto?*'

'Dottor Peroni? I've pieced together those bits of tape you gave me. If you come down I'll play them for you.'

'I'll be right with you.'

Peroni hurried to the room downstairs where the most up-to-date technological devices – or as many of them as the Government budget allowed – were put at the service of police investigation in Venice.

'*Ciao*,' said Peroni's colleague, who was the ringmaster of this hardware circus. 'I warned you it would sound pretty odd. I only hope you can make more sense of it than I can. Sit yourself down.' Saying this he switched on an imposingly intricate recorder.

'. . . thirty metres,' said a voice which Peroni immediately recognised as that of Max. 'Murkier than I'd expected. Bearing to port.' 'Forty-eight,' chimed in either Leo or Teo, 'forty-nine, fifty. That's enough. Turn it off.' '. . . *Dreissena Polymorpha.*' That was Bellini, and the distorted muffling of his voice suggested he was diving. 'They've colonised five big rocks . . .' 'Hegel has scored for Juventus!' Either Teo or Leo, disconcertingly clear, obviously from the shore monitoring centre. 'He took the ball from Siri and smashed it in from a fantastically tight angle! You can probably hear the cheering.' And in fact there was a background noise of cheering from radio or television, but it was immediately interrupted by another voice. '. . . dead ones. They're attached by filaments of byssus.' Willi, diving. Peroni found it more disturbing than he would have thought, this voice from the grave. 'Martini's taking a penalty kick for Sampdoria!' Teo or Leo again from shore. 'Pavoni's got the ball. He's passing to Richter . . .'

The hotch-potch of phrases went on as though it had some sort of surreal logic of its own which, if you only knew the key, you might understand. Peroni listened right through to the end though he knew that, if his theory were correct, he already had all he needed.

'Whatever does that prove, I should like to know?' said his colleague, switching off when it was done.

'It proves,' said Peroni rather over-dramatically, 'that a man was murdered.'

CHAPTER 12

'*Buon giorno*, Dottore,' said the cynical brigadiere. 'Don't tell me you're still wasting time on the English red-head?'

'Her next of kin,' said Peroni coldly, 'has authorised me to pick up some effects of hers which I understand are here. This is her letter.'

Heedless of Peroni's disapproval, the brigadiere glanced at the letter with indifference. 'I'll get the stuff for you,' he said. He disappeared and returned a minute later with Cordelia's light blue canvas hold-all, the sight of which gave Peroni's heart a

141

painful wrench. He emptied the contents on the counter in front of him as though he were upending a sack of rubbish. 'That's the lot,' he said. 'Just check through the list and sign at the bottom.'

Peroni found the contents of the hold-all almost more than he could bear. Doing his best not even to look at them he scooped up the jeans, shirt and gym-shoes she had been wearing when she died and put them back into the hold-all. Then he sorted through the rest. There was her watch, a gold chain she wore round her neck, a lighter (she didn't smoke, but presumably she had domestic uses for it), a tough looking multi-purpose knife, a purse with money and a key. All these things seemed to be somehow physically imbued with the living Cordelia. Peroni put them as quickly as he could into the hold-all, signed and got away. He badly needed a drink. He started to walk through the village in the direction of a quiet back-street bar he knew with Cordelia's hold-all over his shoulder.

His verdict, given a few hours earlier, that the scraps of tape proved a man had been murdered, was bold but not altogether accurate. They didn't in fact prove anything at all, though subject to some checking they might strongly suggest something. If he were in charge of the enquiry they would certainly be enough to have people in for questioning, but as he wasn't and had already tried twice unsuccessfully to bring the official investigators round to his point of view, he knew it would be wiser to hold his fire until he had something inconfutable in hand. And with any luck he should be in that position by the next morning.

But he would need some help. After some reflection he had asked for and got an immediate appointment with the prefect of the Veneto who was a fellow Neapolitan and an old friend.

'A singularly Peroni situation,' said the prefect when Peroni had done talking. 'If I didn't know you so well I should be appalled. As it is I'm just horrified.' He drummed his fingers on the desk for a second. 'Listen, Achille,' he said at last, 'I can't put several hundred men on what amounts to a war emergency footing just because of something you've seen scribbled in a diary. I can only suggest a compromise solution.' He scribbled on a piece of paper and handed it across to Peroni. 'If you ring me at this number any time during the night I guarantee to get you all the backing you need within minutes. All right?'

And Peroni had had to be content with that. He had then driven over to Garda, calling off at San Benedetto di Lugana where he laid on a hired motor-boat for the night. And that done, with several hours still in hand, he had come over to collect Cordelia's poignant belongings.

And now, cutting through the quieter streets behind the lake front, he walked past the house where Cordelia had lived, doing his best not to look at it, and headed doggedly on towards the bar. He came to a low stone archway through which he could make out the architecturally uninteresting outline of the village church. It was just as he was going under this archway that he heard a car backfire close behind him. But there were no cars in the centre of Garda. The explosion reverberated alarmingly in the narrow street and he tried to turn towards it. But his body wouldn't turn. Only then, it seemed, did the impact strike him and he felt as though he had been hit in the back by a hard ball kicked by a child of superhuman strength.

More prosaically, a bullet.

Suddenly everything went wrong. His inner mechanism felt the chaos of a crowded, fast-moving escalator that suddenly halts. His ears roared. Vision flickered alarmingly. Somewhere there was blood. In circumstances of pitiful banality death had jumped out on the hero of a thousand desperate escapades. He felt himself topple forwards. Then felt no more.

Heaven was female. He didn't know he knew this, much less how he knew it, but he was altogether swaddled in femininity. No sight, no sound, no words, no knowledge. Just Woman.

But gradually the sense of being enveloped and lost in a universal and eternal Eve gave way to more specific aspects. Notably breast. He was cradled in a glorious expanse of soft breast. Then smell: a smell of woman as rich and delicious as that of new-mown hay. Then hair. Female hair was trailing across his face like weeping willow on a river bank.

Finally, after a glorious age of all this, the inner mechanism kicked back into some sort of recognisable everyday life and Peroni's eyes opened weakly to see Nausicaa's earth-mother face looming like a tender moon just above his.

'That's better,' she said, making him feel as though he were one of her children recovering from a nasty fall. 'You do lead a dangerous life, don't you? Never let me hear you trying that routine enquiries stuff again. Shot in the middle of Garda! Why, you might have been killed!'

'I thought I was,' said Peroni weakly, wondering at the heavy torpor that enveloped him.

'Nonsense!' said Nausicaa matter-of-factly. 'It's only a shoulder wound. You lost a fair amount of blood and it is quite nasty, but the doctor's already dealt with it.'

In confirmation of this Peroni felt the constriction of bandages around his shoulder. 'Where am I?' he said.

'At our house in Bardolino, of course.'

'How did I get here?'

'I drove you.'

Peroni felt his mind swamped by a wave of somnolence. 'Have I been given some sort of drug?'

Before she could answer this, the door burst open and some half dozen children exploded into the room with a tray which miraculously remained unspilled.

'Put it on the table,' Nausicaa ordered. 'I thought you were coming round,' she explained to Peroni, 'so I told the children to get some tea ready. Cristina, pour it out,' she went on, 'and you, Marco, bring a table over here for the commissario.'

'But I don't like tea!' protested Peroni.

'Nonsense!' said Nausicaa. 'Strong, sweet tea is just the thing when you've lost blood. Alberto, the commissario's tea-spoon is not for digging holes in the carpet!'

'I would really prefer a drop of brandy.'

She looked at him severely, her mouth opening to administer a reprimand, and then apparently changed her mind. 'Oh well, I suppose at your age that's all right,' she said. 'Marco, go and ask Grandpa for the brandy and Martina go and pour the tea out of the window. Antonio, stop staring – the commissario isn't an orang-utan!'

Peroni realised that he was scarcely in a dignified position, draped half upon a sofa and half upon Nausicaa's ample bosom. He tried to pull himself up, but she clamped him firmly back in place saying, 'You're meant to be resting!'

'But how did you come across—?' he was starting to ask when he was interrupted by an anguished yelp from outside.

'Really, Martina,' said Nausicaa, 'you might have looked to see that the dog wasn't there before pouring the tea out. How

144

did I come across you, you were going to say. Well, I'd gone over to Garda for my adult catechism class . . .' (the surprises and contradictions of this woman, Peroni reflected in bewilderment, seemed to be endless) ' . . . and when I came out of church I had to go through an archway to get to where the car was parked. And there you were lying on the ground. Naturally, I assumed you were drunk, but then I saw the blood.'

'But was there nobody about?'

'You mean the person who shot you? Ah, there you are, Marco. Umm! Grandpa's best Courvoisier, I see. You really must be a magician, Achille, the way you've charmed that man. Two glasses, please – we can't let the commissario drink by himself.' As she started to pour, Peroni took the opportunity to get himself into a normal sitting position. 'Chin chin!' she went on, handing him an enormous brandy. 'Here's to a speedy recovery. What was I saying? Ah yes, was there anybody about? No, not a soul. I made a special point of looking because I knew that was the sort of question you'd ask, although, I don't mind telling you, I was terrified out of my wits. But then of course I didn't hear the bang, so he would have had plenty of time to get away. Roberto, stop setting the curtains on fire! And Alberto, I've told you before, you are not to play Operations with your sister!' She rose in a sudden spectacular firework display of wrath. 'Come along all of you, off you go to your rooms! The commissario's been shot and he doesn't want to be pestered by a lot of silly children!' And saying this she herded them towards the door.

While the shooing-out operation was going forward, Peroni struggled through fog-banks of torpor to consider the situation. Had her presence in Garda really been such a coincidence? How was he to know that it wasn't she who had fired at him? Or somebody at any rate whose identity she was aware of? He shook his head and took a large swallow of brandy to quicken the sluggish flow of his mind.

'Aren't they sweet?' she said, returning from the operation. 'Everything goes suddenly flat without them, doesn't it? Yes,' she went on as though he had spoken out loud, 'I suppose it could have been me who shot at you. Or I might be in cahoots with whoever else did. But in that case why should I or Signor X not finish the job off properly? And why should I bother to go and get hold of two burly fishermen to carry you to the car? Not to mention getting the back seat all covered in blood.'

The murk of Peroni's mental horizon was suddenly lit by a lightning flash of memory. 'The hold-all!' he said.

'What hold-all? You are a one for going off at tangents, Achille!'

'A pale blue canvas hold-all – I was carrying it!'

'The English girl's?'

'How do you know—?'

'Don't be so suspicious, Achille. She had it with her when she came here. And you'd hardly be likely to go round with a pale blue canvas hold-all of your own, would you? No, it wasn't there.'

So he had been shot for Cordelia's hold-all. Mentally he reviewed the contents. Taken at face value there was nothing about any of them to warrant such violence. The key? It was an old-fashioned door key, almost certainly of the house in Garda where she had stayed; it would have been far simpler to break in than run all the risks of a daylight shooting.

'But you mustn't worry about that now, Achille,' Nausicaa went on. 'After all you've been through today it's high time for bed.' Was it his own perpetually inflamed imagination or had she given the word an inviting lift? 'You will sleep here, won't you? My husbands have left behind an excellent range of pyjamas.' The prospect was pleasing, but would he be up to it in his condition? Something told him he would. 'Perhaps another drop of brandy first?' She poured hefty slugs for them both.

Another lightning flash of memory zig-zagged alarmingly and by the light of it Peroni saw what he had come over to the lake to do. Bed? His internal chronometer must have remained behind with the shooting. But the lights in the room were all on; the sky, he saw glancing round to the window, was already dark. He looked at his watch. 'It's nearly midnight!'

'That's right. High time we were in bed.' (Another invitation? Oh, why go around looking for trouble when he could be wallowing in that marvellous compendium of all femininity?) 'We're usually all of us sound asleep by now, but the children asked if they could stay up specially because you'd been shot. Come along. We'll go and choose your pyjamas. Though really I think you'll find it's far too hot for pyjamas.'

That, surely, was unequivocal? Peroni tensed with excitement. But at the same time, paradoxically, his mind was lanced with the thought that she was doing it deliberately. All his old suspicions of her came back together with the urgent awareness of what he had come to the lake to do and the near certainty that she was trying every trick she knew to prevent him from doing it.

'I must go,' he said. He stood up as he said it and felt a tearing pain in his shoulder.

'Are you out of your mind, Achille? You can't possibly go anywhere in your state. Sit down at once!' Was there a trace of fear behind the maternal blustering?

'I'm going,' he said, heading for the door and trying not to show the pain he felt. 'All I ask you is to let me use your car.'

'But Achille, this is lunatic!' She was wailing now in the face of what he hoped looked like implacability.

'Yes or no?'

'I'll drive you,' she temporised. 'You can't possibly drive yourself.'

'No,' said Peroni. Under other circumstances he would have welcomed the idea, but now he knew that her presence would be a continual deflection and he didn't feel strong enough to react against it. 'Can I use the car or not?'

'I'll take you to it.'

He had never seen her so submissive. They left the room and the house in silence and walked down the steps to the gravel drive where the car was parked. Still in silence she handed him the keys. He got in and switched on the engine.

'Achille,' she said, 'don't . . .' There was a note of pleading in her voice and, looking up at her, Peroni could make out two enormous tears gleaming on her cheeks in the darkness. 'Be careful!' she said and, turning, ran back up the villa steps.

This time there could be no doubt about the fear in her voice.

CHAPTER 13

As soon as he drove within sight of the harbour, and even in the darkness, the looming mass of the *Proserpina* made itself glaringly conspicuous by its absence. The whole thing was a waste of time: tearing himself away from Nausicaa's siren wiles and the agonising drive through the night. He would have done

147

better to stay in Bardolino and try on all her former husbands' pyjamas. For he was too late.

The *Proserpina* was somewhere out there on the lake carrying out its mission to salvage the Mussolini gold, and with nearly four hours to go before dawn its crew would have more than sufficient time to get the two great cases up, away and into hiding.

Bitterly Peroni realised he would never get at the truth now. With the lever of the Mussolini gold gone it would be impossible to prise open the secret or secrets still concerning Bellini and without them he would be unable to get back to the only thing that really interested him: the facts concerning Cordelia's death.

When he had seen scrawled on the page for today of Bellini's diary '1941 443 waning c.' he had realised that this must refer to sunset (1941), tomorrow's dawn (443) and tonight's moon (waning crescent) which meant that a night trip was scheduled for the *Proserpina*. And in its turn that could only mean one thing: they intended to salvage the Mussolini gold. Hence Peroni's interview with the prefect to rally aid for the capture. But it would be impossible to trace them now: Garda was the biggest lake in Italy and on its vast expanse by night the bathyscaphe – even supposing it was not submerged – could never be traced without a full-scale air-water operation. So thanks to Nausicaa and person or persons anonymous all hope was irretrievably sunk. Feeling hollow and weary, Peroni started to make his way back to the car.

'You'll never find out who killed her now. You won't live that long. Her death will remain an unsolved mystery for ever.'

The man's voice coming out of the darkness from a house Peroni was just passing made him check for an instant in astonishment, until he realised that it came from a late-night television movie somebody had just switched on.

Television.

The word seared blindingly in his brain, making him forget for a moment exhaustion and the throbbing wound in his shoulder. All dives were automatically television monitored, Bellini had said. So there was just a chance he could follow what was going on from the boat-house and maybe get some indication of where they were headed for when the cases were loaded.

148

He broke into an ungainly loping movement which was the nearest he could approximate to running and tried not to think what it would be doing to his bandages and the wound beneath them.

It seemed probable that since the team was one short as a result of Willi's death and since, moreover, they would be wanting to make an immediate get-away with the salvaged gold, the usual monitoring would not be carried out tonight. And in fact when Peroni reached the boat-house it was dark and silent. He set to work on the locks, forcing himself to handle them without speed so as to avoid fumbling and further waste of time.

The job seemed to take an hour, but they finally ceded and he pulled open one flap of the large doors and stepped inside. Nobody, and the bulk of the operation centre with its screens loomed solidly in the darkness.

He went over and installed himself at the panel, gun ready to hand. Then he stared in dismay at the controls. Naïvely he had been expecting a knob or a button on the television part which you turned or pressed as for the eight o'clock *telegiornale*, but this was a computer engineer's adventure playground and Peroni, never mechanical at the best of times, was as adept with computers as a duck in outer space. If only his nephew, Stefano, were here; Stefano was into computers and could do anything with them, from his homework to calculating trigonometrical heliocentric paralaxes. Peroni tried to imagine what Stefano would do with this one and then prodded nervously at some keys and buttons. This had some effect, though hardly the one he was after. Red lights flashed and the whole complex growled angrily at him. The screens, however, remained unresponsive. He prodded some more and the growling climaxed into a deafening banshee wail. If any watcher had not been alerted already by the lights, they certainly would be by this, which must be interfering with the opera performance in the Roman arena at Verona.

Peroni jabbed desperately at the panel, which only made matters worse; the red lights were now dancing hysterically like demons clamouring for human souls and the wailing continued undiminished. Then by sheer luck he touched something which momentarily placated the beast, or more probably set it about devising a yet more deadly means of defending itself. The lights

149

stopped dancing and all went out except for one, which seemed to be watching him in a bloodshot, beady sort of way, and the wail decrescendoed to a low snarl. The screens remained obstinately blank.

It was no good. He stood about as much chance of making contact with the abysses of Lake Garda as he did of swimming there. And then Peroni found himself bargaining with the patron saint of Naples. 'St Januarius,' he muttered inwardly, 'turn on *questa maledetta cosa* and I'll have the fattest candle available in Naples lit before your shrine.'

Childish superstition, the commissario grumbled angrily, and even assuming that a saint would stoop to that sort of haggling, how could a bishop who died in the fourth century be expected to deal with computers? Feeling slightly foolish, Peroni touched two of the controls in front of him and saw the largest of the screens blink smoothly into life.

Sheer coincidence, said the commissario. *Grazie*, St Januarius, said the Neapolitan within.

The *Proserpina* was hovering just above the lake bed, where two slender cylinders had been laid side by side. Then the bathyscaphe passed over these and Peroni could make out nothing in the dim, green, underwater light except for occasional ghostly masses of rock. Then at some distance he perceived two more shapes which at first he thought were also rocks, but as the *Proserpina* drew nearer to them he saw that they were cases. Densely encrusted with molluscs and covered with a sort of woolly looking sediment, but recognisably cases. The Mussolini gold.

'The Mussolini gold!' said a voice right in Peroni's ear. A jerky grab at the gun was halted by the realisation that the programme was audio as well as visual. The words, husky with avaricious awe, had come from a speaker on his left. He hoped that no switch was on for transmission from his end. St Januarius would hardly have slipped up over a silly detail like that, but he determined to keep as quiet as possible just the same.

He hadn't recognised the voice, which meant that it must have been that of either Leo or Teo.

'Lifting equipment ready,' Bellini. The voice had the distorted, hollow sound which Peroni now associated with somebody who was diving.

'Check,' said Leo or Teo.

At the same time a figure Peroni could not recognise with mask, rubber diving-suit and aqualung equipment drifted like a huge fish into view. Propelling itself effortlessly with the flippers, the figure swam forwards and down towards the cases. When it reached them it made an exploratory circle, digging tentatively at the molluscs with some sort of instrument and wiping here and there at the sediment. Then it looked up – directly, it seemed, into Peroni's eyes.

'Something, something embedded,' it said, and Peroni recognised Bellini's voice again. 'Something shifting something grappling four.'

'Check.' Teo or Leo.

Another diver came into view on the left of the camera's field of vision and started to flip towards the cases. He was carrying something which was heavy, but nevertheless trailed like weeds in the water. It took Peroni a second to realise that these weeds were chains. Then when this second diver also reached the cases, he and Bellini started to fasten the chains around them. Their movement reminded Peroni of the first moon-landing: it had the same slow, deliberate, but dream-like quality about it.

'Something touch down,' transmitted Bellini. 'Port something something rocks sandy bottom.'

'Check.'

Slowly the camera started to shift towards the left, moving in a roughly circular direction so that the divers and the two cases stayed more or less centrally within its field of vision. And then quite unexpectedly it blacked out.

Peroni stared at the screen in bewilderment: if the action were cut off now he might once again just as well have stayed with Nausicaa for he would have no clue as to where they were going to surface or what part of the shore they intended heading for afterwards. But even as he thought this he realised that the screen hadn't gone dead. Vision was still being transmitted, but something had completely covered the camera lens. Something black.

Then, as the *Proserpina* continued to move, the black thing distanced from the lens and became identifiable as a human back. A mountainous human back that could only belong to one person. Max. So there were three of them in the water and one in the bathyscaphe.

No sooner had Peroni recognised Max than his attention was

hammered by something he was doing. Or rather a movement he was making which was at the same time both familiar and yet shockingly out of place. Then there was a jet-like movement in the water as though an invisible, supersonic fish had suddenly flashed through the triangle formed by the three men. But it was only when Bellini looked up towards Max that Peroni fully realised what had happened. Alarm seemed to emanate from Bellini's mask and it was almost as though Peroni could see in it the reflection of Max holding an underwater gun.

But if Max had shot to kill he had plainly missed. Indeed, the bullet could not have even touched for if it had pierced Bellini's suit or equipment he would already be in bad trouble and his movements did not betray that particular sort of emergency. He looked towards the third man, presumably in the hope of finding an ally, but as Peroni followed the look he saw that he, too, was holding a gun.

And at the same time Max and the other man started moving in, pincer-wise, on Bellini. With their flippers beating in slow rhythm they made Peroni think of a couple of sharks moving in on their prey.

Then, with a sudden tadpole wriggle, Bellini was away out of sight behind the cases in a bid for escape that was desperate and at the same time surely hopeless. What could he hope to do unarmed against two killers with guns in a situation that was fraught with danger even under normal circumstances?

Even as Peroni thought this he spotted a rapid shadow glide from the penumbra beyond the cases into the ink-black beyond the range of the *Proserpina*'s illumination and almost simultaneously the water was slashed by two invisible bullets, which produced angry little spurts from the lid of the further crate.

Perhaps the bid was not quite so hopeless after all. To carry through their conspiracy – presumably planned to eliminate Bellini as a sharer in the Mussolini gold – the two hunters were utterly dependent on light to find the prey. But Bellini was not in that sense limited. Once out of their sight there was only one direction he needed to go: up. And he needed no light for that. Once on the surface (if discovery or too rapid decompression didn't prevent him from getting there) he stood a chance of reaching safety, as the crates would have been unsalvageable if they had been too distant from the shore. Max was well aware of this and he turned, looking apparently straight up at Peroni, and gestured for the *Proserpina* to join the hunt.

Then, as the camera eye started to crawl forwards and the area of penumbra was pushed outwards, the lake bottom suddenly vanished. It was as though they had come to the edge of an underwater cliff and Peroni stared in horrified awe at the black depths which, sinking down to the bowels of the earth, rejected the *Proserpina*'s illumination as inter-galactic space would reject a candle flame.

Max and his companion halted at the edge of this abyss, obviously uncertain as to what to do next. The pilot of the *Proserpina* must have been uncertain, too, and after a second the lights were tilted upwards so that the awful gulf below them disappeared from view. But the sight that took its place was scarcely less forbidding. Across the chasm, only a few metres away, was what looked like a mountain range of rocks climbing jaggedly up into the blackness above. If Bellini had crossed over to that he would have no great problem in remaining unseen, though the near razor sharpness of the rocks would put him in appalling danger of ripping his diving-suit or damaging his aqualung, both of which were even more terrible purveyors of death than the underwater bullets.

After a couple of seconds, Max waved the man-hunt on, starting himself to flip his way over the great drop below. His companion followed, but keeping slightly behind, obviously reluctant. The progress of the *Proserpina*, too, seemed slow and hesitant, and even Peroni found himself instinctively pulling back in his seat.

They came to the rocks and were forced to pull upwards a good ten metres. From this higher position it was as though they were flying dangerously low over a range of mountains. There was no sight of Bellini and Peroni couldn't help hoping he was on his way up.

Ahead of them, on the frontier with blackness, loomed two particularly high peaks and as Peroni looked at them a tell-tale swirl of movement appeared between them, though it was too dark to see what it was that was moving. Max didn't waste time wondering, but shot straight at the centre of it. Then, as they pushed their tiny republic of light a couple of metres further forwards, Peroni saw that what had been hit was a giant carp. ('The king of the lake,' Bellini's voice echoed in Peroni's memory.)

153

Already the fish was flailing hideously in its death throes, wrenching and jerking with a violence that would have been more than enough to capsize a fair-sized boat on the surface, and at the same time the dark green of the water was staining with the even darker red of its blood, which went on spreading until it imbued the entire lighted area before the *Proserpina*. Peroni stared in horror as the gigantic agony went on; it seemed as though it would last for ever and the threshing of the fish never weaken.

It was like the albatross. Max had slaughtered the king of the abysses, and the abysses would infallibly take their revenge. This thought entered Peroni's mind fully formed before he had time to censor it and now it would not leave him.

'... back to the crates.' Max's voice crackling distortedly through the speaker made Peroni twitch with nerves and realise that the entire hunt until now had been conducted in silence. 'Never something something alive.'

The death struggle of the fish was beginning to show signs of flagging as the *Proserpina* veered slowly round and the two divers started to flip their way back towards the chasm. To Peroni it seemed as though the presage of the lake's vendetta went with them.

As the bathyscaphe churned slowly through the underwater night, he wondered what had become of Bellini. Was he even now rising towards the surface? Or was he sharing death with the giant carp?

The chasm recrossed and left behind, two shapes on the lake bed, just recognisable as the crates, began to loom slowly back into view. And then, as the circle of light edged over them and beyond, Peroni saw that Bellini was neither surfacing nor dead. He was there, crouched in what looked horribly like a foetal position. For a second Peroni thought he must have been mad to be there at all at the lake bottom when he had had the opportunity to escape towards the surface. Mental unbalance, he knew, did sometimes result from prolonged stays in the depths. But as the camera – and with it the hunt – moved nearer, the true reason for Bellini being there became evident, together with the explanation of his foetal posture. He was changing his air cylinder for one of the spares that Peroni had noticed when he had first been transported to the lake bed by the magic carpet of technology. Either his original cylinder had been damaged during his escape or he had run short of air and consequently been obliged to dodge back past his pursuers to their underwater base. He had been lucky to find it by the slender beam which shone from his helmet. Luckier still, expert though he was, to effect the change in his inevitable state of exhaustion and panic. But effect it he had, and he now dropped the old cylinder, kicking himself off and upwards, for the moment still evidently beyond the range of his pursuers' fire.

An incomprehensible roar crackled over the loud-speaker, but Peroni did not need an interpreter to tell him that Max was urging his companions to pursue. The *Proserpina* surged forwards. For Bellini the appalling tension, the privation of air and the sheer physical strain must have been unimaginable, but his upward flight seemed sure and straight. It would be a question, Peroni reckoned, of who could bear the strain longest without the essential halts for decompression.

Then the camera eye suddenly tilted upwards into the dark mass of water above. For a good minute Peroni could see nothing. But at last the bathyscaphe straightened out and Peroni understood the purpose of the manoeuvre. It was to block Bellini's upward flight until the other two could get within shooting distance. And in fact, the prey appeared for a moment in the light below, then disappeared again as the *Proserpina* passed over him. This operation was repeated a couple of times as Bellini swam out from under the craft and started upwards only to be caught in the light and blocked again.

After the third of these operations Max and his assistant appeared level with the *Proserpina* and Peroni imagined they had held their fire until now to avoid the risk of hitting the bathyscaphe. But now Bellini was swimming below, caught like a fly in amber in the full illumination, and both men fired at him almost simultaneously.

It was hard to tell immediately whether they had hit him or not as he continued to move in the water towards the protection of darkness. Max shot again twice and twice Peroni saw invisibility wing through the water. But this time there could be no doubt. Bellini halted suddenly in his progress and his lean body in the black rubber suit arched violently backwards, then went limp. For the second time that night Peroni saw the water stain dark-red.

But, as if they had not seen this, Max and the other man

continued a murderous downward swoop and one of them even fired again. It was as though they were involved in some sort of ritual sacrifice which had started with the death of the carp and from which they could not withdraw even if they wanted.

And then the lake spoke.

Peroni was never exactly sure what happened. It was as though the bed itself had exploded silently. A gigantic spray of sand and rocks seemed to flower up towards the camera in slow motion and in it the two crates lifted and swayed as if they had been cardboard boxes. Max and his colleague were helpless, torn and buffeted in the underwater tornado. Then the *Proserpina*, and with it the camera that was transmitting to Peroni, started to rock, at first gently and then more and more violently. The whole thing was accompanied by a muffled roar over the loud-speaker which continued to crescendo unbearably as the speed of the appalling vortex in the water increased until all semblance of recognisable shapes was lost.

And then suddenly vision and sound were cut off simultaneously and Peroni found himself alone, staring at a dead screen. There was a long silence which somehow, mysteriously, became audible. At first it was little more than a buzzing not unlike that of a humble-bee. Then the bee became a swarm of bees homing in, it seemed, directly on Peroni. Their buzzing grew deeper and louder until it turned into a united roar.

Peroni was so stunned by what he had seen that it was only at this point that he began to link this subjective experience of sound with some objective reality. And then to realise what it might be.

He got up and made for the doors as quickly as his wound would allow him, then pulling open one flap he stared incredulously at the sight before him. A great wave such as he had never seen was moving towards him across the face of the lake, gathering in momentum and height as it came. It had the smooth, crashing force of one of the great Pacific rollers, but it dwarfed even them in size. It was a tidal wave.

He watched it, rooted, until it came within about twenty metres of the shore. Then he turned and half fell into the boat-house, pushing the door to behind him. He was only just in time before the wave exploded and water roared down on the match-box protection of the roof.

Part Three

DEATH BY FIRE

CHAPTER 1

'*Buon giorno*. It's half past ten and breakfast is served.'

The voice was delightful, soft and very feminine. Peroni cocked an eye and found that the appearance matched the voice. She was on the small side with a trim figure set off to perfection by her white nurse's uniform. She had large, tender brown eyes and two dimples which were always ready to betray any professional severity she might assume. She put a tray with fruit juice, coffee toast, butter and strawberry jam on a tray over the bed and helped him to prop himself up on the pillows.

Peroni looked about him with pleasure. His room had a balcony overlooking the lake, which was sparkling innocently in the brilliant sunlight as though it had never even heard of the horrors of the previous night. He decided that a brief stay in the clinic, now that things had been to all intents and purposes cleared up, would be extremely agreeable, particularly if he was nursed by her.

'What's your name?' he asked. She pointed to an identity badge with her surname pinned on to her apron. 'I mean your Christian name,' he said.

'We're not allowed to be on Christian name terms with patients,' she said, the dimples contradicting the formality. 'It's Giovanna.'

'*Ciao*, Giovanna.'

'Eat up your breakfast at once, please.'

The construction of the boat-house had proved sufficiently solid to protect Peroni from the pounding thunder of the tidal wave and when it was over he had gone out to see if there were any rescue work to be done. But the strain had at last proved too much for his wound. He had collapsed and been picked up by one of the carabinieri who had been rushed to the area. Then when the local authorities learned who he was they had offered to recover him in a luxury clinic nearby. Here he had rallied long enough to send a brief report of events leading up to the tidal wave to his colleague in Brescia. He had then had his wound re-dressed, swallowed various tasteless or disgusting things that he was given and finally fallen into a deep and dreamless sleep which had lasted uninterruptedly until the present enchanted awakening.

'Have you heard any news of last night?' he asked.

'I should say I have! Nobody's talking about anything else. The radio said this morning that the wave was caused by seismic activity from Monte Baldo – and to think I go skiing up there!'

'Did it do much damage?'

'Surprisingly little. The radio said it could have been much worse. But three people were killed. Daniele Bellini, the underwater explorer, and two of his team. They were doing some sort of dive when it happened. But another member of the team was rescued – he was in the bathyscaphe. He's been taken to Peschiera Hospital.'

That would be Leo or Teo, thought Peroni. Aloud he said, 'Do you think I could have a telephone?'

'The doctor said you were to rest for forty-eight hours.'

'Telephoning isn't work.'

'I'll see what I can do.'

'And drop in to see me every so often, will you? I have a feeling I shall need a lot of nursing.'

'I do have other patients to look after, you know.' But her dimples said the others wouldn't prevent her from dropping in. 'I'll come back for your breakfast tray.' As she went out Peroni reflected that she would look very nice in skiing costume, too.

Thanks to her persuasive powers, Peroni's position or both, a telephone was quickly installed in his room and he used it to telephone the villa at Bardolino. Aristotle answered and said that both Nausicaa and the general had been out when he reached the villa that morning and that he had no idea where they were.

Then, after some reflection, he called the *Questura* in Verona and asked to be put through to a friend and former colleague there. 'Listen,' he said, after basic news-swapping, 'I need a favour. I want to know everything available about an accidental drowning at Lake Garda some years ago. Apparently there was some talk of an enquiry, but then it was suddenly abandoned. I'm particularly interested in anyone who may have been responsible for getting it shelved. Quite off the record, of course.' He then gave the essentials of Sister Caterina's story and received a promise of information as quickly as possible.

That done he lay back on the pillows and closed his eyes to study the portrait of Daniele Bellini as Cordelia's murderer. There were one or two loose ends, even inconsistencies, but on the whole the portrait was a lifelike one. Would Cordelia's ghost accept it? For the moment he couldn't say, but he was sure she would let him know.

After a medical examination, more medicine (sweetened by the fact that it was administered by Giovanna) and a delicious lunch, Peroni was awakened from a light sleep by the announcement of a visit from his Brescian colleague.

'Er – chocolates,' said the Conscientious Chemist hesitantly, laying a large box of Baci Perugina on the bedside table.

'That's very kind of you,' said Peroni. 'My favourite chocolates.' He also enjoyed reading the amorous quotes from unlikely Chinese philosophers and Nordic poets that were wrapped around them and it would have been rude to add that he would have preferred a bottle of something.

'Well,' went on the Conscientious Chemist awkwardly, sitting in an armchair, 'it looks as though you were right after all.' Peroni waved deprecatingly. 'I can only say,' added the other, 'that at the time we last met it did all seem so obviously straightforward. Of course, now there no longer seems to be any doubt on general lines. However, there is one thing that needs clearing up. So I wonder if you feel up to it . . .'

'I shall be only too glad.'

'It's the tape that worries me. I mean, I know it was faked, but I don't see how they managed to do it when Willi Meyer was already dead.'

'It was you who gave me the answer to that.' This irritating remark, as he knew it would, caused gratifying bewilderment. 'You told me that Willi had been in trouble during an earlier dive in Lake Ledro. So coupling that with the fact that all dives were taped, which Bellini himself told me, I realised how the tape must have been made. They recorded it themselves after they returned from the dive during which Willi was drowned, sticking in the bits from the Ledro recording. Before that, of course, one of them – presumably Bellini – had changed the rubber membrane in Willi's air distributor and when he had started to get into trouble they had just let him drown. And that done, the piecing together of a fake recording was no problem for anyone accustomed to working with tapes. They wrote and

161

acted their own script. But how to prove it? In that I was lucky. Nosing about the boat-house where they had their headquarters I found some scraps of tape at the bottom of a dustbin. Put together they didn't sound very helpful. They had apparently been recorded during a dive and the team member who was monitoring it from the shore kept the others informed about a football match which he was following simultaneously. That was the key. By putting together some of the information (goals, who scored, the teams mentioned) it was easy to find out when it had been played. Sunday, April the twenty-seventh. The same date – as I'd already seen from Bellini's office diary – as the Ledro dive. So the scraps of tape I had were bits recording the genuine Ledro dive which they'd discarded to make the tape of the fake Garda dive. As simple as that.'

The Conscientious Chemist swallowed. 'I'll be needing the tape,' he said.

'They'll let you have it at Venice.'

'Yes, well . . . They've recovered the bodies of Bellini and his two companions, by the way, and the other one is in hospital in Peschiera. I've already questioned him and he's being held for the time being charged with complicity in the murder of Willi Meyer. So that's another end tied up. I shall be making a report to the examining magistrate some time tomorrow. There is of course the matter of the person who shot at you, but as you yourself suggested the only possible indications are that it was done by Bellini or one of his men to prevent you from interfering with the salvage operation. Is that still your opinion?'

Peroni's mind went into slow motion. The previous night, presumably due to exhaustion, he had overlooked Cordelia's hold-all and Nausicaa's part in the business when filing his report to Brescia. Now was the time to make good the omission. He opened his mouth. 'Yes,' he said, 'that is still my opinion.' Then, egged on by the *scugnizzo* within, he went beyond the bounds of good taste. 'I congratulate you on bringing the business to a satisfactory conclusion,' he said.

'Very good of you.' The Conscientious Chemist looked pleased. 'But without your help over the tapes it wouldn't have been half so simple. Well,' he suggested pushing his hand rather nervously at Peroni, 'I must be off. Get well soon.'

When the Conscientious Chemist had gone, Peroni lay in bed examining his conscience. Why had he failed to mention the hold-all and Nausicaa? The answer could only be that in spite of appearances he didn't believe Bellini had killed Cordelia and he wanted to keep to himself the only pointer in another direction, enigmatic though it was.

His telephone rang and he picked up the receiver. '*Pronto?*'

'Achille? *Ciao.*' It was his colleague in Verona. 'I've got the information you asked for.'

Peroni listened. The story did little more than confirm what he had already heard from Sister Caterina with one or two more factual details. From a legal point of view there was an element of doubt about the whole thing and the evidence as it stood would not have been enough to get a conviction, but between the realisation of that and a total abandonment of the enquiry there was a very considerable distance.

'Did you get any hint as to why the whole thing was dropped like a hot brick?' he asked.

'According to my sources,' said his colleague, 'any suggestion that it was dropped like a hot brick would be looked upon as gravely improper. It was eventually decided to take no further action for lack of sufficient evidence. But one of the people I spoke to happened to mention somebody who apparently took some interest in the affair. I thought the name just might interest you. As you said yourself, quite off the record.'

'Of course. What was it?'

His colleague told him. Peroni thanked him and put down the receiver thoughtfully. Was this the indication he had been waiting for that Cordelia's restless spirit was not satisfied? There certainly wasn't evidence to present that in court either, but it was enough to satisfy Peroni.

He edged himself out of bed, limped across to the cupboard where his clothes were hung as neatly as if they had been in a tailor's and started to dress. He was half way through the operation when Giovanna came in.

'Whatever are you doing?' she said.

'Isn't it obvious? No, that was cheap. I have enquiries to make that can't be delayed.'

'But the doctor said—'

'I can't help what the doctor said. Though of course, if I didn't have to leave and if it was only a question of contenting *you*, I would gladly stay for ever.'

The dimples went to work. 'Drink this at least,' she said, 'and

163

promise you'll have that wound re-dressed before evening.' He drank and promised while he finished dressing. 'And now,' she said, 'you'll have to truss me up in a corner or else I shall be in terrible trouble.'

'Pretend that I sneaked out without you seeing me. Cunning before violence any day. I'll back you up.'

'Yes, but I thought the trussing up might be rather fun. Oh, you'd better get out quick before I forget that I'm a registered nurse altogether!'

The carabiniere who was sitting stolidly outside Leo or Teo's room was so young that he put Peroni in mind of the adage that you are beginning to get old when you start noticing how young the policemen are. But his youth would also make him less likely to ask questions about why a detective from Venice should want to interview a man who had already been charged by the local police. Peroni displayed his police card with the aplomb of a Neapolitan street vendor offering a phoney Rolex gold watch and was shown in.

'*Questura*,' he said. 'I've got one or two questions to ask.'

'I've already told your colleague – I'm not answering.'

'Maybe I can make you change your mind,' said Peroni amiably. 'You're charged with complicity in one murder to be going on with and you can get an awful lot of prison for that. But if there was somebody behind Bellini, somebody who ordered the killing of Willi Meyer, and if you helped me get hold of that person then maybe, just maybe, the law might be inclined to deal with you a bit more leniently.'

Leo or Teo was now staring at Peroni. 'What do you want to know?'

'*Did* Bellini take orders from someone?'

'Sure he did. It wasn't difficult to see that. Somebody gave him contacts when he needed them, told him what to do.'

'Who?'

'I don't know. I swear I don't know.'

'How did this person get in touch with him?'

'Mostly by telephone. Sometimes, though, Daniele would go and see him – at least that's who we reckoned he went to see when there were decisions to be made. Sometimes, too, he got letters from him.'

'You say him – you know it was a man?'

164

That puzzled him for a moment. 'No, if you put it like that I don't. We assumed it was.'

'You say Bellini received letters from this person. How do you know they were from the same person?'

'Because he took them seriously. Other letters he mostly threw away.'

'Anything else you can tell me about them?'

He shook his head. 'I never really looked at them – I just saw them occasionally when they were waiting for him. Same sort of envelope – longish, white commercial type.'

'Handwritten address?'

'No, typed – always the same sort of lay-out.'

'Did you ever see a postmark?'

'Never looked that close.'

Peroni twiddled the next question carefully on to his fork. 'Is there anything,' he said, 'anything you heard, anything you saw, that might give some indication of this person's identity?'

A firm head shake. 'Daniele never talked about him and if any of us asked questions he always said to shut up and changed the subject. If anybody wanted to find out something he made good and sure they didn't.'

'Tell me about the murder of Willi – how did that happen?'

The eyes darted about as though looking for a way of escape, then finding none he resigned himself to answering. 'One evening last week Max told Daniele he'd heard Willi promising to tell somebody about the plans for the salvage operation. That was really bad. My brother and I were with Daniele when Max brought the news and we realised at once it meant big trouble. Daniele said he had to go and see somebody – and there were no prizes for guessing it was the same person he always got in touch with when there was trouble. He told the three of us to meet him in his room at two o'clock the next morning. When he arrived we were waiting for him and he said straight away, "We'll have to kill him." And he told us how we were going to do it.'

A two a.m. meeting, thought Peroni. That would have given Bellini time to get there and back to anywhere on the lake, to Verona or a lot of other places. It might be that the person he had gone to see was the same as the person mentioned by Peroni's colleague on the telephone. And equally it might not.

But just possibly there was a way of finding out.

* * *

'Commissario, what a delightful surprise! Or perhaps surprise isn't exactly the right word. My horoscope foretold an unexpected but mysteriously *fertile* visit for this evening. I did not dream it would be you! And you're only just in time – I was on the point of closing. Business matters categorically disastrous towards evening and it's no good trying to fight against that sort of thing, is it? Come in and we'll lock the door – so-o-o – and pull down the blind – so-o. Now nobody will disturb us and we can be cosy and quite unobserved.'

Peroni had the disturbing sensation that he was a sort of latter-day Hansel hearing the key of the witch's front door turn in the lock behind him without even having the moral support of a Gretel for company. He was also disconcerted at the effusiveness of the zodiacal ceramist's welcome. He had expected her to be ill at ease on seeing him and instead she had at once seized the initiative. He opened his mouth to take it back.

'And how *pale* you are looking!' she went on. 'Really quite ill. Come and sit down at once.'

The very words seemed to have a debilitating effect on him so that, for the first time since leaving the clinic, he began to feel strangely unwell. He also noticed with alarm that he was allowing himself to be led towards the little office at the back of the gallery. He tried to pull back. 'I had a slight accident,' he said. His tone sounded defensive which he hadn't intended at all.

'An *accident!*' She made it sound like a major motorway disaster and at the same she propelled him with eerily irresistible gentleness down two steps to the office and into a low, soft armchair which felt like a quicksand. 'You must let me give you something to tone you up.'

'No, no thank you.' Never accept food or drink from a witch.

'I insist.' As if by magic, perhaps it was magic, she produced a bottle of Chivas Regal whisky. 'This is what you fancy, I believe?'

How did she know that? Some stupid magazine article presumably. But perhaps under the circumstances, with this strange sensation of ill-being and the weakness induced by his wound, it was just what he needed. Never accept drink from a witch. He found that a large, chunky glass had materialised in his hand. 'Chin chin!' said the zodiacal ceramist, looking into his eyes.

166

'*Salute*,' said Peroni, using the more formal toast, but drinking just the same.

'So you've come to see me again about my lovely, lamented Cordelia with her torrent of red, red hair.'

'But you said it was black,' Peroni jumped in quickly. That was the launch-pad of the whole interview; if she snatched that away he was as helpless as a mouse.

'No, no, you must forgive me. *You* said it was black. I merely repeated it. You see, I wondered why you were trying to trap me.' For an instant there was an icy glint in her eye, then it was gone. 'So I thought to myself, if the commissario wants to play a game, who is silly little me to stop him? I like games. All sorts of games.'

All nonsense, of course. She had never seen Cordelia in her life and he had neatly trapped her into revealing this. Then subsequently, reporting the conversation to whoever had put her up to making the false report, she had learned of her error and prepared this ridiculous defence against Peroni's return. He tried to shake himself free from the misty torpor that was swirling in his mind, which was difficult in that low, squashy armchair. 'Who told you to tell that story to the carabinieri?' It was meant to sound commanding, but there was something pathetically mouse-like about the result.

'Who told me? Why nobody told me, Commissario. I went of my own free will to the carabinieri because I thought it might be helpful. I take my duties as a citizen very seriously.'

'You never knew Cordelia Hope!' Righteous anger turned into the pathetic irascibility of a tantrum.

'How can you say such wounding, untruthful things? Brief though our friendship was, it was one of the most *rewarding* of my life.'

She said it in such a way as to imply that there had been some sort of lesbian relationship between them and this made Peroni angrier still.

'You're lying!' He tried to roar, but the words came out as inefficaciously as a squeak. Maybe she was turning him into a mouse and there, just inside the cupboard, was the cage which was waiting for him to be popped inside.

'Why are you struggling so hard, Commissario? What are you trying to achieve when all is said and done? Poor, darling

167

Cordelia is dead and you'll never be able to bring her back. She let herself fall from her boat into the water, just as she had told me she would do, and swam and swam until the lake took her to itself for all eternity.'

'She wasn't the type to commit suicide!' Mousier and mousier.

'Oh, *types*! There's no such thing as types in the long run. You can expect anything from anybody if the circumstances are right.' It was absurd, but he was letting himself be caught in the toils of this five lire witch. He was not reacting. He must react. 'You're wasting your time, Commissario. You'll never find out any other truth about poor Cordelia, because there *is* no other truth. Cordelia of the red hair drowned himself.' He couldn't react. His mind was obfuscated. 'You're only looking for complications where there are none. *None*!' There was a steely note of command in the monosyllable, but it was gone instantly and the warm-ice-cream tone returned. 'In the long run you'll only make yourself ridiculous and we should simply *hate* that, shouldn't we, Commissario?'

Maybe she was telling the truth after all. He was certainly spending a great deal of time on the lake, and his position in Venice was strained to the utmost. The *Questore* had been giving him one or two odd looks lately. And even if there were some other truth about Cordelia, how could he seriously hope to find it now? With Bellini officially incriminated a sheer dead weight of circumstances was tugging Peroni away from the enquiry. He had neither the strength nor perhaps any longer even the right to hold out against it.

Then a glint of gold drew his attention to the position of the zodiacal ceramist. She was leaning towards him and one hand was playing with a chain that hung round her neck. Playing, to be accurate, with a little gold figure which hung at the end of that chain and which she had been gently and delicately insinuating into his field of vision and, through it, into his mind.

Although, in his dealings with the enlightened, Peroni professed to scoff at magic, hard experience had taught him that it was a force to be treated warily. It could bite. And the witch was now in the process of weaving a spell around his mind. This was no time for leisurely after-dinner ratiocination about how spells took effect. Something had to be done urgently. But what?

'So why don't we forget all about sweet, dead Cordelia and go out for a little quiet dinner together? There is such a nice little restaurant round the corner, quiet, with an exquisite cuisine, and the owner, who does the cooking himself, is a *very* special friend of mine.'

That meant a member of the same coven, thought Peroni. But what to do? Then sudden inspiration lit up his night sky. If gold images were the weapons, he had his own to hand. Pretending to scratch his chest he felt for the little medal of St Januarius which he always wore, at the same time invoking the aid of the patron saint of Naples. Almost immediately the witch's nose started to twitch as though she could smell something burning in the kitchen and Peroni felt his strength begin to trickle back.

'I'm afraid I can't,' he said. 'I must be getting back to Venice immediately to clear up some work as I have an urgent appointment here on the lake tomorrow morning.' The trickle began to swell.

'An appointment?' Her expression was almost comically baffled and she looked down at her little gold figure as though it were a watch which had suddenly stopped.

'Yes,' said Peroni agreeably. 'You see, things aren't quite as hopeless as you suggest. I daresay you've heard of Daniele Bellini, the underwater explorer who was killed last night.' Staring at him with an expression compounded of rage and bewilderment, she nodded goggle-eyed. 'Well, for some while now it's been increasingly evident to me that if I can find out who was behind him I shall find out who killed Cordelia Hope. Then only this evening I learned that some letters written by this person to Bellini were left in the boat-house which they used as a headquarters at San Benedetto di Lugana. The place is locked up now, but I've telephoned the municipality and they're going to open it up for me tomorrow morning. So,' he pulled himself out of the quagmire armchair, 'if you don't mind I really will have to be on my way. Perhaps we could have dinner some other time.'

Still carefully holding the medal between forefinger and thumb he started to make his way out of the gallery and the witch, her nose now twitching furiously, scampered in painful frustration behind him.

169

CHAPTER 2

Peroni was trying to keep the dead at bay, but in the total darkness this was difficult because you could see them much more clearly. All of them except the only one he wanted to see. There was Bellini staring with jewel-bright eyes into the underwater depths. His lips were moving and in the total silence Peroni was just able to catch what he was saying. 'This is where diving begins to get really interesting. When you reach the confines of the known world. And beyond them the point of no return. D'you know, I often dream of going to meet death one day somewhere beyond that point . . . Beyond that point . . . Beyond that point . . .'

Slowly Bellini receded from the border area where Peroni could see him into the hinterland of death and invisibility and his place was taken by Willi. Willi hopelessly drunk with his ugly features warped by the driving necessity for revenge. 'Three days running she came here,' he was saying, 'right up until just before she was drowned. And I'll tell you something else. She was murdered.' Then the features twisted into pure grief and large, maudlin tears started to pour down his cheeks. 'She was murdered . . . She was murdered . . .'

Then he, too, dwindled into the distance and Max loomed up to hide him from view, his great absence of body hulking massively over the frontier of the underworld. He was searching for Peroni, the bones of his fingers cracking like fireworks in anticipation of a kill. But after a minute he halted, bewilderment suffused beneath the vast sombrero. 'Daniele,' he said, 'there's nobody here. Must be another flaw in the alarm system. Nobody . . . Nobody . . . Nobody . . .'

And just at that moment there was a soft metallic sound which did not come from their world, but from the less substantial one they had left so precipitously the night before. And instantly they vanished like wild animals startled by man, leaving Peroni alone in the darkness of Bellini's little office leading off the boat-house at San Benedetto.

As he had expected, somebody was trying to get in. It was just a question now of seeing whether it was the same person his colleague in Verona had named. He eased his gun into readiness.

Whoever it was fiddled inexpertly with one of the locks, twisting and wrenching. He or she was obviously impatient. Peroni would have liked to have left at least one of the locks open to facilitate entrance, but he realised that to do so would have aroused suspicion, throwing the entire delicate bluff right out of equilibrium. So he would have to wait.

The person went on trying to open the lock for about five minutes. Then there was silence which went on for so long that Peroni began to fear they had decided to give up the attempt and had gone away. But eventually the silence was broken by a muffled explosion of broken glass: they had decided the window was an easier solution.

Peroni was standing just inside the door, which he held open a crack, and through this crack he was able to make out some object of clothing, a coat probably, being used to dislodge and brush away the remaining pieces of glass which were still in the window frame. When this was done the person heaved him or herself up – still too dark to tell whether it was a man or a woman – preparatory to climbing in. It must have taken some effort for Peroni could hear the person's breathing. Then one trousered leg was manoeuvred in, followed a second later by the other, and the person dropped on to the floor and stood there for a moment looking undecidedly about.

The moment, Peroni decided, had come. He pushed open the door with his gun hand, at the same time using the other to switch on the powerful torch he had brought with him. Its beam leapt through the dusty air to pick out the figure of the caller.

'*Buona sera*, Signor Sindaco,' said Peroni, realising as he did so that it sounded hopelessly stagey.

'Who . . . ?' began Bombarone. He was dazzled by the light and, probably for the first time in years, out of countenance.

Carefully circling so as not to turn his back on him, Peroni went to the doors and turned on the switch. Neon flickered into brightness.

'Ah, Dottor Peroni,' went on the mayor, already apparently completely in control of himself and the situation. 'So we meet again, if that doesn't have too operatic a ring about it. How stupid of me. Presumably there aren't even any of my letters

171

here?' Peroni shook his head. 'Well, that will teach me to rely on women, won't it? A remarkable companion in bed – like a very rare *amarone*, to use an analogy we both appreciate – but not to be trusted where shrewd judgement is called for. Pity we haven't got a bottle of *amarone* with us now; however, there's no point in standing around, is there?' As though he were the host, he gestured Peroni courteously to a chair, then sat himself, at the same time waving with the tips of his fingers at the gun which Peroni was still holding. 'There's really no need for heavy artillery,' he said. 'I've never carried one of those things in my life and wouldn't know how to use the damn thing if I did. I can draw on more effective weapons if I care to.' Peroni put the gun down, but for the first time he began to feel a touch of misgiving. Bombarone was, after all, an Italian politician, and the world knows no wilier species; even someone like Peroni who had been schooled in the back-streets of Naples needed to be wary of them. 'But how in the name of Bacchus,' the mayor went on, 'did you get on to my track, if that's how you sleuths put it?'

'I've known for a long while,' said Peroni, 'that there was somebody behind Daniele Bellini. Then I happened to hear of the scandal he was involved in at Bardolino in which a girl was drowned. I made some enquiries and I found out that you had – taken an interest in the affair.'

'Yes, indeed. Delicate, delicate,' said Bombarone as though he were assessing a wine, 'and entirely successful.'

'For Bellini. Not for the girl or her family.'

'One can't be on both sides at the same time.'

'Anyway, your interest in Bellini obviously continued. After all, he was very much in your debt and you are hardly the man to let a situation like that go by unexploited.'

Bombarone shrugged deprecatingly. 'In fact,' he said with evident satisfaction, 'Daniele was already well known for his underwater exploits and I foresaw a great future for him. You'd be amazed how useful and profitable that sort of thing can be for anyone who can command it and knows how to use it. Daniele's activities have brought me contacts and collaboration not only in Italy, but throughout the world. It's the greatest shame they have come to an end. However, to return to more immediate matters, even assuming there were witnesses to our meeting tonight, what possible illegality could there be in giving one's patronage to such an admirable cultural activity as underwater exploration?'

'You used it to salvage the Mussolini gold, which is the property of the state.'

'But Commissario, you're like the frog that jumped too far! For one thing the Mussolini gold is still safe at the bottom of the lake – indeed there's already a lot of nitter natter going on about whether it can still be salvaged or not and when and how and who by. And for another, even assuming Daniele had successfully lugged it out who's to say that I wouldn't have handed it over? I wouldn't of course, I'm not that much of a twit, but who's to say so?'

Peroni began to feel that his sense of misgiving had been well founded. 'You ordered the killing of Willi Meyer,' he said, trying to sound more confident than he felt.

'Strictly between ourselves, so I did, so I did indeed. Mark you, I didn't like it one little bit, but what else could I do? We couldn't have the poor lad blabbing out the details of the salvage to you, could we now? But nobody but the two of us knows that I ordered it.'

'One of Bellini's team is still alive. He can testify that on the night Willi promised to give me details of the salvage Bellini went to see you and returned with instructions to kill.'

'You're jumping too far again. Your run-of-the-mill suspect might fall for that, but not a tricky old lawyer-cum-politician like me. He can testify that Daniele went to see somebody. Not me.'

'I've traced Bellini's movements that night,' Peroni bluffed in what he hoped was a self-assured tone. 'His car is a very distinctive one and I've got two people who saw it outside your house that night.'

'Not bad,' said Bombarone. 'Not bad at all. But not good enough. However,' he went on, holding up a big paw in an oratorical gesture, 'I have undoubtedly slipped on your banana peel and landed flat on my arse. That sort of thing you have to pay for in politics and the law and I'm too old a hand to try to slip out of it. So there are one or two things that need to be said. But really,' he broke off, his eyes flicking about the boat-house, 'I can't believe that Daniele didn't keep a bottle of something or other about the place. Chats like this need oiling. That cupboard over there looks promising.' He went over to it, humming tunelessly, and pulled open the door. 'Ah!' he said. 'What have we here? Grappa – just what the doctor ordered!' He spun round exuberantly and Peroni's hand jumped towards his gun. 'By

Bacchus indeed,' said the mayor, who was holding nothing more deadly than a bottle of grappa and two glasses, 'you're nervous this evening, Commissario. I told you – I've got no time for bang-bangs. We can settle things in an altogether more friendly way than that, I hope.'

Peroni, feeling a fool, sensed that a bribe was looming up just out of sight behind the horizon and he quickly reminded himself that, whatever it was, he must of course reject it.

Bombarone slopped grappa liberally into the two glasses and handed one to Peroni. 'Chin chin!' he said and then took a generous swallow, breathed out noisily and wiped his mouth with the back of his hand. 'Now then,' he said, 'where were we? Yes, the agreement. First of all, cards on the table.' (Did Bombarone ever put his cards on the table, Peroni wondered.) 'You,' the mayor went on, pausing weightily, 'have not got enough hard evidence to convict a greengrocer of selling an onion after hours. But – and this is the nub – you have got enough to make things tricky for me. I should survive, of course, but I'd rather the matter was settled differently.'

Peroni shifted uneasily as Bombarone eyed him. He was cautiously sure of himself when it came to hand-outs, but he felt that the whole situation was wrong. They shouldn't be discussing terms over grappa at all. It was up to him to divert the course of conversation before it flowed too far into dangerous territory. Now.

'I've been giving a great deal of thought,' Bombarone went on in a tone which suggested a complete change of subject, 'to your political ambitions. I think you have the makings of an excellent politician. Excellent. And it so happens that just now I have the say-so for a Christian Democrat candidature that would be the very thing for you. Safe as they come. And anyway, I have no doubt you'd have no trouble whatsoever in getting in under your own steam. Good looking fellow like you. And famous as well. Besides, with all this rubbish people talk about corruption in politics a copper has just the right image for the Chamber of Deputies. Incorruptible. The Champion of Honesty. A vote for Peroni is a vote of probity. I'll be your election manager. And you don't have to throw in your job with the police, either. You keep it with full pay along with deputy's salary. Plus full exes and living allowance when you go to Rome, which is not to be sniffed at either. What do you say to that?'

The proposal had, so to speak, slipped in behind Peroni's defences. A cash bribe he had been prepared for and would have sent spinning away with the contumely it deserved. But this was different. All Peroni's political ambitions, briefly forgotten in the tumult òf the last two weeks, re-asserted themselves in their most beguiling colours. He saw himself sitting nonchalantly cross-legged in the Chamber of Deputies looking bored and polishing his spectacles. (He didn't wear spectacles, but he would get a pair for the job.) He saw himself being interviewed on television. 'With us in the studio we have the Honourable Achille Peroni who is the leading Christian Democrat spokesman on . . .' What? Well, there would be plenty of time to work that out later.

And indeed there was no limit to the heights he might reach. Who could tell? The very Presidency of the Republic itself lay within his grasp. It was a gimmicky sort of office anyway: look at old Pertini – everybody's favourite grandpa and dropping howling gaffes all over the place. Now Peroni saw himself in a vast, gleaming car with a dozen *corazzieri* motor-cycle outriders chatting amiably to the Queen of England on a state visit.

'Well then, how about it? We can nip over first thing in the morning and get the candidature fixed up. You'd have to go before one or two committees later, but that would be just a formality. What do you say?'

What could Peroni say? There was only one answer. Yes. And then the vision of his progress amid cheering crowds towards a state banquet at the Quirinale Palace suddenly flickered and went dim and its place was taken by another of a young, female body lying face downwards in the water with long, red hair stirring as though it had life of its own. And as he looked at it in his mind's eye the face slowly turned and Cordelia looked at him with a mixture of reproach and appeal. Peroni bade a silent farewell to political glory. Or maybe *arrivederci*.

'I shall mention your proposal,' he said in a strictly commissarial voice, 'in my report to the examining magistrate.'

Bombarone flinched as though Peroni had struck him in the face, then instantly regained his composure. 'If that's how you like your *minestra* cooked, as the proverb says, then that's how you shall eat it.'

'The English girl, Cordelia Hope,' said Peroni, 'it was you who sent her to Bellini.'

Bombarone hesitated. 'Yes,' he admitted cautiously.

'How did you find her?'

'I didn't. She found me.'

'Tell me about it.'

'One day about two weeks ago I was told that an English girl wanted to see me. I had her shown in. She announced that she had obtained a copy of a map indicating the whereabouts of the Mussolini gold. First I thought she was off her rocker, but the more she talked the more I believed her. Her mind worked like a man's. Wouldn't tell me where or how she got hold of the damn thing or where it was. Just said she'd heard tell of me as the sort of chap who gets things done and so she'd decided I was the one to organise a salvage operation. Well, it so happened that the day before Daniele had arrived at the lake to carry out a research programme before the platform dwellers congress and I thought it could do no harm to put her in touch with him. If she really did have the map, this was the ideal occasion. She was a bit taken aback when she realised that the organisation she was looking for was already on the scene. Anyway, that was it and along she went to Daniele.'

'And when he'd got hold of the map the two of you decided to kill her.'

Bombarone took another large swig of grappa. 'No.'

'You got rid of her so as to save yourselves paying her a cut of the Mussolini gold.'

'No.'

'You didn't hesitate to kill Willi Meyer to protect it so why should you have scruples about her?'

'She wasn't a threat.'

'She would have expected her share.'

'I would have crossed that bridge when I came to it.'

'Are you suggesting that Bellini crossed it on his own in advance?'

Bombarone hesitated. 'I don't know. Obviously I can't exclude it.'

Was he genuinely ignorant, Peroni wondered, or was he taking advantage of the escape route the possibility offered? That would be up to the police in Brescia to decide. His share he had done.

Outside, the sky was beginning to tinge with the faintest hint of dawn. Peroni swallowed the remainder of his grappa. 'That's as far as we can usefully go tonight,' he said. The two men got

176

up. 'I'll be making a full report of all this and the examining magistrate will act as he sees fit. I must warn you that if you try to leave the country, all exit points will be circulated with your description.'

'No more my style than bang-bang,' said Bombarone. He looked shrewdly, perhaps mockingly, at Peroni. 'Pity,' he said, 'you'd have made a fine Honourable. Oh well, that's the net you've cast and if it's got a hole in it you won't get any fish, will you?'

CHAPTER 3

A photographer's flash froze the instant in which the coffin slid from the hearse. Then the four attendants lifted it and started to carry it under the stone archway into the little cemetery followed by the mourners and a handful of the curious with Peroni bringing up the rear.

Until the last minute he had been in two minds as to whether or not he should attend the funeral of Daniele Bellini. Everything was now in the hands of the magistrature. Or, to be strictly accurate, everything except the discrepancy concerning Cordelia's pale blue canvas hold-all. Time and again Peroni had mentally gone over the contents to see if there could have been anything of conceivable value or importance to anybody. But there was nothing. Obstinately the hold-all remained the one exasperating piece which wouldn't fit into the jigsaw puzzle.

Then by chance he had seen the announcement of Daniele's funeral in the paper and he decided that if he had time he would drive over for the Mass, not so much for any specific reason as to renew contact, even as indirectly as that, with the memory of Cordelia.

He had arrived late when the priest was just concluding a tribute to Bellini's contribution to mankind, and had stood at the back by the font. The congregation was small. The principal mourner was an elderly lady with white hair covered by a black veil, presumably a relative. But it was the two people standing on her right who provided the surprise. The first, rigid as a bayonet and granolithic, was General del Duca. The second was Nausicaa. She was dressed in the deepest black from head to foot, but in spite of that and even with the whole of the church between them Peroni could feel the femininity emanating from her with disconcerting force. Her shoulders were heaving with tears and she mopped constantly at her cheeks with a handkerchief.

At the end of the Mass Peroni waited in his pew for the coffin and the chief mourners to pass. Nausicaa, when she saw him, without for a moment interrupting her weeping, gave him a quick, broad wink. She was the only woman he had ever known who could, without hypocrisy, combine sunshine and rain in the same instant. He had intended to stay only for the Mass, but now curiosity about the presence of Nausicaa and her father impelled him to be present at the interment, too.

The cemetery was small, almost homely, its inhabitants personalised not only by inscriptions, but by photographs. Most of the recently dead were accommodated in loculi in the walls, reaching up from ground level to the top of the wall. One or two of the unoccupied loculi had been opened to receive new arrivals and, as the ground of the cemetery was already full, Peroni assumed that it was to one of these they were heading. But to his surprise the bearers stopped outside a small edifice complete with domes and columns and wrought-iron gates which now stood open. So Daniele was to be buried in a family tomb.

As the coffin was carried in, Peroni edged nearer until he was able to see inside. A niche had indeed been opened in readiness. But what really took him aback was the name which he saw repeated on each of the closed niches. Del Duca. The fact that Nausicaa and her father had been with the principal mourners had not prepared him for this. It could only mean that Daniele was a member of the family.

Accompanied by final prayers from the priest and sobs from Nausicaa, the coffin was edged into the niche and a man in jeans started sloshing on cement preparatory to lifting in the slab. Peroni's mind whirred frenetically in an attempt to work out the possible consequences of this new development. The disquieting thing was that, seen from one angle, it didn't appear to change anything at all while, seen from another, everything was altered. The facts remained substantially the same, but the characters all shifted their positions with relation to each other. And at the centre of this new grouping, or so it seemed to Peroni, was Nausicaa, holding all the others in the coils of her femininity.

Now the man in jeans and a colleague lifted the slab into place and the group around the tomb experienced that sudden collective tension which is produced by a man's final disappearance from human view. Then as the man in jeans started expertly smoothing cement into the cracks between the slab and the outer sides of the loculus, his colleague layed out the wreaths that had been in the hearse rather as though he were stacking tins in a supermarket. The tension slackened into a general atmosphere of 'Well, that's that' and the little crowd of mourners began to break up.

General del Duca, Nausicaa and the elderly lady remained for a moment staring at the still blank slab. Then Nausicaa kissed her hand and briefly fondled the stone before the three of them turned and left the tomb. With the general and Nausicaa supporting the lady by each arm they made their way slowly towards the gate and although, following at a respectful distance, Peroni could not catch a murmur of sound, they were going through the motions of talking.

Outside, little knots of mourners were hanging around chatting in voices still subdued, but with an air of relief at returning to everyday life and imminent lunch. Not far from the cemetery there was a stately, old-fashioned car from which there emerged a chauffeur who opened the back door. The elderly lady got in followed by the general and the car drove off in a dignified and sedate manner, leaving Nausicaa standing on the pavement with her hand raised in salute. Peroni approached her.

'*Ciao*, Achille . . .' she said vaguely as though returning from another world. '*Ciao*, Achille,' with more vivacity. 'I let them go off with the car as I thought it would do me good to walk back. Lies, lies, lies. When I saw you in church I thought a trip somewhere with you would be just what I needed when the whole thing was over. Which was extremely silly of me because you're a busy and important man with a hundred better things to do than waste your time with prolix and tearful women. What a funny word, *prolix*.'

'I've got nothing better to do than going out with you,' said Peroni, thinking at the same time that she was in a distinctly odd mood.

'However, I can perfectly well walk back to the villa myself,' she went on, apparently not having heard him. 'It'll serve me right. And it was very kind of you to come to the funeral.'

'It wasn't really particularly kind,' said Peroni. 'I didn't know that he was connected with your family.'

'Oh, yes, didn't I tell you?' she said vaguely and then broke off, staring at him. 'Did I hear you say that you *could* come out with me?'

'You did.'

'How perfectly marvellous! You must forgive me if I sound a bit distraught – funerals do that to me. Particularly the funeral of someone so close . . .' She swerved away from the subject. 'But your presence will work wonders.' Again she stopped and looked down at herself disapprovingly. 'I can't come out with you dressed like this, can I now?' She thought. 'Yes, I know what I'll do. Come along.'

She set off towards the centre of the village, taking him by the hand as though he were a recalcitrant member of her brood. 'You won't mind waiting outside, will you? I don't like being watched. Like larvas. Or should that be larvae? Anyway, I shan't be long.' She came to an abrupt halt, both in speech and motion. 'How stupid of me!' she said, now swellingly maternal. 'I quite forgot about your wound. I shouldn't be dragging you along like this. How is it?'

'Much better. I just have gauze and sticking plaster now.'

'Are you quite sure?' She eyed him suspiciously. 'Anyway, we shan't rush – there's no hurry.'

'I tried to telephone you the day after,' said Peroni, 'but you were out.'

'Yes, I was, wasn't I? Papa and I went to see Daniele's poor mamma – that was her we were with at the funeral . . .' Again she veered off. 'And I was very worried about you that morning, too. Now I'm going in there.' She indicated a shoe shop. 'You sit down and rest. I'll be as quick as I can.' She put Peroni down at a *caffe* table and went off, leaving him in a state of irritated bewilderment and pleasant anticipation. What was this maddening, irresistible woman holding back? Why was she avoiding the subject of her relationship with Daniele? Why had she and her father gone straight off to see his mother after the tragedy?

Typically, her idea of being quick was elastic, but the result was worth it and when she emerged from the shoe shop Peroni goggled at her in delight. It was a simple, but effective, transformation. She had shed into a bag she was carrying the little black hat and veil, the jacket, shoes and stockings she had worn to the funeral so that her hair was liberated into its usual state of cheerful anarchy and her magnificent torso swelled sensuously in the low-cut blouse she had been wearing beneath the jacket. And in place of the shoes, she had bought a cheeky pair of sandals decked with gaudy bits of coloured glass which should have looked awful but didn't. Only the black skirt remained, but that, far from being funereal, was now positively slinky.

'Am I all right?' she said. 'Papa would certainly say that I look like a strumpet. And he,' she added mysteriously, 'should know. Have you got your car here? Because in that case I suggest we buy ourselves a picnic lunch and drive over to Costermano.'

'Costermano?'

'We used to have a villa there.' Peroni remembered the general having mentioned it. 'Come to that, we still do, but it's really no more than a shell. I always used to go and play in the garden there when I was a little girl and I've always loved it. It's a place I go to when I want to be alone or think. Or lick wounds.'

'Daniele's death?'

'I only take very special people there.'

'Husbands?'

'Not necessarily. Let's get the lunch.'

Her choice of that was as idiosyncratic as everything else about her: two bottles of San Benedetto wine, a packet of figs, some smoked cod, a couple of balls of spinach, a bottle of ketchup and an enormous loaf of crispy bread. She put this motley alimentary assembly into the bag along with her funeral attire and they set off for Peroni's car.

'I wish you'd tell me about your relationship with Daniele,' said Peroni when they were driving away from the lake and into the hills.

'The dead don't like us talking about them all the time.'

They drove on in a silence which was uncharacteristic of both of them.

After about twenty minutes' drive they stopped outside high moss- and ivy-covered walls with rusty, iron gates through which could be seen a dark and riotous garden almost large enough to be considered a park, and beyond that Peroni could just make out bits of the façade of what promised to be a magnificent specimen of the Veneto villa. Nausicaa fished about with a sort of cheerful pessimism in the capacious handbag she

181

also had with her and came up eventually with a key which she used to unlock the padlock on a chain that served to keep the gates closed. And they stepped into a sort of earthly paradise which was both lulled and vivified by a sonic tapestry of birdsong.

'When I come in here,' said Nausicaa, 'I always think of that poem by the Englishman – what's his name? You know the one who wrote about cats – where he says, "Quick, said the bird, find them, find them, Round the corner. Through the first gate, Into our first world, shall we follow The deception of the thrush? Into our first world." This is my first world.'

'I thought you only read the worst scandal magazines.'

'In front of the children,' she explained enigmatically. 'Look!'

Suddenly a vista had opened up in the trees before them to the hills, beyond which they could just make out, in a dip, the lake winking at them in a conspiratorial way. 'I always thought this was a place for some sort of prehistoric ritual,' she said, 'maybe human sacrifice. Oof!' She shed the two bags and curled herself on to the grass like a snake with her back against a tree.

'Tell me about Daniele,' said Peroni, sitting beside her.

'Oh, why do you go on so? You'll make me think you're jealous.'

'Is there any reason why I shouldn't know?'

'Pandora's box. Curiosity and the cat. The Apple itself. Let's have lunch.'

Contrary to all Peroni's expectations, the dire mixture of food she had brought turned out to be delicious. After another fishing expedition in her bag she improbably came up with a Swiss knife bristling with appurtenances and capable of anything from the simplest tasks to delicate brain surgery and boring artesian wells ('Useful with children'). She used this to construct two mighty sandwiches with cod, spinach, figs and liberal doses of tomato ketchup. 'The children love them,' she said and, unlikely though this would have sounded half an hour ago, Peroni had to confess that he agreed with the children. Using the same knife, Peroni uncorked the two bottles of San Benedetto and what with the sandwiches and the heat they had no difficulty in emptying both of them.

Then, replete, they lay back on the grass and Nausicaa hummed a little tune Peroni couldn't quite place, as though she were crooning to an infant. It was all very pleasant, but Peroni felt lust beginning to prickle like goose-flesh. His eyes would not leave the swelling uplands of breast and the delicious lowlands described with such tacit clarity by the tight, black funeral skirt. He longed to nuzzle and lose himself in that rich and fertile landscape of femininity. He raised himself on one elbow. 'Nausicaa?'

'Umm?'

'Tell me about Daniele.' The question was out before he was aware of it, bowled from the murky depths of his subconscious.

'Yes,' she murmured tenderly in answer to what he hadn't said and then, as his actual words reached her, 'Oh, Achille, must you?' She pulled herself up into a sitting position. 'Very well,' she said, 'but don't say I didn't warn you. Daniele was my brother.'

'Your brother!' He wasn't quite sure why it should sound so sensational.

'Well, my half-brother. His mother was Papa's what-do-you-call-it. And he must have had a particularly soft spot for her because he took Daniele very seriously and was always getting him out of trouble.'

'You knew then about the business—'

'When that poor girl was drowned – yes. Papa had endless worries over that, but he got hold of a very good lawyer – Bombarone, you probably know of him – and everything was all right in the end.'

Peroni stared at her in amazement. 'You call that all right?'

'Daniele was always weak by nature.' Her eyes were broodingly maternal. 'A strong person wouldn't have got himself into a position like that. And after all, it wasn't his fault that the girl was drowned. It was an accident.'

'You believed that?'

'Well, of course. He would never have murdered her!'

'What makes you so sure?'

'Because I knew him. He was silly, vain, boastful. I told you before, Achille, he had a lot in common with you. But he wasn't a killer.'

Peroni eyed her with mounting irritation. Did she really believe what she was saying, he wondered. 'And the English girl,' he said, 'don't tell me it never occurred to you that he killed her, too. You were frightened when I suggested to you that she'd been murdered!'

'I do wish you wouldn't go on like Perry Mason! You're getting me all flustered. Yes, of course I was frightened. I'd have been a fool not to have noticed the similarity between the two deaths, and I was frightened for him.'

'You were frightened that he'd killed her! You still think he killed her!'

'No! I know he didn't!'

'How can you be so certain?' She was silent. 'You knew she'd been in touch with Daniele?' She nodded. 'You knew that it was in your villa she photographed the map showing the position of the Mussolini gold?'

'What?' she looked genuinely bewildered. 'In our villa?'

'You didn't know that Mussolini entrusted the map to your father?'

'He did? Well, the cunning old man! Of course, he's always been a roaring Fascist, but in all these years he's never let on to anyone about a map – certainly not to me and I know most of his little secrets. But however did she get it?'

'Aristotle let her in one night,' said Peroni reluctantly, feeling that he shouldn't let himself be deviated. 'She found it and photographed it.'

'Well, well, well! If Papa knew that, he'd personally roast Aristotle alive on a grid. I suppose,' she went on in a tone of understanding, 'he did it for love?'

'But you knew about the Mussolini gold?' Peroni insisted, refusing to be further deviated.

'No!'

'Nausicaa, you're lying!'

'Yes then. I did know. Daniele told me. But he certainly didn't know where she'd got the map from any more than I did.'

'And that was why you tried to keep me with you on the night of the salvage operation. You were acting for him to stop me interfering!'

'Not only that! I was worried about your wound. I am human, Achille!'

'You gave me some sort of drug, too!'

'I thought you needed rest!'

'So how can you go on pretending that he didn't kill her? He had no intention of giving her a share in the Mussolini gold and so he drowned her in the lake!'

'He didn't – I swear he didn't!'

'How can you possibly know?'

'Achille – don't go on! Please! You don't realise what you're doing!'

'How can you *know* that Daniele didn't kill Cordelia Hope?'

'All right then, if you insist. I know that he couldn't have killed her because that night he was with me. All that night.'

Peroni stared at her for a second uncomprehendingly. Then he understood, and the understanding was worse than he would have expected.

'I told you not to go on,' she said very softly. 'I told you it was Pandora's box.'

Peroni got up and walked off through the trees, his soul weighed down by dead lust. And not only that, for there was a new weight of guilt and remorse. Cordelia's death had not after all been revenged in the depths of Lake Garda. Her ghost was still unlaid. And what hope was there now that he would ever be able to lay it? In spite of grave obstacles and handicaps he had followed the path through to the end. And the end had turned out not to be the end after all. Or rather it had turned out to be a dead end. Blind alley. *Vicolo cieco.* Where could he possibly go from here?

He came out into an ample clearing before the villa and halted, staring dully at it. It was indeed a superb piece of architecture. Or rather had been. The façade was intact, if somewhat dilapidated, three storeys high with balconies on the first floor and even fragments of what looked like eighteenth-century frescoing. The door and most of the windows were nailed up with wood, but some of the first- and second-floor windows had been left open and Peroni could see through them, mostly to sky and trees, but here and there to bits of wall. The building was a shell.

Then as he continued to stare at it there filtered into his mind the idea that it was trying to tell him something. Something important. And he was too obtuse to see it. A dim-witted Neapolitan donkey, all ears and bray and not a grain of intuition.

And then he saw it. Or rather, as he reflected with something like satisfaction, he didn't see it, and that was the whole point. And now at last he understood what Cordelia's letter should have told him. The alley was not so blind after all and maybe somewhere there in the darkness at the end of it Cordelia's ghost would find rest at last.

CHAPTER 4

The ivy, Peroni noticed, clung less tightly to this particular bit of the wall as though somebody had recently pulled it aside. If his guess was right, that somebody was Cordelia and he had a shrewd suspicion as to what she had found. A couple of seconds later the suspicion was confirmed. There in the stone-work beside the door was a carved sun with an expression of benign joviality and wavy stone rays emanating from it. He put the strands of ivy back in place and started to make his way round the side of the house.

At the lake front everything was very quiet. There was the ramshackle boat-house with a somewhat decrepit but service-able craft moored in it and the water was still gently lapping the narrow, pebbly shore as though the lake were trying to show that it was the tamest and least dangerous of creatures. The vegetation seemed to be even wilder and more luxuriant than the previous time Peroni had been there. He looked carefully about him, but there was no sign of anybody. French windows, however, were open leading into the house and after some hesitation he went up to them. '*Permesso*,' he called. '*Permesso*.' There was no answer and after waiting for another second he stepped inside.

The room was large, dark (protected from all light even on the sunniest of days by the profusion of growth outside) and in an incredible state of chaos wrought, not by intruders, but by years and years of neglect. The furniture looked as though it had come from the scrap-heap of a junk shop: broken wicker chairs, debowelled armchairs, a table with one leg missing, propped up by a box on a stool and bearing the remains of not one but a whole series of skimped, wretched meals, an upended bookcase with books scattered about it like rubble. In one corner stood an ancient, broken harp with its strings curling desolately in the air. Here and there were glass cases with stuffed animals in them and one or two pieces like the gilt mirrors, the wreck of a handsome grandfather clock and some photographs in silver frames which indicated that the owners had once been well-to-do. The dominant feature of the room and that which was least affected by the reigning decay was a large and magnificent stone fireplace with last winter's ashes still in the grate and an ornate coping in which the same sun Peroni had found under the ivy outside had been carved. It must have been some sort of family crest. But of the owner there was no sign.

'*Permesso* . . .' Peroni tried again.

Only the dusty silence of the large room answered him. And then a sound which might have been that of a mouse stirring in paper crept up to him from out of the silence. It came, he recognised, from a half-open door opposite the fireplace. He crossed over and looked in.

The room was a sort of study and on a sofa by one wall a figure was lying asleep covered by a coat, its face moon-pale in the darkness. The sound Peroni had heard was the breathing of this figure. He went in and knelt by the sofa.

'Signor Pagani,' said Peroni, touching his shoulder, which felt like that of a bird's skeleton. At the congress the old man had evidently been ill. Now he was dying and the smell he was giving off was so overpoweringly foul that Peroni had to make a powerful effort not to vomit. 'Signor Pagani . . .' Peroni tried again. And then, just as he was deciding that the only thing he could do was call a doctor, the white face turned towards him and the eyes flickered and looked up at him. For a long moment they were vacant. Then recognition seeped painfully into them.

'Signor Commissario.' The voice was an agonising croak. 'You must forgive me . . . Yes. I was expecting you.' With what looked like a superhuman effort he pushed aside the coat that covered him and started to struggle into a sitting position.

'Lie down,' said Peroni. 'Let me get you something.'

'No, no. You are my guest.' Even in the shadow of death there was a certain authority in the way he said it. 'A glass of sherry? I have nothing . . . You will take sherry?'

'Let me get it. Where—'

'No such thing. If you will be so good as to give me an arm . . .' Incredibly he managed to stand up and Peroni saw that he was wearing the same cotton suit that he had worn to the opening of the congress, though now it was badly creased and stained.

Somehow, clutching for support at pieces of furniture and

stopping every so often for breath, he managed to make his way out of the study and across the other room to what must once have been an elegant cabinet standing beside the fireplace. With difficulty he opened its one remaining door and got out a bottle from which, spilling more than he poured, he succeeded in filling two glasses.

'Very well,' he said, 'I will concede the point and allow you to carry them. My hand is not as steady ... We'll go into the study. It's more comfortable, or shall we say less uncomfortable ... Yes ...'

When they were back in the study and seated and Pagani had drunk a little sherry, an almost imperceptible glow of colour returned to his skull-like features. 'Now,' he said, 'I imagine that you wish me to tell you how I killed that unfortunate English girl.'

'It's what I came for.'

'This will be my confession. I don't believe in priestly confession; all such ritual is shutting one's eyes to the naked fact of death while the supreme destiny of man is to look death in the face without flinching. But confession without fear or favour to a gentleman and an officer like yourself – that is valid. So ...' He paused for breath and to drink more sherry. 'Let me make it clear,' he went on, 'that I do not look upon my actions as in any way wrong. The true hero is above right and wrong. I simply had no alternative. I was in the position of a soldier who kills in battle. I was acting in pursuance of a sacred trust.'

Peroni had heard it all before: it was the grandiloquent clap-trap of Fascist heroics, the third-rate jargon of bullies trying to make up with melodrama for their own inability to think honestly. And in this apparently civilised man it was even more horrible than the disease that was destroying him physically. 'Go on,' said Peroni, bracing himself against the moral and physical putridity.

'Last time you were here I told you that the girl came to see me to enquire about a document or documents left with my family by the Duce immediately before he left the lake for the last time. I told her, as I had told Churchill before her, that my family had already escaped to Switzerland. But the girl returned here a few days later.'

Peroni had known she must have done, but he could not suppress a shudder at the thought that he had at last started to walk down the dark corridor that led to the truth about her death.

'I was returning from the village in my car shortly after midday when I saw her coming out of the footpath which leads from this house to the main road. It is a private path which was opened up by my family and there would be no reason for her to be in it if she had not been here. When I reached home I saw that the lock of the French windows had been forced open. I should have had a better one put in, but there is nothing of value in this house.' He paused. 'Except for – some documents. And even then I was confident that she would not have found them. They have a better protection than any lock could afford. And indeed when I looked they were still in their place. Or, rather, they seemed to be in their place. For a closer examination showed that my burglar alarm had been tampered with – the girl was more skilful than I had imagined – and they had been moved. I always leave them in such a way that I can tell if even a single sheet is a millimetre out of place.

'I drove back to the village in time to see her arriving there, so I parked the car and followed her. It was not difficult to do this unobserved in the crowd of tourists. She went first to a photographer's shop – a twenty-four-hour development service – and I observed her through the window as she took a reel of film from her bag and handed it over the counter, receiving a ticket in exchange. She next went to a travel agency where again taking advantage of the crowd I was able to hear her making a flight booking for London the next day. At first it seemed they were all full up, but then the girl at the desk managed to get a cancellation. After that the English girl went to a *caffè* by the lake front.

'I was in a dilemma. She had evidently photographed the documents and was leaving the country the next day . . .'

Now the strange patchwork of Cordelia's mood that last day was explained, thought Peroni. She had achieved her objective which accounted for the exhilaration, but at the same time she was going back to England. 'I shall leave him with real regret,' the words of her letter came back to him. 'But I shall leave him.'

'I didn't wish her any harm,' Pagani was going on, 'but I couldn't let her do that; it would have made me guilty of treachery. But was there any way in which the situation could be saved? I considered the problem for a long time while I observed her and I was contemplating an attempt at persuasion when she was joined by a man. A man whom I later recognised to be you. I don't need to tell you what happened during the following hours for you were with her all the time.'

Peroni remembered the curious sensation he had had of being watched that afternoon. The end had already been lying in wait for her.

'She finally left you at the harbour and went out with her yacht. I knew that this was my last opportunity. I drove back here, got out my motor-boat and went out on to the lake. It wasn't difficult to find her. I drew alongside her yacht and asked if I might board. She agreed – reluctantly. I accused her of having photographed the documents and she did not deny it. I said if she would give me the negatives I would take no further action. She refused, adducing spurious, hypocritical motives for the action: the documents, she said, belonged to history and I didn't have the right to keep them to myself. I insisted, but she refused again. So I had no alternative. I could feel that the wind was getting up, which meant that a storm might be on us at any minute. There wasn't much time. I hit her once quickly on the side of the neck. I had been taught how to strike blows like that in special training with the Giovanni Fascisti and she can scarcely have had the time to realise what was happening. Then I let her go into the water and held her under with a boat hook until I was quite sure she was dead.'

There was a horrible matter-of-factness about his ruthlessness; it was as though he were giving an account to his superiors of an operation successfully carried through to its conclusion.

'I then got back into my own motor-boat and returned home. By then the storm had started and I was just able to make out the shape of her sail in the distance by a flash of lightning.'

There was a silence which Peroni eventually broke by prompting him: 'And the photographs?'

'Yes . . .' Pagani's thin, dry lips shifted into something that might have been a smile. 'I knew that, since she intended to leave the next day and since the shop offered a twenty-four-hour service, the prints would be ready next morning. Fortunately, I had used the shop myself on various occasions so I knew its ways. I jammed a used film into my camera in such a way that it could only be removed by opening the machine, which would have to be done in the darkroom if the film were not to be exposed. Then I went to the shop in the late morning when there is little business and after making sure it was empty I entered. I explained the problem to the woman and then when she was in the darkroom I went behind the counter where the developed

190

films are kept and quickly found the envelope with the girl's name on it. Unfortunately, this time my calculations were inaccurate . . .'

There was a marked note of irritation in his voice as he said this. The fact that he had drowned a young girl in the lake without a trace of mercy left him indifferent but, even now that he was dying, he was nettled that his calculations should have been wrong.

'The photographs were not what I had expected at all,' he went on. 'They were no more than tourist snapshots.' There was a hint of contempt in his voice as he said this. 'So where were the real negatives? I had observed her uninterruptedly, so she couldn't have left them somewhere without my knowing. I wondered if they might be in her yacht. I went to the harbour that night and searched it, but there was no trace of them. That left only one possibility – she must have had them somehow with her, perhaps in that large bag she carried. And I was quickly able to discover from village gossip that the carabinieri were keeping that until it was collected by some relative. I started to keep watch on their headquarters from a bar nearby and eventually it was you who came.'

'And you shot me.'

'I had no alternative,' he repeated with monotonous insist-ence. 'It's lucky I didn't have to kill you.' With an inner shudder Peroni realised that if another bullet had stood between Pagani and the hold-all he wouldn't have hesitated to fire it.

'And the negatives were in it?' But even as he said it, Peroni realised where they had been.

'At first I thought not. But a closer inspection showed she had put them inside a lighter.'

A micro-film of course. He had been culpably bone-headed not to have thought of it. 'And where are they now?'

'I destroyed them immediately.'

Naturally. So that just left the originals. Where could Pagani have hidden the originals? The originals of what, come to that? Peroni assumed he knew, but only anonymous documents had actually been mentioned. 'We are talking about the Churchill–Mussolini correspondence, I imagine?' he said.

Pagani looked at him quickly and paused as though even to admit it were a betrayal of his trust. 'Yes,' he said at last and something in his tone made Peroni suspect that the answer had been dictated as much as anything else by a desire that at least one other person in the world should know of the unique honour that had been bestowed on him. 'Yes.' He relished it.

'But you told me your family had already escaped to Switzerland when the Republic of Salò fell. So how did you get hold of the correspondence?'

For the second time Pagani's lips were moulded into something like a smile. 'My family had already escaped,' he said. 'I had not. I refused to go. A Fascist does not escape. I stayed on here to fight until the end, if necessary to die with the Duce. I lived here alone, only going out by night to forage for provisions. Nobody ever guessed I was here. But one night about ten days after my family had left . . .'

CHAPTER 5

Pagani huddled on a sofa in the front room, trying to keep warm inside a heavy military greatcoat. The cold was about the worst thing he had to put up with. The absence of his family was a positive benefit; he had never liked them and they had never liked him, seeing nothing more than his insignificant physical appearance and not even guessing at the heroism which he knew lay within, only waiting for the occasion to blossom forth in all its stern and glorious magnificence. Besides, his family were traitors. Since Mussolini's rise to power his father had always declared himself a Fascist, had been high in the councils of the party and had even had the supreme honour of being part of the Duce's immediate entourage on various occasions. And now, just when all hope seemed to be lost – the supreme moment for loyalty and sacrifice – he had scuttled pusillanimously off to Switzerland. Good riddance.

Nor did Pagani mind the isolation from the rest of his fellow human beings. He had never made any real friends and he was ill at ease with other people, being frankly perplexed at the things which motivated them: love, money, comfort, food . . . They were animals guzzling in the trough without any conception of glory. Only in the Giovanni Fascisti had he found the sort of people he sought and they had mostly ignored him because of his puniness. What would they think if they could see him now – living here by himself, an unknown, constant challenge to the decadent world, each night an adventure as he went out to search for food without being seen, without even letting anyone suspect that he existed.

And all the time waiting for the summons. For he knew beyond any doubt that it would come one day. What it would demand of him he had no idea; he only knew that the task would be a supreme one. Ever since he could remember he had been dogged by a sense of destiny and now, in this empty house, cut off from the world, it haunted him more obsessively than ever.

He went to the ornate, gilded mirror in which his mother always used to be surreptitiously admiring herself and looked at his own reflection. His face – lean, with a small black beard and eyes that glowed in the darkness – seemed to confirm his thoughts. It was the face of a hero.

If only it were not quite so cold. He didn't dare light a fire for fear the smoke would be noticed and his presence detected. He pulled the greatcoat more tightly about him. Fortunately the warmer weather was not far off.

And then he heard the sound of a car engine, the crunch of tyres on the gravel, and saw the light of headlights through the chinks in the closed shutters. He picked up the heavy service revolver which he always kept to hand. If this were the moment, if he were to die now, he would not die alone.

He ran out of the room, up the stairs and into the large, icy cold, old-fashioned lavatory which held so many memories of childhood struggles with bowels and bladder. All the windows in the house were shuttered and barred except for the high window in this room, which was too small for anyone to get in at and had no shutters and was consequently used by Pagani as a look-out post. He climbed on to the seat and peered out.

The car was a small one, a Balilla, and it had stopped just outside the front door. Pagani was puzzled. Had somebody somehow discovered his presence? But who? And how? And above all, if it were so, what were they intending to do? He prepared himself to run up to the attic where he had made himself an emergency hiding-place in the rafters.

The door on the driver's side of the car opened and a man in military uniform got out. An officer of some sort. But instead of

193

coming directly to the front door, the man walked round to the other side of the car where he opened the passenger door and a second figure started to climb out, heavier than the first and making a considerable effort. He was wearing a grey, somewhat slovenly greatcoat which hung loosely about him like the clothes on a scarecrow. He had no cap on and was quite bald. He was carrying a briefcase.

It was as this second figure started to walk, or more accurately to shuffle painfully towards the front door, that Pagani recognised him. There could be no doubt about it. The man was tired, maybe ill, but he was unquestionably Mussolini. With a searing inner flash Pagani knew that his moment of destiny had come.

As he left the lavatory the first knock sounded below. He ran down the stairs in the dark, heedless of the danger of tripping, heedless of everything except destiny. In the hall he scooped up a torch and hurled himself towards the door as the second knock sounded. He started to fumble with the locks and chains. It seemed to take an age to get done. Then finally when the last lock had been turned he pulled open the door, briefly shone the torch on his own face as a gesture of reassurance and respect and raised his right hand in the Fascist salute.

'*Saluto* al Duce!' he said.

Mussolini responded with a tired, perfunctory gesture. 'Who are you?' he said.

'Pagani, *eccellenza* – the son of Livio Pagani.'

'Your father?'

'He's gone, *eccellenza*. Escaped to Switzerland with the rest of the family. Only I stayed behind. To fight for you, *eccellenza*, for Italy and for Fascism until the end.'

But Mussolini didn't seem to be listening any longer. He shook his head like an old bull plagued by flies. 'Then it's no good,' he said, more to himself than Pagani. 'Who can I trust? Who can I trust?'

'You can trust me, *eccellenza*! Anything my father could do I can do. More! He ran away – I stayed behind.'

This time the words seemed to get through and Mussolini looked at Pagani with new interest. 'We'd better go inside.'

Pagani stepped aside, then closed the door and ushered Mussolini into the front room, getting a chair, which was waved away. Mussolini put his briefcase down at the table and gave Pagani one of those looks which his supporters used to claim could reach to the depths of the human soul; it now looked more like a baffled, rather petulant stare. 'Are you willing to be on call whenever I may need you?' he said finally.

'*Eccellenza, si*!'

'To risk your life?'

'*Eccellenza, si*!'

In the old days Mussolini would have rewarded such devotion with glowing words; now he merely humphed. 'Very well,' he said, picking up the briefcase, 'I shall have to risk it. This briefcase contains documents – letters – letters written to me by Churchill – copies of letters written by me to him. The future of Italy, of the world, may depend on these letters. They prove beyond doubt that my sole and unwavering concern has always been the well-being of the Italian people. That is why many people want to obtain them and destroy them in order to represent me as the enemy of my country. If they succeed I am finished, but if I am able to produce these documents at the right moment, then my justification will shine forth like the sun and I shall lead Italy again to the glory of a new Roman empire!' This thought worked on Mussolini like a heroin injection on an addict in the last stages; for a moment his eyes shone again, his voice took on a confident ring, his frame seemed to swell and fill out the greatcoat with jutting pride. Then almost immediately the effect wore off; he shrank again, his eyes filmed over and he seemed to forget what he had been talking about. 'Yes,' he said, looking at Pagani as though he were trying to remember who he was. 'What was I ... Yes, the documents. Tomorrow I am leaving the lake. I am going ...' he stopped as though that, too, had slipped his mind '... to a secret destination with the few men who have kept faith. I cannot take these. We might be stopped, robbed. It's too dangerous. What I am asking you to do is keep these documents in a safe place of hiding until I need them. And then you must bring them to me wherever I may be. Can you do this?'

'*Eccellenza, si*!'

Mussolini attempted another soul-piercing look, then gave him the briefcase. 'Remember,' he said, 'this is the highest trust I have ever placed in any man.' The glory of it soared in Pagani's mental sky like a million fireworks. 'The future of Italy is in your hands. Above all, whatever happens, whatever the cost, never let these documents fall into other hands!'

'I will defend them with my life!'

'Bravo,' said the Duce. 'Bravo.' He thrust his hand warrior-like at Pagani. 'And now I must go.'

Pagani stood to attention, clutching the briefcase to his side, as Mussolini left the room, then followed him out to the front door and opened it for him. The engine of the car was switched on and the headlights briefly picked out the two of them in the frame of the door as Pagani saluted Mussolini once more.

'Whatever happens,' said Mussolini. 'Whatever the cost.' Then he walked to the Balilla, climbed in and was driven off.

Pagani shut and locked the front door. Then he stood silently in the dark hall, alone for the first time with the destiny of his lifetime.

'. . . I continued my clandestine existence for another two years. It seemed safest for the documents and anyway I had come to prefer the life. But as Italy adjusted itself slowly and painfully to a shameful peace I realised that people were beginning to show some interest in this house. My parents, I knew, had been killed and I was the only surviving heir. If my absence continued, sooner or later somebody would try to get possession of the house, so it seemed advisable to "return". This I did in nineteen forty-seven, starting at once to lead the quiet, somewhat boring life I have lived ever since. But it didn't matter greatly. I had known glory such as the vast majority of mankind cannot even imagine and now I had my duty. I was a soldier at my post. I still am. That is all there is to say.'

There was silence in the room. What to do now? Arrest him? Hand him over to an often inept and long-drawn-out human justice when he was already to all intents and purposes submitted to a divine one? But what alternative was there?

Then Peroni wondered about something else. The Churchill–Mussolini correspondence was one of the great question marks of history. If he could get hold of it he would not only be accomplishing for Cordelia the task she had set herself, but he would also be setting off the most clamorous avalanche of publicity that even he could possibly desire. The only problem was where Pagani had hidden the documents.

'If you will permit me one more glass of sherry before we go it will give me strength for the journey and I will then put myself at your orders . . .'

'Let me—'

'No, no, no. I have not far to go and I prefer to be my own master and servant until the end.' Once again Pagani pulled himself up painfully, collected the empty glasses and started to shuffle out of the study and into the other room.

As Peroni watched him he had the impression that there was some sort of anomaly. It had filtered itself into his subconscious while the story of Mussolini's last visit was being told. Something to do with the room. Something almost imperceptibly wrong. But what?

His eye ranged about the study where he was sitting but, whatever it was, it was not in there. Which meant that it must be in that other, larger room where Pagani was continuing his semi-crippled progress. Peroni shifted his position to command a fuller view of it.

The harp? The grandfather clock? No. They might indeed be hiding-places, but there was nothing anomalous about them.

The stuffed animals? Nobody would think of them. Peroni observed them one by one – macabre, glassy-eyed mockeries of wildlife – and then rejected them, too.

His eye went back to Pagani, who had by now almost reached the cabinet. The cabinet? True, it only had one door but, though that was unusual, it was hardly, in that house, out of place.

Now Pagani was putting the two sherry glasses on the mantelpiece. Why on the mantelpiece. Suddenly, without yet understanding why, Peroni knew that the anomaly was part of the fireplace. But which particular part of the fireplace? The grate? The chimney? No again.

The coping?

Yes, the coping – the stone sun! One of its crooked rays was more in relief than the others, raised above the surface of the carving. Like a handle. The Mussolini–Churchill letters were inside the coping, protected by that primitive, grinning sun-god.

Peroni rose with the sudden knowledge that something had to be anticipated, prevented. Pagani's hands were moving about the coping urgently and powerfully as though all the life-force remaining to him were concentrated in them. What was he trying to do? Peroni started to move forwards and was immediately blasted backwards.

The sun had exploded.

A sheet of flame belched from it with a roar towards the surrounding furniture and the bricks of the fireplace seemed to bulge out very slowly like the stomach of a fat, stone god bursting. Pagani was swaying apparently quite peacefully at the centre of the pyre, wrapped in flames, and there was a darkness at the centre of his body.

It took Peroni a second to realise that this darkness was a briefcase and, even as he looked, it began to dissolve like black ice melting. One or two burning wings scattered from it and instantly shrivelled. And finally as the brightness of flame penetrated the darkness more and more, Pagani slowly collapsed, still clutching it as though it were a wound, or a child.

CHAPTER 6

'I think we'll ask for some more coffee,' said the Conscientious Chemist.

'Grappa, too, while you're at it,' put in Peroni.

They were sitting in an office at the carabinieri headquarters, where they had gone after finally leaving Pagani's house with the fire extinguished, the remains of the body removed and as many of the facts as possible cleared up on the spot. The officer in charge of the firemen had confirmed what Peroni had already imagined: that the explosion had been caused by a rudimentary but powerful bomb fitted inside the coping – the burglar alarm referred to by Pagani which Cordelia had detected and de-fused, almost certainly without realising what sort of alarm she was playing with. 'It was lucky for you,' the fire officer had added, 'that you were in the other room and you were simply knocked over by the force of the blast. You could have been badly hurt.'

Of the Churchill–Mussolini correspondence nothing remained but charred fragments. 'Whatever happens,' Mussolini's final charge had hung almost palpably on the air of the soggy and blackened ruins of Pagani's home. 'Whatever the cost.' It had been obeyed.

'There's just one thing I don't understand,' said the Conscientious Chemist when the drinks had arrived. 'What put you on to Pagani in the first place?'

Peroni took a ruminative swallow of grappa. 'It's simpler,' he said with uncharacteristic modesty, 'if you ask what put Cordelia Hope on to Pagani. I've done little more than follow her, and I'm bound to admit that she was usually quicker off the mark than I was. She had the photograph of the map showing the whereabouts of the Mussolini gold, right? She went to Bombarone for advice about salvaging it and he sent her to Bellini. But the crux of the whole matter is that she was the only person who was not after the Mussolini gold at all for its own sake. She wasn't interested in money, but as a historian she was passionately interested in the Mussolini–Churchill letters and she followed the salvage operation for just as long as she believed it was leading her to that. As soon as she realised it was no longer doing so she abandoned it.'

'But how did she realise it was no longer doing so?'

'That was where I was so slow. I had the same evidence before me as she did, but I didn't reach the same conclusion. You remember she went to see the antique dealer in Verona and he described to her how the gold was loaded into the cases? Well, it was clear from that that *only gold* was loaded. No documents. When she understood that she cut loose from Bellini and started off on her own again. The letter she wrote to her aunt – I told you about it, remember? – should have told me that. It spoke so clearly of the whole Bellini episode in the *past*. It was no longer part of her life. But there was something else it should have told me. I felt it as soon as I read the letter, but I couldn't put my finger on it. And yet it was the key to the whole thing.

'The address. The single word 'Costermano'. But I didn't realise the significance of it until I happened to go there by chance on the day of Bellini's funeral, and while I was there I saw something, or rather I didn't see something, which made the whole thing clear.'

Peroni knew he was overdoing the Poirot-in-the-library-at-the-end scene; it was a recurrent temptation of his and one he could never resist. 'When Colonel Volpi described the night before Mussolini's departure for Como and his visit to a villa on the lake with a briefcase, he mentioned seeing, by the light of the headlights when Mussolini came out of the front door, a stone sun carved in the wall of the house. Now both of us, Cordelia and I, assumed that Mussolini had handed over the map that night to the del Duca family who then lived at their Costermano villa. The description of the young man with the beard fitted del Duca's son, Gervaso, whose portrait both of us had seen. And the fact that Cordelia did find the map with his family seemed to bear this out. But when she realised that the documents were not with the gold she went the next morning to Costermano and saw the same thing as I did: the villa is a shell, but its facade is still intact and on it there is no carved sun. So then she went back to Pagani's house and found the sun there – underneath the ivy by the front door.

'Once you know that the rest is easy to work out. Mussolini indeed entrusted the map to General del Duca some time before the fall of Salò. Then the night before he left for Como he took the Churchill correspondence to the only other leading Fascist family on the lake – the Pagani family. The parents had escaped, but the son was in hiding there, and no great wonder if we took Colonel Volpi's description to apply to the del Duca son. A lot of young Fascists in those days did have short black beards. It was a fashion.'

Without being able to say why, Peroni felt uneasy. Everything was cleared up. The adventures of the lake were over. Venice was waiting impatiently for him. Why then did he feel so reluctant to leave?

He sat at a bar table, ordered himself a drink and tried to puzzle it out. But it was only when he looked about him that mental light began to dawn. Without realising what he was doing he had sat at exactly the same *caffe* table he had taken that morning nearly three weeks earlier when he had first met Cordelia over a lost contact lens. And there beside him her empty chair told him why he was uneasy and reluctant to leave the lake.

Her ghost was still unlaid.

Yet what could he do? The truth had been revealed. Those whose part it was to die had died and the rest had more or less resignedly taken up the business of day-to-day living. What could he do?

His eyes shifted from the chair to the only other material object in sight connected with Cordelia. The *Spaghetti Western*. It was still moored there in the little harbour with its indefinably cheeky and adventurous air.

'Whatever happens don't you dare waste our lessons.' Her voice sounded almost as though she were sitting on the chair next to him. 'I'm docking the *Spaghetti Western*, so take her out whenever you can. She'll appreciate it.'

Was she somehow still lingering there in the customs and passports area of the Kingdom of Death waiting for him to go sailing again? It was childishly superstitious, but then the Neapolitan within was childishly superstitious, too.

He paid for his drink and walked across to the yacht. Then, having cast off, he let her glide without sound or effort out on to the lake.

It was a perfect, velvet-soft evening. Darkness was beginning to fall and lights like fireflies were coming out as far as he could see along the shore. The *Spaghetti Western* handled superbly, instantly responding to the smallest touch, making him feel like a master yachtsman. Maybe, indeed, he was a master yachtsman and it had only needed those brief lessons from Cordelia to bring it out.

As he sailed out into the open lake he met a playful little wind which tugged like a kitten in the sails, putting his newly realised skill into yet higher relief.

'You see, I haven't given up sailing at all,' he found himself saying to Cordelia-who-wasn't-there. 'I just haven't had the chance till this evening. But now that everything's settled I shall come back whenever I can. Who knows? I might even go into the ocean-going class like that Englishman they made a lord or something.'

This rather silly little speech was interrupted as it was borne in on him that the playful little wind was turning boisterous and the tugging at the sails had become a buffeting. The *Spaghetti Western* began scudding fast over the lake, tipped over almost to the surface of the water, and Peroni found that he was having increasingly less to do with its speed or direction. And it was the second of these which gave him the greatest cause for alarm. For far from going towards the already distant shore line, the yacht was heading for the centre of the lake, which also appeared to be the centre of a fast-brewing storm. What he could see of the water was a sullen steely grey, humping into ugly waves which spat foam at him. He tried to keep calm and carry out the instructions Cordelia had given him for similar eventualities.

The sail was flapping like an enormous flag while the yacht

headed directly into the wind. Cordelia would probably have told him to tack which meant, he seemed to remember, zig-zagging at a 45 degree angle to the direction of the wind. How do you calculate 45 degrees in a storm? He tried to turn the bow, but the *Spaghetti Western* somehow wouldn't respond.

'Small sailboats,' he heard her voice inside his head maddeningly cool, 'can easily capsize in dirty weather.' And that was what she was doing.

'Shift your weight!' The now almost nightmare weather conditions lent the words an illusion of reality. 'Shift your weight? And slack off the sail!' He tried to obey, but all he succeeded in doing was to make the sail slam across the boat, knocking him down into the hull.

'Oh, really! Talk about butter-fingers – I'll have to do it myself. Just hang on tight and don't panic.'

Although he knew it was absurd, this time her voice bucked off the label of illusion and during the next few minutes everything except common sense said that Cordelia was in the yacht with him. She didn't take the blindest bit of notice of him, but as on that other occasion she gave the impression of being everywhere at once, trimming the sail, jibbing, tipping her very absence of weight to right the dangerous tipping of the *Spaghetti Western*.

And somehow she did right herself and start to sail shorewards across the wind, lifting out of the water and planing on the surface at a speed of something like twenty-five kilometres an hour.

For how long Peroni hung on tight, clutching at the side of the hull, he never knew, but eventually this suspension of time came to an end and he found himself alone in the yacht and out of the storm, sailing on smooth water towards the lights of Garda harbour.

'You should be able to handle her yourself now. *Arrivederci*, Achille . . .'

The voice was receding into the land of illusion again, but Peroni had the conviction now that Cordelia's ghost was laid at last. He turned his head in the direction from where the words had seemed to come.

'*Arrivederci*, Cordelia,' he said.